THE HOLLOW CHASE

Also by Cap Daniels

The Chase Fulton Novels Series
Book One: *The Opening Chase*
Book Two: *The Broken Chase*
Book Three: *The Stronger Chase*
Book Four: *The Unending Chase*
Book Five: *The Distant Chase*
Book Six: *The Entangled Chase*
Book Seven: *The Devil's Chase*
Book Eight: *The Angel's Chase*
Book Nine: *The Forgotten Chase*
Book Ten: *The Emerald Chase*
Book Eleven: *The Polar Chase*
Book Twelve: *The Burning Chase*
Book Thirteen: *The Poison Chase*
Book Fourteen: *The Bitter Chase*
Book Fifteen: *The Blind Chase*
Book Sixteen: *The Smuggler's Chase*
Book Seventeen: *The Hollow Chase*
Book Eighteen: *The Sunken Chase* (Summer 2022)

Books in
The Avenging Angel – Seven Deadly Sins Series
Book One: *The Russian's Pride*
Book Two: *The Russian's Greed*
Book Three: *The Russian's Gluttony*
Book Four: *The Russian's Lust* (Summer 2022)

Other Books by Cap Daniels
We Were Brave
I Am Gypsy (Novella)
The Chase Is On (Novella)

THE HOLLOW CHASE

CHASE FULTON NOVEL #17

CAP DANIELS

The Hollow Chase
Chase Fulton Novel #17
Cap Daniels

This is a work of fiction. Names, characters, places, historical events, and incidents are the product of the author's imagination or have been used fictitiously. Although many locations such as marinas, airports, hotels, restaurants, etc. used in this work actually exist, they are used fictitiously and may have been relocated, exaggerated, or otherwise modified by creative license for the purpose of this work. Although many characters are based on personalities, physical attributes, skills, or intellect of actual individuals, all the characters in this work are products of the author's imagination.

Published by:

** USA **

13 Digit ISBN: 978-1-951021-32-0
Library of Congress Control Number: 2022934082

Cover Design: German Creative

Printed in the United States of America

The Hollow Chase

CAP DANIELS

Chapter 1
Subject Matter Experts

November 2005

The man wearing jeans, a skintight black T-shirt, and boots looked more like a fashion model than a gunfighter, but despite his polished exterior, he produced a pistol from some mysterious location on his body and raised the weapon—one-handed—closed one eye, and yanked the trigger twice. Blood exploded from the upper body of his target some twenty feet away, the wounds high on his chest. The victim fell to a knee, drew a throwing knife from his boot, and sent it soaring through the air toward the gunman. A third concussive shot from the man's pistol rang out, and the bullet struck the airborne knife, sending it tumbling through the air in a flurry of sparks and sounds of ringing metal on metal.

A voice, authoritative and excited, filled the air behind me. "Cut! Perfect! I love everything about it!"

Desperately trying to contain our laughter, Stone W. Hunter and I twisted in our canvas-bottomed director's chairs and shuddered at the ridiculous episode we'd just witnessed. The screenwriter who'd written the scene leaned in and pinched an inch of fat—that hadn't existed a year earlier—from my side like a good Southern Baptist mother controlling her wayward child during

Sunday-morning service. "Chase Fulton! If you two can't behave and be quiet, they're going to throw you off the set."

My brilliant, beautiful, but incensed wife, Penny Fulton, had written the story, but I prayed she wasn't responsible for the atrocity we'd just witnessed.

"We're trying, sweetheart, but that was atrocious. Gunfights don't work like that. And shooting the knife out of the air? Come on . . ."

Penny's eyes flashed upward and filled with disappointed realization, so I turned to see what had her attention. A strange little man wearing a sweater vest and sporting a terrible attempt at an adolescent mustache stood only inches away. The only thing more ridiculous than the scene we'd just sat through was the man's attempt to appear menacing. "Pen, your guests are disrupting the shoot."

Did he just call her Pen?

There are few things my partner and brother-in-arms, Stone Hunter, loved more than seeing Penny treat me like an errant child, so he threw up a hand toward the soundstage. "Shoot? Ha! That thing you just did out there started with *sh* and ended with *t*, but nothing about it qualified as a *shoot*."

The woman more beautiful than any actress in Tinseltown scowled, and I was convinced if she could get her hands on the throwing knife, she'd carve me and Hunter into cat food. "Julian, I'm sorry," she said. "They were just leaving."

Julian? What a perfect name for the impish little character.

He stared at us as if his role as second assistant director—according to the badge dangling from the lanyard around his neck—gave him the power to throw us off the set.

I elbowed my partner and turned back to Julian. "I'm sorry, Jule. It won't happen again."

To my amusement and Hunter's delight, Julian stomped a foot and turned a shade of red no human should ever be capable of accomplishing. I caught the laughter in my throat before it escaped, but Hunter couldn't hold it in.

If Penny would've had a switch, she would've spanked her problem children all the way to the car, but before she could explode, an unexpected savior came to our rescue.

Famed Hollywood actor-turned-director Robert DaSilva stepped beside his second assistant. "Is everything all right over here?"

Julian drove a finger through the air, alternately pointing between Hunter and me. "These two . . . ugh!"

I wouldn't have turned around to see Penny's face for a billion dollars at that moment. I didn't fear her switch. Decapitation in my sleep would've, no doubt, been her punishment of choice.

When Hunter spoke, I panicked. He said, "We're sorry for being a disruption, but that ain't how gunfights work."

Julian threw his clipboard into the air. "Oh, really, Mr. Gunfight Expert? Just exactly how many gunfights have you been in?"

As much as I hated what Penny was going through in that moment, I was like a kid at Christmas waiting to hear what my partner was about to tell the boy wonder.

Hunter scratched his chin and peered skyward. "Hmm, I can't remember all of them, but in the past two years, I'd say at least seven or eight. Does that sound about right to you, Chase?"

Hands flew to hips, and Julian clenched his fists.

Oh, this is about to get good, I thought.

But DaSilva laid a hand across the little man's shoulder. "Relax, Julian. These two are, shall we say, subject-matter experts. In fact, I'd love to know how you two would envision this scene playing out."

It was Penny's turn to drop her clipboard. The loving, considerate, good-husband part of me knew I should've turned to my favorite screenwriter for permission to proceed, but the gunslinging, knuckle-dragging, door kicker in me couldn't let the opportunity pass.

Hunter and I slid from our big-boy chairs and headed for the bright lights and imaginary world of the soundstage.

The pretty-boy actor tossed me the pistol as he ambled out of the lights.

I caught it, and his arm, at the same instant. "If you'll treat these things like they're always loaded, it's impossible for anyone to get hurt."

He pulled away. "It's a prop gun. If you knew anything about *the business*, you'd know that."

"Arrogance is tough to overcome, and experience is the only real teacher. If you'd have spent any time defending the country that made you a millionaire, you'd know that."

Certain I'd never teach Tight Shirt Tommy—or whatever his name was—anything about the reality of firearms safety, I hobbled my way toward what the director called "first position." The hobble came courtesy of the fourth prosthetic right ankle and foot I'd worn in the previous year after losing my foot during what I believed would be the final tactical operation of my career. Since the accident, I'd been relegated to stable hand, boat washer, and full-time Bonaventure bourbon boy. The prop gun in my hand was the closest thing to a real weapon I'd held since December of the previous year.

An errand boy plucked the throwing knife from the stage, dusted it off, and handed it to Hunter. My partner looked at the dull chunk of metal in his hand and traced the fishing line tied to the handle and leading somewhere into the darkness above.

So, that's how they got it to fly away as if Pretty-Boy Bobby had miraculously managed to hit it with his imaginary bullet.

I released the magazine from the prop gun and discovered it to be loaded with a convenient stack of blank nine-millimeter rounds. A quick check of the muzzle revealed a plug with an opening the size of pencil lead to allow expanding gasses to escape when the blank fired in the chamber.

I turned on my carbon-fiber and titanium heel. "Ready, partner?"

He shrugged. "Sure. I'm just waiting for somebody to yell 'Action!'"

The director obliged, and I pretended to draw the weapon from a make-believe holster on my hip. My turn was anything but tactical since I hadn't yet mastered the whole fake-foot balance thing, but I regained my posture, kept both eyes open, gripped the weapon with the strong, two-hand grip every soldier learns on day one in firearms training, and pressed the trigger.

The recoil felt real enough, and I reset the trigger as the hunk of polycarbonate in my hands bucked and returned to its first position. With the sights covering my target for the second time in less than a second, I pressed again, and Hunter melted to the ground exactly as a man with two nine-millimeter holes in his upper chest and two coffee-can-sized exit wounds in his back would do in the real world.

"No, you amateur! You've got to throw the knife!" came the voice of Hollywood Harold . . . or whatever his name was.

Hunter rolled from his back onto his side. "No, you make-believe, wanna-be gunfighter. Nobody has the ability to throw a knife after catching two in the chest, but that's not the lesson here. Did you see how Chase held and fired your *prop* gun?"

"Yeah, I saw, but that's not how it's done in the movies. Unlike you, I'm required to make the shot and still look like the leading man I am, and that's done with one hand."

"When was the last time you fired a real gun?" Hunter asked.

"I don't believe in guns."

"You don't believe in guns?" Hunter laughed. "I can assure you they exist whether you believe in them or not. I've sent a couple million rounds through them and even caught three incoming rounds—one of them high on my chest. You could've given me a dump-truck load of throwing knives, and I wouldn't have been able to launch any one of them more than a foot."

The actor huffed. "I'm morally opposed to guns. They should only be in the hands of police officers and the military."

Hunter hopped to his feet. "Morally opposed to guns? Is that what you said?"

"That's right. Guns are part of the problem in this country."

My partner repositioned the hat on his head. "So, let me get this straight. You're morally opposed to guns, yet you'll make a movie with one and cash the check, all the while looking like the leading man you are. Is that about the size of it?"

I was secretly pleased it had been Hunter who sent the crushing blow and not me, but there was little doubt I'd still catch some of the fallout.

DaSilva stopped me before I arrived back at my chair beside my horrified wife. "Is that really how it happens?"

Hunter stepped to my side as I said, "Real gunfights between people who've been trained to shoot are typically over in seconds, they never happen one-handed, and shooting a flying knife out of the air is preposterous. People hide, cry, and wet their pants when bullets start flying."

The director alternately stared between the soundstage and me. "I appreciate the education, but it would be hard to get a hundred million people to pay to see a movie like that. As much as I'd like to make this scene as realistic as possible, I'm afraid I'll have to stick with the fiction we created."

"I understand," I said. "Your way is a lot more exciting, and I agree . . . No one wants to see a real gunfight."

Hunter let out a chuckle. "And next time somebody throws a knife at me, I think I'll try to shoot it down."

Chapter 2
Playing for The Bear

Penny sat in her favorite chair, overlooking a canyon in the Hollywood Hills, her pencil scratching at a bound stack of papers.

I stared at the professional version of my wife, the side that dived headlong into every project she started, especially when that project was becoming a major motion picture. "What's happening over there?"

She looked up and bounced the pencil against her lower lip. Her look said mischief more than anger, so I pressed on.

"Are you still mad about the shoot this afternoon?"

She let out a soft chuckle. "No, the shoot didn't do anything to make me mad. It was the two of you who did that."

"What? The director called us subject-matter experts."

She rolled her eyes. "Well, you two are certainly experts when it comes to playing 'embarrass the writer on set.'"

"I guess it would be better if Hunter and I didn't come back to the set, huh?"

She bit the pencil. "Oh, you don't have to worry about that. The screenwriter just revoked your set passes."

"But . . . you're the screenwriter."

She made a toy gun with her pencil and thumb. "You're smarter than you look. Now, go play with Hunter or something. I'm busy."

"Busy doing what?"

"Marking up tomorrow's script. We're starting early."

"Hollywood early or real-world early?" I asked.

"Ten o'clock early."

"That's what I thought . . . Hollywood early."

She waved the back of her hand in my direction. "Shoo! Go away. You're disturbing me. I don't pester you at your job while you're out chasing bad guys, do I?"

I raised my prosthetic foot and ankle. "I'm not sure I have a job anymore. I'm really not fit to chase anybody—bad guys or otherwise."

She swallowed hard. "Seriously, Chase, I really need to work."

I rested my prosthetic foot back on the floor and stared at it. Beneath long pants and boots, everything looked perfectly normal —until I stood and walked.

The past year of my life had been an exercise in reliving the aftermath of the first catastrophic injury of my life in the final game of the 1996 College World Series. Back then, every dream I had was to catch for the Atlanta Braves, and I'd checked all the boxes to turn that dream into my reality. I was the only player in NCAA history to have earned the Buster Posey Award for catcher of the year twice. I threw out more runners attempting to steal than any catcher in SEC history. I was the NCAA Division 1 College Baseball Player of the Year, and in my final year at UGA, I received the Dick Howser Trophy for collegiate player of the year. Catchers are rarely first-round draft picks into the major league, but until the day my world came crashing down around me in a collision at home plate, I was destined to beat the odds and don the blue and red hat of an Atlanta Brave on draft day. Of course, being a catcher to my core, I would've worn the hat backward.

The collision at home plate left my right hand and wrist broken so badly, it would take five major surgeries and months of physical therapy to return it—to the closest condition possible—to a normal, healthy, right hand. A hand and wrist, though, aren't weight-bearing appendages. Ankles and feet, however, are something quite different.

I could walk on my fake foot, as Hunter called it. Most days, I could even run a few strides without falling, but not a second of my life passed without debilitating phantom pain. The day before I lost my right foot forever, I could run a five-minute mile in boots and run almost continually at an eight-minute pace without panting. The scars of nearly a decade of gunfights, fistfights, knife fights, airplane crashes, and explosions were the trophies of my career as a covert operative instead of a major league catcher.

Back at Walter Reed National Military Medical Center almost a year earlier, I abandoned the wheelchair in minutes, the crutches in hours, and the cane in days. I would accept the scalding brand of an amputee, but never the stamp of disabled. The first foot they gave me was little more than a pirate's peg leg. It was stiff with a rigid ankle and made no attempt to masquerade as a real foot. I clomped along on that miserable thing while the prosthetic lab at Walter Reed in Bethesda, Maryland, built an articulating ankle, and fi-nally, a third iteration with pneumatic shock absorbers to soften the clomp.

Having never worn the uniform of a soldier, the fact that I was a patient at Walter Reed was bizarre enough, but singing "I left my foot in Western Africa" to the tune of "I left my Heart in San Francisco" apparently made the doctors and nurses fear I'd lost not only my most distant limb, but also my sanity. Little did they know I'd never had an abundance of sanity to lose.

The day the doctor wearing an Army uniform declared me and my new plastic foot to be as well as I'd ever be, I limped out of the hospital with a singular goal—to locate and hire the best prosthetic lab in the world, regardless of the cost. My life would not be spent dragging a government hunk of garbage attached to the stump of my right leg.

The lab, it turned out, wasn't at the Mayo Clinic or Johns Hopkins, as I'd expected. It was smack-dab in the middle of the most unlikely state in the country, at the University of Alabama at Birmingham. The hospital at UAB boasted some of the finest medical minds on the planet, as well as a prosthetic research facility second to none.

I expected my first visit to the lab at UAB to consist of an hour of talking to a nerd in a lab coat. Instead, I met Doctor Michael Smithfield, who extended his gargantuan hand and said, "Nice to meet you, Chase. Call me Ham."

"Ham?"

He shrugged. "Yeah, you know, like Smithfield ham. I picked up that cute little moniker my freshman year at Alabama playing for Bear."

"You played football for Bear Bryant?"

"Yeah, I was an offensive lineman until I folded my knee backward in eighty-three against Georgia." He paused almost imperceptibly, then asked, "Where'd you go to school?"

I froze and suddenly wished I'd brought Mongo with me for the appointment. The second largest human I'd ever met just told me how my alma mater ended his football career.

"Um . . . it's a little school you've probably never heard of."

As if driven by some invisible yet irresistible force, his smile broadened into a wide, toothy grin. "I'm just messing with you, Chase. I know where you went to school, and my son's looking hard at Georgia. He's one of the best high-school catchers in the country."

"You've got to be kidding. Is he really looking at Georgia?"

"Yeah, and my knee hurts a little more every time he mentions going to school over there. Needless to say, his mom and I are pushing hard for him to Roll with the Tide in Tuscaloosa."

I measured the probability of me being able to fight off Mongo's twin brother and decided to roll the dice. "If he doesn't have the grades to get into Georgia, I guess he'll have to settle for Bama."

Thankfully, his grin remained. "Seriously, though, I think he's going to end up at Vanderbilt. No offense to either of our schools."

"They've got a great program up there," I said. "It's hard to do any better than Vandy when it comes to a baseball school."

Ham pulled out a framed picture from the credenza behind him and slid it across the desk. "That's my boy. The filthy one second from the left."

I picked up the picture and studied the five players in the photo. Nostalgia washed over me as I remembered the pictures of me and the four infielders who started every game in '96, the year we won the College World Series. "Good catchers are born dirty, and they never grow out of it. I could ruin a pair of uniform pants in three games."

Ham said, "Unlike you and me, though, the game is his fall-back plan. He's going to be a doctor like his old man. That's why I say he'll end up at Vandy. He knows he's good. In fact, he's even a little cocky about it. I think a runner from third will clean his clock when he starts playing real ball in the SEC, and it'll knock some of that cockiness out of him."

I held up my hand laced with scars and full of pins and screws God never put there. "After my collision, I had the cleanest clock in the game. But I kept my cockiness intact."

"My son and I were at that game, you know."

"My game? When I got hurt?"

He nodded. "We've been to Omaha to see the College World Series every year since he started playing little league. Next time you come to Birmingham, I'm sure he'd love to shake that magic hand of yours—if you have time."

I grinned. "I'd like that. Maybe we can toss a few and see if I've still got the arm to gun 'em down at second."

He replaced the picture on the credenza. "Hop up on the table, and let's have a look at your leg."

I dragged my clunky foot across the floor and took a seat on the paper-covered exam table.

Ham removed my shoe and the prosthetic. "Where did you get this dinosaur?"

"It's standard government issue."

He let the foot slide from his hand and into the stainless-steel trash can in the corner. The look on his face spoke of confusion, and he lifted my file from his desk. After thumbing through the first several pages, he looked up and shook the file. "This doesn't say anything about you being military."

"I'm not in the military."

He narrowed his eyes. "Then why are you wearing a government-issue prosthetic?"

"It's a long story."

He crossed his arms. "I've got plenty of time."

"Maybe so, but you don't have the clearance or the need to know. Suffice it to say, I do a little contract work overseas for the government from time to time. Or at least . . . I used to."

He pursed his lips. "Contracting, you say?"

I gave him a nod. "Something like that."

"Since you won't tell me your story, let me tell you mine." Ham took a seat on a rolling stool that looked like a toy beneath him. "When I busted up my knee in that game against that little school I've never heard of, I thought my life was over. All I was inside my head was a football player. I'd never thought of being anything else until they replaced my knee with something just about as worthless as that piece of garbage foot they gave you."

I said, "You had to have your knee replaced from a football injury? I've never heard of anything like that."

He knocked on his kneecap with his knuckles. "The team doctor said it was probably just ligament and tendon damage, but the X-rays told a different story. The ligaments were trashed, but I also crushed the top of the tibia and fibula. Those are the two bones of the lower leg here and here." He pressed against each of the bones in my leg, just above the amputation.

"What they stuck in me was a joint designed to carry the weight of an eighty-year-old man less than half my size. Trying to learn to walk on that thing turned into the best motivator of my life. I changed majors from criminal justice to pre-med and biomedical engineering. When I finished my undergrad at Alabama, I came to school here at UAB and earned my MD and PhD. I'm now a board-certified orthopedic surgeon and the director of the prosthetic research laboratory. I designed an artificial knee joint that was light years ahead of anything else on the market, had it installed, and became my own crash test dummy. I put that knee through the wringer, redesigned it twice, and became patient zero for the best prosthetic knee available anywhere in the world. I no longer get hit by three-hundred-pound defensive linemen every time somebody says 'Hike," but this knee could take it . . . even if the rest of me couldn't."

I listened to his story with the fascination of a child. "Can you build me a foot as good as your knee?"

He shrugged and motioned toward the trashcan. "I don't know. But I know I could carve one, with a dull knife, out of a stick of stovewood, and it would be better than that thing."

* * *

I spent the remainder of the day trying on new feet and ankles. The doctors, physical therapists, and technicians videotaped my stride, measured my legs, and spoke to each other in words I'd never be able to pronounce or understand.

When my day at the lab came to an end, Dr. Ham and I ended up back in his office. "Well, Chase, I've got some good news, some better news, and some news between those two that won't sound so good to you."

"Let's have the bad news first," I said.

He held up a finger. "Not so fast. That's not how I do things. I'm a good-news-first guy, so we'll start with that. You'll leave today with a prosthetic that's a thousand times better than the one you came in with."

"That's definitely good news."

"But it's not the better news. The better news is this. I can make you a foot and ankle that will, in time, fool your brain into believing it's the foot you were born with, and you'll be able to run and jump and play like the other little boys."

I chuckled at his attempt at doctor humor. "Great! How long will that take?"

"It'll take about a month to construct the prosthetic, but you can expect about the same amount of time it took for you to learn to walk the first time for you to become confident and comfortable with the foot."

"What do you mean, the first time?"

"You were probably around a year old when you learned to walk the first time, so it's reasonable to expect it will take about a year for you to learn how to fully integrate your prosthetic into your life."

"A year?" I said with far more fervor than I should've expressed.

Ham held up both hands. "Don't shoot the messenger. Even though we all watched *The Six Million Dollar Man* in the eighties, that was science fiction back then, and it still is today. We'll build you the best foot on Earth, but unfortunately, your body will continue to reject it and see it as unnatural for a long time."

"So, that's the bad news, then? It'll take a year to get used to it."

He shook his head. "No, that's just an inconvenient truth about it. Before I break the bad news, I need to know who performed the amputation."

"The doctor from the American Embassy in Gabon."

He scowled. "Gabon? Like Gabon in Africa?"

"Exactly like that."

"Was he an orthopedic surgeon?"

I shrugged. "I don't know. I was unconscious, and honestly, I don't even know if the doctor was a man or a woman. Why does it matter who did it?"

He pulled off his glasses and sighed. "It matters because whoever did it likely had never done it before. The amputation was done too close to the ankle. It is structurally impossible to construct a prosthetic with the necessary stability with only inches for attachment."

I let his words wash over me, and my stomach turned. "You're going to cut off more of my leg, aren't you?"

He cleared his throat. "That's up to you, but let me show you something first."

He pulled up an X-ray on his computer and turned the monitor so I could see. With his pen, he pointed toward the bones of my lower leg. "As you can see, the fibula—that's the smaller bone—extends past the terminus of the tibia. It's far more complicated than this, but for now, let's say the fibula is more important for balance than structural support. Holding up the two hundred pounds above it is the job of the tibia. The ideal location for the amputation is four to six inches below the top of the tibia, with the fibula being shortened a few millimeters above that."

Unable to focus on anything else, I asked again, "You're going to cut off more of my leg, aren't you?"

He slid his glasses across his desk and pinched the bridge of his nose. "If you want extremely good results, yes, it is necessary that I relocate the amputation, and in doing so, I will construct a nearly perfect site for the prosthetic connection."

"Extremely good results?" I said. "What if I want excellent results?"

He lifted his glasses and returned them to his face. "Have you ever heard the term *osseointegration*?"

I shook my head.

He said, "*Osseointegration* is a procedure in which an abutment—essentially a threaded rod—is surgically implanted inside your tibia and protrudes through the skin of the amputation site. Your prosthetic will then be attached to the abutment by way of a threaded coupling fixture. This is still an experimental procedure, but we've had extremely good results, and I think you're the perfect candidate."

"What happens if it doesn't work?"

"That's the beauty of the procedure," he said. "If it doesn't work, I'll remove the abutment, and we'll return to a conventional attachment."

"I have only one question. When can you do it?"

"Which one?"

"The osseointegration," I said. "The only thing better than having a stump is having a stump with a metal rod sticking out of it. While you're at it, why don't you stick a couple of bolts in the side of my neck so I can be Herman Munster for Halloween?"

Chapter 3
Losing Another Foot

Just as Dr. Smithfield had described the planned result, I awoke from surgery with a metal rod protruding from a new stump, and another foot—twelve inches, not the appendage—had been amputated from my lower leg.

"Does it hurt?" were the first words out of Penny's mouth when she stepped through the curtain and into the post-surgical recovery suite.

With a goofy, groggy smile on my face, I said, "Nope . . . Can't feel a thing."

The second voice I heard belonged to Clark Johnson, my first partner and current handler. "How's it going, Stumpy?"

My narcotic-induced grin continued. "Stumpy? Really?"

"Yep, Stumpy the One-Footed Wonder. Wasn't he one of the seven dwarfs? Sleepy, Dopey, Doc, Stumpy, and Sneezy?"

I returned my out-of-focus gaze back to Penny, the only sober, sane one in the room. "Hit him in the face with something hard . . . please."

She leaned down and kissed my forehead. "Hit him hard? Or hit him *with* something hard?"

"Both," I said as Dr. Smithfield stepped through the curtain, his massive frame blocking out all the light from behind him.

Dr. Ham laid a meaty paw on my shoulder. "How are you feeling, Chase?"

"A little drunk."

"Good. We'll keep that buzz going for the next several hours. The surgery went perfectly well, and I couldn't have asked for a better patient."

Unable to stop grinning, I asked, "When can I walk?"

He laughed and gave me a pat. "We'll get to that, but for now, just rest. We'll put a little weight on the leg tomorrow and see how it feels. As soon as the anesthetic wears off a little more, we'll move you up to your room. The nurses tell me there's an unruly bunch—including a guy who's bigger than me—up there waiting to see you. I'm looking forward to meeting him."

I nodded through the haze. "Yep, that'd be Mongo. And the rest of the guys are Hunter, Singer, Disco, and . . ."

He chuckled. "It sounds like a bunch of imaginary friends to me. Don't you hang around with anybody with a real name?"

I gave his hand a squeeze. "Just you, *Ham*."

"Touché," he said as he stepped back through the curtain.

"Are you cold?" Penny asked, pulling a blanket across my stomach.

"I don't know. Maybe . . ."

She giggled. "You don't know if you're cold?"

"I don't even know if any of this is real. For all I know, I could be dreaming."

She leaned down and planted the most luxurious kiss on my mouth, then she whispered, "Does that feel real enough?"

I was then smiling for a thousand reasons that had nothing to do with anesthesia. "Kisses like that from you will always feel like a dream."

Before I could slobber on my gown anymore, a pair of orderlies stepped into the space, and a third pulled back the curtain against its long, curving track. The sound reminded me of my toy cars on the plastic track Santa Claus delivered when I was seven. The next experience reminded me of being hurled through space when the fluorescent lights whizzed past as I was rolled beneath them. The wheels of the bed were nearly silent, giving the impression of flight. A turn, and an abrupt stop inside a silver box, left me bewildered and nauseous until the familiar ding of the elevator finally yanked my gooey brain from its fog. "Oh, an elevator."

"Yes, sir. We're in the elevator and taking you up to your room. Do you feel okay?"

The disembodied voice filled the box, but I hesitated to answer, fearing the words had come from inside my head instead of from the lips of someone else.

Perhaps sensing my confusion, one of the orderlies leaned down and met my stare. "Are you feeling okay, Mr. Fulton?"

"No, not really. I think I may . . ."

He produced a long bag with a blue plastic funnel affixed to the top and placed it into my hand. "If you feel like you're going to be sick, hold this over your mouth."

Fortunately, the contraption never became necessary, but I had my moments of doubt. Perhaps two more minutes—or possibly two weeks—passed before one of the orderlies stepped on the locking mechanism of my bed, hung an IV bag, and asked, "Is there anything else you need?"

"I'm thirsty," I mouthed.

Penny held out a plastic sippy cup emblazoned with UAB Medicine across the side.

I took it and sipped the warm water through the attached nozzle. "Thank you."

She ran her fingers through my hair and dabbed at the corner of my mouth. "How are you feeling?"

I squinted against the light. "I wish people would stop asking me that. I feel like somebody cut off my leg and installed a metal rod while I was asleep. How would you feel?"

Singer, the Southern Baptist sniper stepped to my bedside. "It's good to have you back."

"It's good to be back," I said, looking around him at Penny. "I'm sorry I got grouchy."

She smiled, and I melted just like a thousand times before when I saw her smile and forgot the rest of the world existed.

A nurse wheeled a cart into the room and connected all sorts of things to my body. In that moment, the only one I recognized was the blood pressure cuff, but she appeared pleased with her work and made a few notes on a clipboard she pulled from the foot of my bed.

"Dr. Smithfield ordered some pain meds, so I'll inject them through your IV. You'll probably fall asleep quickly after that. So, if you want to tell anyone good night, now's the time."

A face came into focus in front of me at the same instant the warmth of the pain meds found the vein in my arm. "Hey, Okhotnik."

Hearing the Russian word for *Hunter* come out of my mouth left me with a thousand questions pouring through my head.

Why did I speak in Russian? How much more of my body—of me—can I sacrifice before there's nothing left to give?

Sleep took me the instant after Hunter said, "We've got a mission."

When the human mind dreams, it isn't bound by any laws—natural or man-made. It casts off its limitations and soars without limits . . . almost. Something inside the unconscious mind—perhaps it's the devil himself—still allows us to fail in the misty world beyond sentience.

Hunter's declaration of a mission gaffed its claws into my brain and sent me back onto the battlefield, but not a battlefield of old, where men stood hip to hip with their brothers and face to face with their enemies and fired musket balls, one every forty seconds, until lead, powder, or blood was run dry. Mine was a battlefield of silence, deceit, and cunning. I didn't fear the coming musket balls propelled upon white smoke and the roar of flashing powder. If I had a fear, if I knew hesitation and cowardice and dread, it was my hatred for the silenced round fired from the darkness by the hand I would never see, the face I would never confront, and crack of the whip I would never feel.

I died a million deaths in my dream—deaths of indescribable agony and deaths of peaceful silence. I slipped from the realm of the living into the darkness of the transition between the bounds of Earth and the freedom of eternity, reliving my every failure, my unending weakness, and my every sin against man, woman, myself, and my God. I begged for Singer's faith in the moments of darkness, in the moments of fear and dread and emptiness. I prayed for Hunter's strength in the moments I longed to lie on the bitter ground and cease the fight. I beseeched whatever power stood before and above me for the wisdom to know if my sacrifice, my fight, my life were in the right, on the side of the light, and not aligned with the darkness of those I despised and toiled to end. Would I someday be given the magnificent gift of knowing I had stood when it was right to do so, and bowed and stepped aside when honor and goodness demanded my subjugation?

The battle before me rose and fell in waves of fury and solace, roaring and silent, dark and light. The men I loved as if we shared the same blood clashed with our foe, and fell when struck, but always returned to their feet as if driven by a strength and might beyond themselves, as if propelled by the hand of God. I knew their faces as if they were my own, but my sword was absent when it should have flown beside those of my brothers. The places where I should have run and stood and fought and bled were empty, but they fought on without me, more valiant and fearless than I'd ever seen them, more determined and undefeatable than they'd ever been with me at their side.

Had I been anything more than the burden of my own mass, my own ignorance, my own incompetence? Were my brothers, my team, my family stronger without me? Had my tortured, depleted body become only weight they need not bear? Had my vessel, now empty and void and hollow, become only a shell of former humanity? Had the day come when my weapon would never again feel my grasp, when my mortal enemy would never be forced to feel my blade, my ire, and my will?

A hand that is little more than a machine, and a leg forever gone, likely incinerated into smoke and ash, were the tokens of a life lived with my eyes fixed on the goal and my will unbreakable and resolute. It was over, I was finished, and yet the battle raged on as if having never known the fall of my feet, the metal of my blade, or the sting of my bullet. It was fought long before me and would be fought until eternity. I had become a broken remnant of the fight that cannot be won, the battle that can never end. Ending came only to its victims, its defeated, its cast-off bodies like mine.

Chapter 4
The Goods

I awoke to the sound of soft baritone humming from the darkness of my room. As my eyes adjusted to the absence of light, I scanned the space, uncertain of where I'd been and where I was. The glow of a monitor to my left cast shadows through the room, and a thin beam of light cut its way from beneath the door. Turning toward the gentle humming, I discovered a silhouette standing by the window and staring out into the darkness.

I licked my dry lips. "Singer?"

He turned, stopped humming, and stepped toward my bed. "I thought it was about time for you to join the land of the living. From the sound of things, those drugs they gave you stirred up some humdinger of a dream. You've been wailing and moaning for hours."

I rubbed the sleep from my eyes and stretched, twisting at the waist. The movement drove my stump against the mattress and sent flaming arrows up my spine. I gasped and jerked to reposition in my bed, but the pain kept rising and exploding with every passing second. Singer took two more strides toward my bed and reached down for my arm with his right hand. With his left, he thumbed the nurse call button.

I covered his hand with mine. "It's okay. I just twisted on my leg—or what used to be my leg—and it got my attention."

Before he could respond, a nurse stepped through the door, bringing light from the hallway with her. "Is everything okay, Mr. Fulton?"

I twisted and wriggled to find a comfortable position. "Yeah, I just put some pressure on my leg and . . ."

She pulled the cover away and flipped on a fluorescent light above my head. "Let's take a look." She removed the bandage and studied the wound. "You've had a little bleeding, but that's normal. I'll redress it and get you some more pain meds. Don't go anywhere. I'll be right back."

She left my leg exposed, and I stared down at the protruding rod. I looked up to see Singer staring as well. I said, "It's hard to believe, isn't it?"

"These things happen in our line of work."

"That's not what I meant. I was talking about the metal abutment that's part of my body now."

"Oh, yeah, modern medicine is remarkable. Maybe we can get Mongo to build you a machine gun to mount on that thing."

I smiled for the first time. "If anybody could do it, he'd be the one."

Singer chuckled. "That guy's something else. How does anybody get that smart?"

"Maybe he made a deal like Solomon. You know . . . for wisdom instead of riches."

Singer grinned. "You've been reading the Bible, haven't you? I'm proud of you."

"Don't be proud. I learned that in Vacation Bible School when I was a kid."

"Regardless," he said, "it stuck with you. I think Mongo may have made a better deal than even King Solomon, though. He got riches, strength, and wisdom. That's the trifecta, if you ask me."

"Where'd he go to school?"

Singer shook his head. "I don't think he went to school. I think when he's not bench-pressing Volkswagens or pulling you out of a hole, he's reading." He pulled a chair close to my bed. "Are you going to tell me about those dreams?"

Part of me was too ashamed to admit where my brain had gone in those dark hours brought on by the narcotics, but Singer's faith and innate ability to sort through the garbage in my head, and to make sense of the demons that danced in there, gave me the reassurance that anything he and I discussed would, forever, stay only between the two of us.

"I think I'm done." I pointed toward my stump and abutment. "I'll never be able to . . ."

In his typical wisdom, he said, "That's up to you. And whatever you decide is the answer you'll have to live with."

My initial reaction was to scoff. "That's psychobabble."

He shrugged. "How long has it been since you've thrown a baseball?"

"I don't know, but what does that have to do with anything?"

"I wasn't there, so I've only heard the stories, but from what I *have* heard, you did more damage to that right hand of yours than anybody could come back from."

"I didn't come back from it. It ended my career, no matter how much they cobbled it back together."

"Could you throw a ball now if you tried?"

"Sure I could, but I wouldn't be much of a ballplayer with only one foot."

That accident with your hand may have ended your baseball career, so you missed the draft and never got to play in the big leagues. After a couple of years, though, you could throw a baseball again, and you could learn to throw it just as hard and as accurately as you did when you gunned down more base stealers than anybody else. Why didn't you go back to the game then?"

I swallowed the lump in my throat. "To be honest, I didn't think about it. I was an operator by then, and that's what was important."

He snapped his fingers. "Exactly. That's my point. Maybe God never wanted you to play baseball. Think about it. How many lives would you have saved as a ballplayer?"

"I'm afraid I don't know what you're talking about, and I don't blame God for anything that's ever happened to me."

He looked up toward the door and held up a finger. The nurse turned and disappeared back down the hallway. "I'm not suggesting you're blaming God for anything, but how many human lives have you saved in the last ten years as an operator?"

"I don't know. But I know how many I've taken."

He continued. "Did you learn anything about King David in Vacation Bible School?"

"I know the story about Goliath, the giant."

"That's just our introduction to David. What he did after killing Goliath is what made him Israel's greatest king. He did everything wrong. He was an adulterer, a murderer, and probably spent a lot of time with a cup of wine in his hand. But God loved him anyway. In fact, He called him a man after His own heart."

"What does any of that have to do with me?"

"That's up to you, too," he said. "I can shoot, and I can sing. You can lead, and you can teach, but you've got one more asset that maybe makes you a man after God's own heart."

He had my attention, so I listened intently when he said, "You believe."

Perhaps it was the hangover from the pain meds, or maybe I just wasn't smart enough to follow. "Believe in God?"

He nodded. "Well, yes, but that's not all. You believe in what you're doing. It's even more than that. You know what you're doing is right. Believing is great, but *knowing* is something special." He waved a hand beneath my stump where my foot used to be. "It doesn't matter what isn't here . . ." He then laid the same hand on my chest. "What matters is what's here, and in here, Chase . . . You've got the goods."

The nurse returned wearing gloves and rolling a cart. She carefully cleaned my wound, applied ointment, and rebandaged the site. Watching her work, it occurred to me that Singer had done exactly the same: He'd listened, inspecting the wound inside my psyche. He cleaned the wound by helping me understand the questions from my dream. And he bandaged my wound by encouraging me to deal with my new hurdle the same way I'd overcome the hand injury. Mongo may have been the smart one, but I think Singer, somehow, got a double helping of wisdom.

When she disposed of the leftovers, the nurse gave me a genuine smile. "Are you ready for some more pain meds?"

"Do you have anything that won't make me sleepy?"

"We have Tylenol, but that won't do much to hold off the pain. Dr. Smithfield ordered the narcotics. It's not good to let the previous dose completely wear off before we issue the next one. It's better to keep them in your system. I can call the hospitalist if you want, but—"

"No, it's okay. Just give me what Dr. Smithfield ordered. I could probably use the rest."

She produced a syringe and forced the drugs into my IV. The warm, familiar feeling of the medicine crawling through my veins and making its way to my heart sent me turning to see my friend and counselor. "Thank you, Singer."

He patted my shoulder. "You never have to thank me, Chase. We're family, and family takes care of each other."

As my eyelids turned to lead, I whispered, "Oh . . . Hunter said . . . a . . . mission."

Singer nodded and flipped off the light above my head. "Yes, we've got a mission, but it can wait. For now, we're all here to look after you."

Chapter 5
We Have a Winner

By the end of the week, Dr. Smithfield had proven to be a man of his word. The first foot he built for me was a Corvette compared to the Soap Box Derby car they'd stuck on my stump at Walter Reed. It hurt every time my new heel struck the floor, but it hurt like a real foot. I could deal with the pain. It was something I understood.

I'd never been out of shape. When I left high school, I believed I was in the best shape I'd ever be. I was 6'4" and 190 pounds. At the end of my freshman season at UGA, I'd added twenty pounds of lean muscle, shaved thirty seconds off my mile, and bench-pressed 305. The day my world came crashing down around me in Omaha, Nebraska, I was stronger than every member of the team and only slightly slower than our lightning-legged shortstop. When I graduated from The Ranch, I was even stronger and faster than I'd ever been. Since that day, I'd held myself to a demanding standard. No one outworked me on the battlefield. I fought harder, swam farther, and dug deeper than everyone around me, especially my enemy. All of that changed the day I left my foot in West Africa.

The lean muscle I'd worn for fifteen years softened as I learned to walk with a robot hanging beneath my right knee. Running was out of the question, swimming wasn't an option, and bicycling bored me to tears. But boredom was the least of my sorrows. Watching my team train up in preparation for a mission I would watch from the sidelines left my heart shredded inside my chest.

Ginger, the only analyst on Earth more talented than Skipper, was back in Silver Spring, Maryland, but Skipper stayed behind. She claimed she needed to be in the ops center to gear up for the coming mission, but Penny had a different theory.

"You know she's staying because she's worried about you, right?"

"There's no reason for her to worry," I said. "I'm getting around just fine, and she's probably right. The team does need her involvement while they ramp up."

My wife and chief nurse rolled her eyes. "You're delusional, but you've got a great big pieced-together family worried sick about you."

"It's not easy," I said. "I'm not good at being sidelined."

She sighed. "I know, but you've got plenty to do while you're healing and learning to use that new foot."

"Of course, you're right. I'm looking forward to getting back in school. I've wanted to get some post-grad work under my belt since I left Georgia."

"I'm sure that'll keep you busy. How long will it take to get your master's?"

"I don't know, but I plan to get my PhD at some point. We'll see how it goes."

She let out a laugh. "When was the last time you didn't accomplish something you set out to do?"

"It's not really an accomplishment. I just have to write a few papers, sit still for a while, and pay my tuition."

"I think there's a little more to it than that, but I have faith in you."

I pulled her against me for a long, warm hug. She shied away from my prosthetic, and I silently wondered which one of us would be the first to accept it as part of our life.

She leaned back and looked up at me. "I've got some writing to do. Can you find something to keep yourself busy for a couple of hours before dinner?"

I motioned up the stairs with my chin. "I think I'll sit in on the preliminary mission brief upstairs—if they'll have me."

She gave me a kiss and a gentle shove. "You own the house containing the ops center. They *have* to let you in."

I gave her a wink. "I think you're on to something there, Mrs. Fulton. Now, go get your writing done. The whole world is clamoring for a second screenplay out of you."

She moved silently down the hall and into her office with soundproofing almost as solid as the walls of the ops center. I stood at the bottom of the two flights of stairs and glared upward, dreading the clip-clop of dragging my foot up the steps. Involuntarily, my finger pressed the call button for the elevator, and I gained another pound.

On the third floor at Bonaventure, I pressed my thumb against the small, oblong reader and waited for the mysterious red light to compare my thumbprint to the seven others held inside the electronic sentry's digital brain. The amber light illuminated, indicating the first checkpoint had been successful. The next guard required a ten-digit access code entered in fewer than ten seconds after the thumbprint was accepted. On the other side of the door, a tone sounded, and a red light glowed above the access door to warn the occupants of the ops center that the door would soon open, breaking the seal between the security of the room and the space outside.

I met the time limit with my code and waited for the telltale click that would follow six seconds later. The window of time was designed to allow Skipper, or whoever happened to be in command of the ops center, to darken the displays, cease conversation, and cover any classified material on the conference table.

The fifteen seconds it took for me to access one of the most secure facilities in any private residence in the country gave me time to further question my place on the other side of the door.

Will I have anything meaningful to add to the discussion? Do I truly have a bona fide need to know about what's being discussed, debated, and planned? Will someone inside recognize my lack of legitimacy and kick me out of a room in my own house?

My fear was relieved when Mongo looked up from his place at the head of the table. "We wondered where you were. Get in here. We need you."

The giant rose, surrendering the chair I'd occupied since the construction of the ops center after an arsonist burned the two-hundred-year-old house that had been in my mother's family since its original construction.

I held up a hand. "Keep your seat, Mongo. It belongs to you now."

He grimaced. "No, it'll never be mine. But I'm honored to keep it warm until you're back to full strength."

"Don't let me interrupt," I said.

"You're not interrupting. In fact, we were just talking about you. We could use your insight on this one. I'll let Skipper bring you up to speed, and we'll continue from there."

I pulled out a chair opposite Mongo and met the eyes of the men and women who'd been my brothers and sisters-at-arms.

Disco, the most recent member of the team, nodded first. "It's good to see you, Chase. Welcome back."

"I'm not back," I said. "I'm just a consultant at best."

He let out a huff. "Ha! We'll see about that."

Disco had come aboard the same time we bought the Citation jet. His pocketful of aeronautical licenses and his career as an A-10 Warthog pilot made him the perfect fit to fill some holes we had on the team. Although Clark and I were well-qualified pilots, Clark's upward movement into the role of handler instead of operator left him behind on most missions, and my primary responsibility was to lead the team when the bullets started flying. I didn't need to be tied to a cockpit when I should've been returning fire.

Singer, the Southern Baptist sniper and my personal spiritual advisor, filled his roles flawlessly.

Mongo, the team leader in my absence, was a commanding presence, at least initially, based solely on his size. At six feet eight inches tall and approaching three hundred pounds, he was impossible to ignore, but his mass was far from his most impressive trait. His intellect and overwhelming ability to retain massive volumes of information most people would forget made him a leader on and off the battlefield. Those of us who'd fought alongside him would never hesitate to follow him into the fire.

Stone Hunter, the one man who'd be my partner when and if I leapt into the fray without the rest of the team, came with an equally impressive résumé. His experience and training as an Air Force combat controller, working alongside Army Special Forces and Navy SEALs on battlefields across the globe, more than qualified him for his position on our team. His major strengths were his prowess in the water, coupled with his absolute fearlessness in the face of danger. If he had a weakness, it would be his refusal to retreat, even when outnumbered and outgunned. I would fight beside Hunter without hesitation against any foe willing to draw his blade against us.

The woman at the briefing console of the ops center was the heart of our team. She'd demonstrated an innate ability to operate as the team's analyst under the tutelage of Ginger, one of the world's most elite intelligence analysts. Skipper's command of technology and her ability to manage unbelievable amounts of information efficiently and effectively made her the one irreplaceable member of the team. The fact that she was the daughter of my beloved baseball coach from UGA only made her more important in my life. She was sassy, brilliant, and sometimes demanding, but finding someone to fill her shoes was a task I prayed I'd never have to undertake.

Mongo pointed a meaty finger toward the screen. "Give Chase the condensed version."

Skipper's fingers danced across the keyboard like those of a concert pianist on stage at Carnegie Hall. "Take a look at this map," she said. The screen came to life with an aerial shot of Central America. "It shows the northern coast of Colombia, specifically the port city of Barranquilla."

I said, "Yeah, I know Barranquilla. I went to Carnival there with my parents when I was ten or eleven."

She groaned at the interruption. "Okay, anyway. Carnival is what the city is known for, but it's one of Colombia's busiest port cities. The reason Barranquilla is on our radar, though, is because it's the mouth of the Magdalena River. There's an up-and-coming drug cartel run by a guy named Macario Mateo. He's a particularly nasty boy, but we'll go into that later. For now, what you need to know is that his right-hand man is an American named Simon Benoit. Simon, as it turns out, is quite the gifted engineer and naval architect. I'm still working on his real name and background, but for now, all you need to know is that he designed and built several minisubs that aren't all that mini. They're capable of carrying fifteen thousand pounds of cocaine. Just so you'll know, that much cocaine has a street value in the States of around half a billion dollars."

She paused for a drink as I tried to digest the number. "How many of these things are there?"

She recapped her water bottle and held up a finger. "Now, that's the right question, and the answer is . . . we don't know. We don't know exactly how they work yet, but here's what we and the DEA believe. The minisubs are the most mechanically and technologically advanced submersibles ever used in drug trafficking. Simon Benoit, the engineer, is an undisputed genius. We believe he designed and built these things to be almost undetectable, and here's the kicker. If they are detected and captured, they blow themselves up before authorities can defuse the explosives built into the hull. We've captured two of them. The first one lasted thirty hours before it blew itself to bits, killing four DEA agents and two Coast Guard officers."

"What about the second one?" I asked.

"We were a little more careful with that one. We quickly X-rayed it, photographed it, and took samples of the payload. It was pure, uncut, Colombian cocaine. We towed it into shallow water off the Florida Keys and waited for it to kill itself, which it did twenty-two hours after we captured it."

"Why was there such a difference in delays between the first and second self-destruction?" I asked.

"We don't know that, either, but thanks to the topography of the ocean floor in the shallow water off the Keys, we recovered about fifty-five percent of the debris. Some of it was small enough to be carried by the current or disappear into the sandy bottom. Here's what the big-brained folks at ATF and DEA came up with . . ."

She slid a binder across the table, and I unwrapped the rubber band holding it closed.

Thumbing through the reports inside was agonizing, so I closed the file and turned to our own big brain. "What does this mean, Mongo?"

He said, "It's pretty simple, really, but it's ingenious. The hull of the sub is actually two hulls, twenty-two point five inches apart. In that void, our boy Simon built a massive battery. The entire hull of the sub is its power source. Previous, less-sophisticated versions had more conventional batteries stacked and wired in series, but this thing is leaps and bounds ahead of anything we've seen before. It's pretty sexy, if you think about it. Instead of piling batteries wherever they could find a spot, they built the boat out of batteries."

"But even that's not enough power to get fifteen thousand pounds of payload to the States all the way from Colombia, is it?"

"No, it isn't," Mongo said, "but it's enough to give it a lot of capabilities the earlier versions didn't have, like GPS and INS."

"What's INS?"

"INS is inertial navigation system. It detects the direction and velocity of the sub while it's underwater, giving it the ability to always know roughly where it is and what course corrections are required to hit its waypoints and final destination."

I raised an eyebrow. "So, this thing is the smartphone version of the narco-sub?"

"That's one way to put it," Mongo said. "But it's more than that. You may have seen the notes about the umbilical in the file. Nobody seems to know what it's for, but I have a theory."

"I'd put money on your theory over anything the government guys can come up with, so let's hear it."

He said, "It's not really a theory yet. It's more of a hypothesis. I believe the umbilical is a hawser and a charging cable."

I leaned in. "You have my attention. Don't quit now."

He turned to Skipper. "Forgive me for jumping ahead."

She waved a hand. "By all means, the floor is yours."

He said, "These things are sailing down the Magdalena River from the town of Magangué. They may do it by themselves, but more likely, they're towed by a small boat assisted by the gentle current of the river. When they hit open water in the Caribbean, they come to life and travel northwest toward the Caymans. Based on the rough calculations I've done, the minisub can likely travel about eight hundred miles before running out of juice. That's when the umbilical comes in. I think the thing goes almost dormant at a depth of maybe fifty feet and floats a homing buoy. The signal is picked up by a small freighter or a big commercial fishing vessel. Of course, the captain and crew of the surface vessel are in on the scheme and either paid well or threatened badly. The cartel is known for both. I think a surface ship picks up the umbilical and tows the minisub while simultaneously charging the massive battery. When the battery is back to life, they cut it loose, and it continues its pre-programmed route to South Florida."

He stopped talking as if I were supposed to say something prophetic, but instead, I said, "Let me guess. Our job is to catch one of these things and figure out how to keep it from blowing itself up."

Skipper hit a key on her computer, producing a sound like a ringing bell at the check-in counter of a no-tell motel.

Hunter said, "Ding! Tell him what he's won, Johnny."

Chapter 6
No, Earl. No!

"That's why you're in charge," Mongo said. "Your head gets to the finish line a little before everyone else's."

I rolled my chair back a couple of feet and threw my prosthetic onto the table. "Perhaps that's why I *was* in charge before they stuck this thing on what's left of my leg. Now the team's all yours, Mongo. Besides, you and Skipper are the big brains in this outfit."

Mongo laughed. "Don't get too excited about retirement, big boy. I'm just filling in until you get back in shape."

Hunter leaned over the table as if inspecting my leg. "Speaking of shape, yours is expanding a little. You might want to lay off the cupcakes before you start getting soft like Clark."

I threw a pencil at him. "Take your shots at me, but don't pick on Clark when he's not here to defend himself."

He knocked the pencil from the air in true Bruce Lee fashion and said, "Clark can take it, but if you keep getting fat, you're going to have to increase the capacity of that elevator of yours."

"Let's talk about the minisubs," I said. "I'll roll you down the stairs later."

I pulled the binder from the table and thumbed through the specifications we knew. "How deep do we think this thing can go?"

Mongo scratched his chin. "We don't really know, but I have a theory on that, as well."

"I knew you would," I said.

He held his hands about two feet apart. "The hull of these things is almost two feet thick, so the actual crush depth is probably hundreds of feet. The batteries are mostly gel, so they're not compressible. That gives the hull incredible strength. We don't have enough data yet to understand the circuitry, but I'd put money on the fact that there's a run-deep-and-hide mode written in the code."

"What does that mean?" I asked.

He continued. "If I were building them, I'd include a process to let the sub know when it was being tracked by sonar. If it detected a sonar lock, I'd make it shut itself down, start a clock, and sink."

"A clock?" Hunter said. "Why would it need to start a clock?"

Mongo said, "So it would know when to come back to life. It has a limited amount of compressed air on board to blow the water ballasts and return to the surface. The limited amount of compressed air is why I doubt it runs very deep. The deeper it goes, just like when we're scuba diving, the more air it takes to blow its ballasts. I didn't see anything in the radar images that indicated an onboard air compressor, so they're limited in the number of times they can dive and surface. Diving is easy. It just opens the ballast doors and takes on water, but getting rid of that water takes air pressure, and a lot of it."

I said, "That brings us back to my original question . . . with some modification. How deep do you think these things run when they're operational?"

Mongo said, "The winch cable they use to float the locator buoy is sixty-six feet long. We recovered the entire cable, unscathed, after the second one we caught. That means when it's ready to recharge and be towed, it's no deeper than sixty-six feet at the location of the winch."

I slapped my palm onto the table. "Listen to my question, and answer it with a number. How deep do you think these things run when they're operational?"

Mongo grimaced. "Fifty feet, but there are a lot of factors . . ."

"Perfect," I said. "Don't make this more complicated than it is. Now, how much noise does this thing make when running at fifty feet deep?"

Mongo curled a finger, and I slid the binder across the table to him.

He stuck his head containing the big brain of his into the binder. When he emerged, he said, "Not much. Maybe forty to sixty decibels. That's about the volume of normal speech—a little louder than we're talking now."

I asked, "Just out of curiosity, how loud is a nuclear submarine?"

To my surprise, Hunter spoke up. "Ninety to a hundred and twenty decibels, depending on its configuration and maneuvers. The more it changes direction in the water, the louder it gets, but it's never louder than a car horn, except when it's blowing ballasts. That gets really loud."

I cocked my head. "How do you know this stuff?"

"You know how much I love the water, and I read a lot. You don't know my life. Don't judge me, Cap'n Peg Leg."

I turned to Mongo, and he nodded.

"Hunter's right."

"Forgive me for doubting you," I said. "But the peg-leg thing was a little hurtful. I'm sensitive, you know."

Hunter rolled his eyes. "I'll try to be more thoughtful in the future . . . or not."

"We'll come back to your sensitivity issues in a minute, but for now, I need to know if these things are loud enough to track with hydrophones."

It was Mongo's turn to show off again. "First, you have to understand that sound is measured differently in water than in the air. Generally, scientists agree that sounds measured underwater are based on the reference intensity of the sound wave with a pressure of one micropascal, while sound moving through the air is generally agreed to be measured based on an intensity of twenty micropascals. Therefore, what we have to . . ."

I glared across the table. "I'm going to take my foot off and beat you to death with it if you don't start answering my questions in English. Plain old regular English."

Mongo bit his lip to suppress his laughter, but no one else in the room did. When the decibel pascals—or whatever they're called—calmed down, Mongo said, "Yeah, it's loud enough to track with high-quality hydrophones, but they'd need to be *really* good, like the ones on the towed arrays of our military subs."

"Now we're getting somewhere," I said. "I've got a crazy idea."

"Those are our favorite kind of ideas out of you," Hunter said. "Let's hear it."

"First, I have to know if anybody in this room is smart enough to build an electromagnetic pulse generator."

Hunter lowered an eyebrow, and Mongo stuck a pencil in his mouth, but Skipper grinned and said, "That's why I love you, Chase. You're exactly the right amount of crazy. Yeah, we can build one, but we don't need to. I've got a guy who'll sell us one."

Singer, who'd been silent until that moment, said, "I've got ten bucks on Mongo."

Everyone in the room turned to face our sniper.

Hunter said, "What are you talking about?"

Singer grinned. "I don't think Chase can beat Mongo to death with his prosthetic while hopping around on one foot. That, and I bet Mongo can build a better one than we can buy."

Mongo said, "Sure, I can build one, but making it waterproof is the problem."

"How about your source, Skipper? Are they waterproof?"

Instead of answering, she held up a finger before turning away to her keyboard. Seconds later, she swiveled in her chair. "How big? How many? How soon?"

Every eye in the room turned to me.

I said, "I don't know, but here's my idea. If we can find this thing and track it, maybe we can catch it with DVPs, attach some lift bags, blast it with an electromagnetic pulse generator, and let it die. When we fry its circuitry, it won't know to blow itself up. That means we can study it all we want without being afraid of it."

Mongo shuddered. "First, you're completely insane, and only you and Hunter are crazy enough to chase one of these things with a diver propulsion vehicle. Second, that's not only brilliant, but also the craziest plan I've ever heard."

Hunter snapped his fingers. "How big is an EMP generator?"

Everyone turned back to Skipper, and she began typing. After a minute of conversation with her source, she said, "They're big . . . and heavy. What's the minimum voltage we'd need to stop this thing?"

Mongo closed both eyes, and the wheels started turning. Seconds later, he thumbed through the binder. "Fifty kilovolts with a duration of six seconds."

Skipper typed and waited. When the response came, she spun back to face the table. "Seventy pounds, and three feet by two feet."

I locked eyes with Mongo. "Are you sure fifty kilovolts are enough?"

He nodded. "Definitely, but that box is an anchor in the water. There's no way to get a DPV to pull it fast enough to catch the sub."

I could almost feel the blood pumping through my body. The excitement of putting a mission together was almost enough to forget I wouldn't be the one in the water chasing the minisub. As good as it felt, the sickening truth of my inability to rejoin the team in the field left me feeling like I'd been stabbed.

"Are you okay, Chase?" Mongo asked. "You don't look so good all of a sudden."

"I'm okay. I just don't like how it feels to be left behind." Before anyone had time to respond, I said, "Ask your guy if he can make a streamline version that looks like a missile."

Her fingers flew across the keyboard.

Mongo said, "If Skipper's guy can't build it, we can take his stock version and adapt it. Earl can build anything I can design, so even if he can't do it, we can."

Skipper shook her head. "It's a no."

"How many do we need?" I asked no one in particular.

Mongo said, "At least three."

"Order five. How long will it take for them to get here?"

"They're a hundred grand apiece!" she said.

I eyed Mongo. "If you have one to play with, can you build more?"

He smiled and nodded.

"Order six," I said. "And get them here ASAP. Clark will pay for them."

Skipper placed the order, and I dialed Earl's number.

She answered with a line that was pure Earl. "This better be Stud Muffin."

"It's me, old girl. How's it going?"

"I'm lovin' on my man, so this better be good."

"Thanks a lot, Earl. That's not a picture I needed in my head. I've got a job for you, if you're up for it."

"You're just jealous 'cause you're too young to know what good lovin' really is. What's this job of yours?"

"Again, I don't want to think about you and Cajun Kenny getting your lovin' on. I need you to build a couple torpedoes for me."

"Torpedoes, you say?"

"Well, sort of," I admitted. "I want to put an EMP generator inside a streamline container so I can tow it through the water with a diver propulsion vehicle. Can you build something like that?"

"Sure I can, Baby Boy, but there ain't no need in towing the thing. I can put a motor in it."

"That's why I love you, Earl. How long will it take?"

"I don't know. It depends on a lot of factors, like how long my man intends on keeping me on the edge of paradise."

"Stop it! I'm going to throw up. The machines will be here in two days." I turned to Skipper, and she nodded. "Yeah, two days and Mongo will draw up what we need."

She said, "I'll have this fine man of mine melting like butter in ten minutes, and I'll be ready to go to work as soon as your gadgets get here. I'm not far away, Sugar Britches. I'm at Kenny's house, so just let me know when you're ready for me to start welding."

"Go do whatever you do to Kenny, but don't hurt him. I'll call you in a couple of days."

"He likes it when Momma hurts him just a little."

"No, Earl. Just no! There are limits to what I'm capable of filtering out."

Chapter 7
Time to Call Daddy

I hung up and tried to brief the team on the conversation with Earl without gagging. I managed to leave out the colorful parts and keep my breakfast in my stomach.

I asked, "Can you plot eight hundred miles northwest of Barranquilla for me?"

Skipper sent the map of the Caribbean back onto the screen and plotted a rhumb line from Barranquilla to the Yucatan Peninsula with five hash marks in the northern third of the line.

"What am I looking at?" I asked.

"Just what you asked for, plus a little more," she said. "The rhumb line is the likely course of the subs, and the hash marks delineate every one hundred miles from six hundred to a thousand—just in case Mongo's range prediction of eight hundred miles isn't spot on."

I said, "Would you look at that? This is starting to look like a trip to the Caymans."

"That's quite convenient," Skipper said, "but we don't think the surface support vessel comes from the Caymans. It's more likely that it comes from someplace on the Yucatan Peninsula, most likely around Cancun. This makes the most sense if we're going with the charging-while-towing theory."

I watched the scenario play out in my mind's eye. A surface support vessel designed to look like a commercial fishing vessel or small cargo ship could leave Cancun, sailing southeast and listening for the beacon. "Tell me about the beacon they float."

Mongo grinned. "Believe it or not, we have one. The DEA guys were smart enough to chop it off the winch cable and have it analyzed. It works like an emergency position-indicating radio beacon, but not on the typical frequencies. If they floated a marine EPIRB, every vessel in the area and every airplane overhead would react. The latest and greatest EPIRB, as of nineteen ninety-eight, broadcasts on four hundred six megahertz and sends both a distress call as well as a precise location through both geostationary and polar-orbiting satellites. The one we plucked off the second sub we captured was even more high-tech than those."

"What makes them more high-tech?" I asked.

Mongo took on his professorial look and leaned toward me. "It's complicated. I'll use small words so you can keep up."

"Singer may win the bet . . . I may not be able to beat you to death with my foot, but that won't stop me from trying."

He smiled. "You don't want to risk breaking that foot of yours. It's really not *that* complicated. Every carrier wave in a radio transmission has a pair of sidebands that contain information using the carrier wave as the vehicle."

"You've not lost me yet," I said. "I understand sidebands, so keep going."

He said, "This Simon Benoit guy is a lot smarter than the average bear. He's found a way to hang things that I'm calling side-sidebands above and below the original sidebands that can only be heard and deciphered by a receiver that's specifically designed to receive the side-sideband signals. That's where he's transmitting the position data. It would appear only as slight static in the background of a conventional receiver. When we catch these guys, I call dibs on Benoit. I want to dig around in his head before he goes to prison."

I tried to digest what Mongo had described. "How did we catch the two subs if we can't decipher their transmissions?"

"Frankly, we got lucky," he said. "The first one hit a Coast Guard cutter when it surfaced in relatively shallow water about a hundred miles north of Key West. The second one was reported by a fishing boat when it apparently snatched their purse seine net not far from the spot where we picked up the first one."

"We can't count on luck," I said. "We have to manufacture our own. How long will it take you to build a receiver that can talk to the EPIRB?"

Mongo shook his head. "I can't do it, but the guys who worked for Dominic and built the radios and jamming equipment for the Mark V could do it. Does Clark still have them on retainer, or did they disappear with his dad?"

Skipper spoke up. "We've still got them. I'm calling them now."

I said, "When you get them, put them on the phone with Mongo. He can explain what we need. Then, get a time estimate."

She nodded, and Mongo spun in his chair and rolled to the console by her.

Hunter eyed the room and rolled beside me. Barely above a whisper, he asked, "Are you getting wet on this one?"

I'd almost forgotten about the load of titanium, carbon-fiber, and electronics hanging from what remained of my right leg. I let out a long sigh. "No, I'm not going."

He said, "There's nobody else good enough in the water, and I can't do it alone. Between managing the EMP generator and chasing the sub, if it runs, it's a two-man job at best. We're going to need another SEAL."

I shuddered as the memory of the six SEALs who'd given their lives on the previous mission poured through my head. "I can't do it."

Hunter nodded. "I know, but by the time they work the kinks out of that foot and you get back in shape, you'll be back in the water where you belong."

"That's not what I meant. I can't ask the SEALs to come with us again after what happened last time."

"I get it, but Mongo's too big. Singer's too important on the surface. I don't even know if Disco knows how to dive. And Clark's spine can't take the stress if we have to wrestle with that thing underwater. Who else is there?"

I called across the table. "Disco, do you know how to dive?"

"You mean, like scuba diving?"

"Yeah, exactly like that."

"I learned a long time ago," he said. "But I've not done it in years. Why?"

"We're looking for volunteers," I said.

Skipper handed a headset to Mongo and rolled toward Hunter and me. "What are you guys talking about?"

"We need at least two combat-level divers if we're going to chase down one of those subs. Normally, that would be Hunter and me, but . . ." I waggled my prosthetic in front of her.

"I wish I could do it," she said.

"Me too, but there's a big difference between exploring coral reefs and the kind of diving we're talking about."

She put on her conspiratorial look. "What about Anya?"

I didn't hesitate. "No, for a thousand reasons. The first two are we don't know where she is, and she's too much of a wildcard for team ops. There's no way to predict if she could keep her head inside the team bubble long enough to make it through the mission."

Skipper checked over her shoulder. "Actually, only one of those things is true. I know where she is, and I know how to contact her."

I shook her off. "It's still a hard no. There's too much on the line. We can't have her going rogue on this one."

"I'm with Chase," Hunter said. "She's great in the water, but if she goes off the reservation, it's my life on the line down there."

Skipper stared at the floor for a moment before looking up. "What about Tony?"

Hunter asked, "Who's Tony?"

I stared back, wide-eyed. "Tony? Clark's brother, Tony? You're former boyfriend, Tony?"

She smiled part of a sincere smile. "Yeah, that Tony. He's good in the water, and you know he's itching to get back in the game."

"What do you mean, *back* in the game?" I asked.

"He's out of the Coast Guard and running a ferry boat to Ocracoke Island on the Outer Banks. He's scrubbing barnacles off boat hulls to make some extra cash."

Hunter knocked on the table. "Who's Tony?"

Skipper rolled her eyes. "Jeez, try to keep up. He's Clark's younger brother, and he was a rescue swimmer in the Coast Guard for seven years. He's like a fish in the water. And . . . he and I had a *thing* a few years ago."

Hunter gave her the hairy eyeball. "A *thing*? Like Chase and Anya's *thing*?"

She shoved him. "No! Not like that. He's never been a Russian assassin."

Hunter threw up his hands in surrender. "Don't bite my head off. I was just asking. So, how good is he in the water? Has he been to the combat diver's course in Key West?"

"I don't know, but probably. Should I give him a call?"

"Not yet," I said. "I think it's time to call Daddy first."

Skipper said, "I think you're right. He should be out of his Pentagon thing by now."

"Pentagon thing?" I asked.

"Yeah, he had some bigwig Homeland Security briefing or something. That's why he wasn't in on this powwow. I'll hit him up as soon as Mongo gets off the phone with the geeks."

No sooner than she'd said the words, Mongo pulled off the headset and laid it on the console. "They're in, but they need to get their hands on the EPIRB. Do you think you can make that happen?"

I said, "I can't, but Clark probably can. He's hobnobbing with the big brass as we speak."

To my surprise, Mongo didn't question the hobnobbing. He said, "Okay, they're standing by and ready to move at a moment's notice. They seemed excited about the job."

"I'm sure they did," I said. "That's right down their alley."

Skipper took command of the room. "We're calling Clark to brief him up and get him on board. If anybody needs to hit the head or get a drink, now's the time."

Mock salutes came from around the table, but no one moved.

Thirty seconds later, Clark's voice came over the speaker. "It's about time you called. Do we have a plan?"

"We've got *most* of a plan," Skipper said. "But we still have a few missing pieces only you can put in place."

"Let's hear it."

She said, "Here's the *Reader's Digest* version. We need your dad's tech geeks to build a radio that can hear and decipher the EPIRB the subs use. Mongo has them standing by, but they need to get their hands on the transmitter from one of the subs. The last I knew, it was in the custody of the DEA. Can you get them access to it?"

"Sure, no problem. What else?"

She continued. "When we build the radio, we plan to get to the sub before the surface-support vessel gets there. The timing may not work out, but even if it doesn't, that okay. We'll tail the tow vessel until they cut it loose again. After that, we can find it with the sonar from the Mark V. Here's the good part. Are you ready for this?"

"Spit it out!" Clark demanded.

"We're going to put two divers in the water with DPVs and an electromagnetic pulse generator. They're going to chase down the sub, kill its electronics, float it, and deliver it to whoever you say the appropriate authorities are. I guess the Coast Guard or DEA."

"Slow down," Clark said, "I've got three questions. First, where are we going to get a waterproof EMP generator? Second, besides Hunter, who's the other diver? And third, this was Chase's crazy idea, wasn't it?"

She said, "First, we aren't getting just one. Six of them will be here tomorrow or the next day. Second, we've got two possible options for a second diver—Anya or your brother Tony. And third, of course it was Chase's idea. Other than you, he's the only one insane enough to come up with a scheme like this."

Clark clicked his tongue against his teeth. "I like everything about it except Anya and the part about turning the sub over to somebody else. Count her out, and count Tony in. He calls me every other day begging for work."

"Does that mean you can get the EPIRB in the geeks' hands?" I asked.

"Don't worry about that. It's a piece of cake. How soon will you be ready for Tony?"

"We're ready now," Hunter said. "I'll need a good week in the water with him to train up before we go wheels-up."

"He'll be there as soon as Disco gets back from picking him up on the Outer Banks."

"Give me a contact number, and I'll be airborne in thirty minutes," Disco said.

Skipper scribbled Tony's number on a scrap of paper and slid it to our chief pilot.

I asked, "Is there anything else?"

Clark said, "Yeah, there's one more thing. If you were the one who came up with the idea of having Anya jump in on this one, I'm ordering you to punch yourself in the throat as hard as you can."

Chapter 8
It's Funny to Me

Disco made a grand entrance by sliding our Amphibious Cessna Caravan onto the North River and drifting her to a perfect stop, kissing the edge of the floating dock with her port side float. I watched the show from one of my favorite spots on the planet—the grand gazebo housing the eighteenth-century cannon Clark and I pulled from the mud and muck on the bottom of Cumber-land Sound.

A pair of green duffel bags were the first things to emerge from the Caravan and land with thuds on the dock. The bags were followed by a pair of well-worn boots attached to the two *healthy* feet of ferry captain and former Coast Guard rescue swimmer Tony Johnson. I didn't have to look behind me to know who'd just emerged from the kitchen door and bounded down the gallery steps.

Skipper met Tony before he'd made it off the dock. For a moment, the scene resembled that of a sailor, home from war, right up to the instant when they *didn't* kiss. The glow in Tony's eyes said he wanted to, but Skipper had matured and grown more cautious about everything in her life in the years since the two had seen each other. The misunderstanding that drove them apart was all but forgotten, and the little voice in my head told me the two would soon be inseparable again.

I stood from my Adirondack chair, situating my new foot beneath me before striding from the gazebo.

Tony stuck out a hand without dropping his bags and tried not to look down at my leg. "You don't know how much this means to me, Chase. I really appreciate the opportunity."

I shook the hand and caught a strap from the bag on his right shoulder. "I'll take one of these. And you may change your mind about being happy to be here by the time Hunter gets finished with you."

"Who's Hunter?" he asked.

The approaching footfalls behind me said I wouldn't have to make the introduction. Stone W. Hunter stepped beside me and eyed our newest potential teammate from stem to stern without saying a word.

Tony stuck out his hand again. "You must be Hunter. I'm Tony Johnson."

Hunter ignored his hand and pointed across the river. "See those two rags hanging in the marsh grass out there?"

Tony withdrew his offered hand and turned. "Let me guess. We're racing across and back to see who can get back on this side with his rag first."

"Close, but no cigar," Hunter said. "You'd better beat me back here with both of them, or it's going to be a long, wet bus ride back to your ferryboat job."

Before Tony could react, Hunter sprinted for the dock. He beat the rescue swimmer into the water by at least five running strides, but Tony didn't appear concerned. He dived from the end of the dock and sliced into the water like an Olympic swimmer. When he resurfaced, he closed on Hunter by at least half the lead my partner held when he left the dock.

Having spent hundreds of hours in the water with Hunter, I didn't envy the next fifteen minutes of Tony's life.

Skipper shook her head. "What are they doing?"

"Establishing a baseline," I said. "Hunter needs to know how comfortable Tony is in the water."

"But that's a race—not a comfort test."

"It only *looks* like a race. Just watch."

Skipper and I stepped aboard *Aegis*, our fifty-foot, custom sailing catamaran, and climbed to the upper deck to get ringside seats for the coming melee.

"He's catching him," she said.

"He's *letting* him catch him."

She laughed. "I don't think so."

Almost before she could finish her thought, Hunter vanished beneath the surface of the black water. In his determination to catch my partner, Tony didn't seem to notice Hunter's absence in front of him, but that was about to change.

Seconds later, it was Tony's turn to disappear, but not by choice. Knowing what was coming, I watched Hunter's hand and forearm protrude from the water beside Tony's head, hook his neck, and drag him below the instant before Tony would've rolled his face out of the water for his next breath.

Skipper gasped.

I said, "Get a deep breath, and try to hold it until they come back up."

She frowned in confusion before realizing what I'd suggested. When it occurred to her, she inhaled deeply and held her breath. I made no effort to compete with the men in the river or the analyst by my side. A glance at my watch told me one minute had passed since Hunter vanished and forty-five seconds for Tony. Hunter had the decided advantage, having taken a long, full breath before descending, but Tony's breath was depleted before being dragged under.

A minute and a half passed, and I turned to Skipper as her eyes bulged and her face turned red.

The need to breathe overtook her. She let out the breath she'd been holding and gasped for a fresh replacement. "I hope Tony doesn't hurt him."

"Oh, they're hurting each other, but they're each learning a thousand things about the other." I checked my watch. "They've been down for two minutes. It's about time to see at least one head."

"Just one?" she said, panic creeping into her tone.

"Don't worry. It'll be Tony's head."

Right on cue, Tony's face—mud-covered and confident—emerged above the inky surface. He took two deep, loading breaths and descended back into Hunter's playground. The water roiled above the two combatants as a pair of bottlenose dolphins surfaced downstream, moving directly toward the battle. Perhaps one of the dolphins was Prowler, the U.S. Navy–trained dolphin who patrolled the sound outside Naval Submarine Base Kings Bay in search of things that shouldn't approach the top-secret facility.

I returned my focus to the site of the battle and watched my partner's body roll, face-up, and out of the water with Tony's arm laced forcefully around his midsection.

Skipper leapt onto her tiptoes. "Oh, Tony's got him. I told you he was going to win."

I playfully elbowed her. "Tony just allowed Hunter to get a breath, and that was the worst thing he could've done."

Clearly cheering for her former love, Skipper squeezed the rail, leaning over to yell her encouragement. "You've got this, Tony! Keep fighting!"

Another two minutes passed, and a muddy hand rose from the water, slapping at the surface in a wasted attempt to find purchase. I'd played that game with Hunter more times than I cared to remember, but I'd never forget the burning in my chest and the rising panic in my head as I realized my exhausted body required more oxygen than it could find, and I just wanted the fight to end. I believed that was exactly where Tony had found himself.

"Don't worry," I said. "Hunter won't let him pass out. They're too far from shore. He can't revive him in the water. If he was going to let him black out, he'd drag him to the bank first."

She couldn't take her eyes away from the last spot we saw Hunter roll to the surface. "I think Tony might let Hunter pass out, though." I silently laughed and propped up against the corner of the rail. "Some popcorn would be nice. I love shows like this."

She slapped at my knee. "Stop it. This isn't funny."

"Oh, it's funny to me because I've been there too many times to count."

Another glance at my watch reassured me the battle was coming to an end, so I scanned the surface, expecting to see Tony's head pop up any second. I was rewarded with exactly what I expected. Tony's head and shoulders emerged, driven by Hunter's lift. That's always how he ended the episode—shoving his student into the air so he could refill his lungs and recover from the exercise.

Unlike I had done the first time when Hunter put me through my paces in the water, Tony took one breath, spun on the surface, and spotted the two rags still hanging in the marsh grass twenty yards away. A second breath preceded his powerful swimming stroke toward the trophies. Hunter would never admit to being impressed by anything the Coastie did in the water, but I was pleased and surprised by his determination, if nothing else.

Hunter nonchalantly emerged and took a long clearing breath, followed by shorter normalizing inhalations. He dragged a hand across his face to clear the black mud from his eyes. Obviously expecting to see Tony treading water inches away, my partner spun through a full revolution in search of his student, only to find him powering toward the rags. He slapped the water and let out an obscenity as he buried his face back into the river and kicked toward the objective.

As much as I hated to admit it, Tony was faster than Hunter on the surface. His extra height and reach made the difference. Hunter's size made him hard to handle in a wrestling match. He could squirm clear of even Mongo's grasp, but Tony's six-foot wingspan made his swimming strokes longer and more powerful.

When the Coastie reached the rags, he checked over his shoulder to find Hunter two strokes behind. He snatched the rags from the grass and kicked against the mucky bottom, propelling himself southward with the gentle current. Instead of staying on the surface where his speed would be a clear and unsurmountable advantage, he dived beneath the surface, choosing stealth over speed, and I grinned.

The same instant Tony vanished underwater, Hunter stopped stroking and looked up, hoping to find the rags, but their absence sent him into another water-slapping fit. He looked across the river at Skipper and me on *Aegis*'s upper deck. I gave my partner a signal with an ever-so-slight tilt of my head downstream. He likely didn't need the hint from me since Skipper was staring south of my partner and bouncing on the balls of her feet.

Hunter turned south and scanned the surface in vain. Tony wasn't leaving so much as a bubble for Hunter to chase, but that didn't stop him. He kicked and stroked to the south, occasionally gliding beneath the surface for a few seconds before returning to the top and continuing the pursuit. As his frustration grew, demonstrated by his ever-increasing radical search pattern, he dug harder and faster with every stroke.

Hunter lived up to his name, scouring the surface and probing the depths, while Tony continued somewhere none of us could see. My partner came to a water-treading stop in the middle of the river and yelled, "How long has he been down?"

"Three and a half," I shouted back.

Hunter spun through another complete rotation, scanning in every direction. "If he doesn't show in half a minute, splash the boat. We've got to find him."

"Skipper, stay here and watch for him to surface. I'm going to get the RHIB into the water."

I hopped down the ladder and clomped across the cockpit deck to the davits holding the rigid hull inflatable boat. I lowered the boat and clumsily crawled aboard. The engine came to life at the touch of the key, and I shot a glance upward. "Any sign of him yet?"

Skipper shook her head as panic overtook the look of excitement she'd worn a minute before. "No. Chase, you've got to find him!"

I checked the time and didn't like what I saw. Four minutes is too long for anyone to remain submerged, even if they are an elite rescue swimmer. Shoving the RHIB away from *Aegis*'s stern, I added power and pointed the bow toward my partner. In twenty seconds, I scooped Hunter from the water and deposited him on deck.

He shook off the water from his face. "Are you sure he went downstream?" I nodded, and he said, "Hit the sonar wide scan. That's our only chance of finding him."

"It's already scanning. Point the way," I said over the hum of the engine.

He motioned across the water slightly downstream from the Bonaventure dock. "Give it a burst, then neutral. We don't want to chop him up with the prop."

I gave the throttle a shove and then pulled the engine into neutral to stop the propeller from becoming a SaladShooter. Staring down at the sonar while Hunter scanned the surface of the river, I said, "Got him!"

Hunter leapt from the bow and landed his eyes on the sonar screen as I drove my finger against the figure on the display ten feet below the surface.

My partner shook his head. "That's not him. That's the two dolphins that were playing with us. How long?"

"Just over five minutes," I said. "But he could still be . . ."

Hunter said, "No, I beat him up pretty good. If he's still in the water, he's blacked out. I knew I was pushing him too hard."

I didn't want to believe Hunter was right, but it was undeniable. Nobody could survive a submerged fight with him and then spend five minutes underwater. The horrible thought of the drowned body of Clark's brother tumbling lifeless along the bottom of the North River sickened me, but the terrible realization that Anya was now our only option felt like a double kick in the gut.

I looked up in desperation, hoping Skipper had spotted Tony from her elevated vantage point. I prayed to see her pointing into the water somewhere downstream, but it wasn't to be. Instead, she'd stopped watching the river and turned away to face her once and future love standing behind her on *Aegis*'s upper deck, covered in mud, dripping wet, and holding a pair of rags in his teeth.

Chapter 9
SODA

Hunter and I motored back to *Aegis*'s stern and hoisted the RHIB back onto her davits.

Tony leaned over the upper deck rail. "I hope I didn't hurt you, Mr. Hunter. Is that as rough as it's going to get?"

Hunter didn't look up. "If you ever call me mister again, I'll show you just how rough it can get. Get down from there before Chase shoots you for getting his boat dirty."

Tony stepped over the rail and dived into the water. With his fingers spread wide, he scrubbed most of the mud from his face and hair before climbing onto the dock, where Skipper met him with the freshwater hose. He pulled off his boots, pants, and shirt, and took the nozzle from her hand. Skipper stood, mouth agape, and stared at the filthy, water-soaked, mostly naked man.

Hunter snatched the hose from Tony and washed off most of the mud from his clothes, then he cast a thumb toward his student. "Check it out, Chase. Have you ever seen a grown man without any bullet holes in him?" He tossed the nozzle back to Tony and stepped toward him.

The look in Tony's eyes said he was at least a little afraid of what Hunter was about to do.

Instead of shoving him back into the water or giving him his first bullet hole, Hunter traced the outline of Tony's sculpted abs with his finger. "Wow! Those are real. How many sit-ups can you do?"

Tony shrugged. "I don't know . . . maybe a couple hundred in two minutes. Why?"

Hunter nodded as if thoroughly impressed. "Great! That'll come in handy next time we get into a sit-up battle with a gang of raping, burning, pillaging terrorists. Don't you think so, Chase?"

I gave him a look. "Have you seriously never been shot or stabbed?"

The swimmer frowned. "No. I've never been shot or stabbed. Have you?"

Hunter and I chuckled, and I said, "Stick around. That'll change. Oh, and you might want to think about not skipping leg day at the gym."

Tony looked down at my prosthetic. "You may call it *leg* day, but the rest of us call it *legs* day."

Hunter's laughing fit forced him to take a knee. When he caught his breath, he said, "Oh, now, that's funny, kid. You're going to do just fine around here."

I motioned toward the house. "You two jackasses get cleaned up and put on some clothes, for God's sake. I'm buying dinner."

Skipper stepped in front of me, grabbed a handful of my shirt, and growled, "Don't you dare get him shot!"

Hunter climbed backed to his feet and threw an arm around Tony. "Come on, kid. I'll wash your back, and you can help me with my hair."

Skipper scooped up Tony's filthy clothes and followed him and Hunter up the steps to the back gallery.

Disco untied the Caravan from the dock. "Come on, Chase. Let's take this thing back to the airport."

It occurred to me that I hadn't been in the cockpit of an airplane since I lost my foot, so I pointed down at my robot.

Disco huffed. "You can still push a rudder pedal with it, can't you?"

"I guess we'll find out."

He climbed across to the right seat, and I lugged myself up the ladder to the left. Even sitting still at the dock, it felt amazing to have the yoke in my hands again.

Disco tossed a laminated checklist into my lap. "Are you going to make love to it or fly it?"

I grinned like a kid at Christmas. "Maybe both."

The turbine spun up, and I lit the fire. Taking advantage of the Caravan's reversing propeller, I backed us away from the dock and pointed the nose down the river. With the before-takeoff checklist complete, I added power and felt the workhorse accelerate beneath me.

We climbed out over Cumberland Sound. A pack of wild horses galloped along the shoreline of the island, and a few of them glanced up to see the giant noisemaker disrupting their dinner, but most of them ignored us.

I soaked in the magnificence of flight and forgot all about my missing parts. I leveled off at a thousand feet above the water and started a gentle turn toward the airport. As I scanned for other air traffic in the area, I felt and heard the turbine stop making power. My eyes were instantly back inside the cockpit, and my right hand flew toward the throttle, prop, and condition levers.

Disco slapped my hand away. "Simulated turbine failure."

My late-afternoon joyride had just turned into a biennial flight review, and the airplane headed for the water. An aircraft as heavy as the Caravan, with amphib floats hanging beneath her, made a terrible glider. She fell like a rock, and I picked out a landing site.

In that moment, I swore I could feel the right rudder pedal beneath my boot-clad, manmade foot.

The approach was steep, but I put us on the water as gently as anyone—including Disco—could.

As we settled into the water, he said, "Good. Power is restored. Show me a confined area circling takeoff, but hold it a foot off the water."

I performed the maneuver and flew with the keels a few inches off the water.

"Nice," he said. "Now land the left float but keep the right one flying."

I landed the floats individually to his satisfaction.

"Not bad. Now, fly the RNAV-two-two approach into Fernandina Beach."

I climbed away from the Sound and called the controller. "Jacksonville Approach, Caravan two-zero-eight-Charlie-Foxtrot one mile east of Saint Marys, request the RNAV-two-two at Fernandina Beach. It'll terminate to a VFR miss to the northwest."

The controller's voice came through my headset as if she were sitting right beside me. "Caravan two-zero-eight-Charlie-Fox squawk zero-two-five-four and Kilo is current at Fernandina."

I pressed the button. "Roger, zero-two-five-four in the box, and we have Kilo, eight-Charlie-Fox."

I loaded the approach into the GPS, and the controller said, "Eight-Charlie-Fox, radar contact position as reported. Cleared to the Fernandina Beach Airport direct IFWOC. Cross IFWOC at two thousand, cleared RNAV-two-two approach."

I replied, "Cleared to the airport direct IFWOC. We'll cross at two. Cleared approach. Eight-Charlie-Fox."

I activated the autopilot, and Disco immediately pulled the breaker to disable it. "Oh, no, you don't. Fly it by hand."

I flew the approach exactly by the plate and climbed away from the airport to the northwest.

When the tower controller switched us back to the approach controller, Disco keyed up. "Departure, eight-Charlie-Fox is back with you off Fernandina. We'll cancel instruments and continue VFR to the northwest."

"Roger, zero-Charlie-Fox. IFR cancelation received, squawk and maintain VFR. Good day."

Disco turned to me. "How's that foot?"

"It almost feels real."

He nodded. "Good. Take me home, and we'll get you a soda."

"A soda? When was the last time you saw me drink a soda? They're called Cokes here in the South, by the way."

"I'm from Tennessee," he said. "I know what they're called, but I'm not talking about a Coke, Fly Boy. I'm talking about a Statement of Demonstrated Ability—a SODA. I'll write the letter, and we'll get the flight surgeon to reissue your medical. With that new foot of yours, I don't see any reason why you can't safely operate anything that flies."

Although it should've, the thought of my prosthetic preventing me from meeting the aeromedical standards for flight hadn't entered my mind.

"Just to be certain, let's hover the chopper around a little before you go see the flight doc. But I have no doubt that you'll do fine."

I landed at what used to be the Saint Marys Municipal Airport before the city council sold it to Clark and me. The paperwork was still in the works, but it would eventually become Bonaventure Landing private airport.

We towed the Caravan into her hangar and tugged out the Bell 412. I demonstrated my ability to taxi, hover, takeoff, fly, and land with the contraption almost as complex as the chopper attached to my leg.

"Did that feel all right?" Disco asked after I set the helicopter down on its cart.

"Felt fine," I said. "Thanks for doing this. I needed the time back in the sky. It was good for my sanity . . . if I have any left."

He pulled off his headset and unfastened his buckle. "We need you back in the cockpit almost as much as we need you back in the field with us. Pardon the pun, but this is just *step* one."

"Oh, so now you're jumping on the pun train, too. I thought you and I had something special, but clearly you're on *their* team."

He chuckled. "I thought you said we're not a team. We're a family."

"I'd never say anything meaningful like that. Now, get out of *my* helicopter."

It wasn't graceful, but I managed to climb down from the cart without falling on my face, and Disco pulled the chopper back into the hangar.

When he returned, he said, "While we're talking about *your* airplanes, I'm sure *your* Mustang misses you."

After making my way into the hangar, I looked up at the beautiful old warbird and remembered the first time I'd ever seen her. My mentor and favorite psychology professor had owned her when she wore the nose art of *Katerina's Heart*. She became mine when he made the final takeoff of his life and left the P-51D Mustang to me in his will. My first time inside the cockpit was a day I'd never forget. Dr. Richter stuck me in the front seat and flew me from Athens, Georgia, into a world I never knew existed—a world that would become mine, or perhaps a world that would ultimately own me.

I slid my hand across the leading edge of her elegantly powerful wing and let my fingers slip inside the openings where the 30-caliber machine guns had once lived, breathed, fought, and won over the skies of Europe in 1945. Three of the four holes now housed plugged barrels of mock machine guns that couldn't fire a shot if they had to, but one still housed a live thirty-cal machine gun with which I'd single-handedly taken on a Russian spy ship off the coast of Georgia—the American Georgia, not the Black Sea Georgia—and survived . . . barely. What was left of the tattered, torn, wounded, and weary airframe and her twelve-cylinder power plant pouring black smoke brought me all the way home in what should've been her final day on Earth. But fate, good fortune, and a brilliant mechanic, Cotton Jackson, brought her back from death's door in grand fashion. Dr. Richter's glamorous nose art depicting the only woman he'd ever loved—the beautiful, dark-haired Soviet KGB officer, Katerina Burinkova—was replaced by the equally beautiful Penny Thomas wearing a mischievous smile above the banner of *Penny's Secret*. The Cold War took Katerina from him, but I prayed the two of them were sitting beside Heaven's most beautiful river, holding hands and drinking tea with honey, without the dark cloud of communism hanging over their heads.

Looking up at my wife smiling down from the cowling of the Mustang, I wondered if *my* war would take me from her. Perhaps, it was already doing so . . . one piece at a time.

Chapter 10
Something Complex

The security system alerted me to a pair of vehicles coming up the tree-lined drive, and I stepped outside to find the delivery driver and Earl arriving simultaneously. Earl wasted no time establishing her dominance. "Pull around the north side of the house, and follow the drive to the shop. Unless you're unloading them yourself, you need to back in as close as possible to the doors."

I had nothing to add, so I waddled down the stairs and followed the driver toward Bonaventure's shop. Earl unlocked the door with her key that I didn't remember giving her, and she hit the lights. Seconds later, she sent the heavy sliding doors along their tracks and directed the driver with a mysterious collection of hand signals, leaving me grateful not to be at the wheel of the truck. Soon, the hiss of the airbrakes echoed off the concrete block walls of the shop.

Before the driver could slide down from the cab, Earl had the roll-up door on the back of his truck ascending with a rattle and the forklift I didn't know we owned heading for the opening. With skill I never knew she had, Earl eased the forks beneath the first pallet and had it situated on the floor of the shop in no time. The second pallet required a chain to pull it into the forklift's range, but just like the first one, she made short work of the process while the driver stood in disbelief of one woman's ability to do so much so quickly.

I stepped beside him. "Not bad, huh?"

He exchanged glances between me and Earl and laughed. "Yeah, you could say that. We could really use her at the warehouse."

"You couldn't afford her," I said. "Besides, a woman as beautiful as her tends to disrupt the workflow in male-dominated workplace."

The driver stared at all five feet and two hundred pounds of the best diesel mechanic and metal fabricator I've ever met and shuddered. He shoved a clipboard toward me. "Whatever you say, man. Just sign here."

I chuckled along with him and signed his paperwork. He and his truck disappeared without offering Earl a job in the warehouse.

I pulled the doors closed and watched Earl unbox the first electromagnetic pulse generator. She carefully cut the cardboard away, revealing a solid black metal box with a single electrical cord protruding from one corner and a small panel on the front with four buttons and a digital screen. The contraption was bulky, rectangular, and anything but waterproof.

Earl pocketed her knife, stepped back, and scratched her head of short gray hair protruding in every direction. She let out a guttural sound of disapproval and stared down at the contraption. "I'm afraid I may have let my dollar mouth overload my nickel ass on this one."

I let the statement bounce around inside my head a few times before saying, "I know I'm going to regret asking, but what on earth does that mean?"

She alternately scratched her head and the part of her anatomy she apparently thought was only worth a nickel. "It means I said I could do it before I saw how much work it'll be. If it was anybody but you, Baby Boy, I'd throw in the towel and walk away. But I told you I'd do it, so I will, even though I was in the mindless throes of passion and intimacy with my man when I said it."

I plugged my ears. "No! I was on the verge of getting that picture out of my head, and you just ruined it for me. I'm going back home and scrubbing out my ears. You just do . . . whatever it is you do out here, and turn at least one of those things into a submarine."

The remainder of my morning was spent convincing the flight surgeon I was still medically fit to fly. Just as he'd promised, Disco provided a letter supporting my Statement of Demonstrated Ability, but he went further than that. He sat right beside me and described the flight review he'd put me through, leaving no detail unexplored.

The flight surgeon listened intently, then pulled off his glasses. "I want to see you do it."

"See me do what?"

"I want to see you fly. Do you have access to an airplane, Mr. Fulton?"

I gave Disco a sideward glance. "I think we can round one up. Do you have any particular airplane in mind?"

The doctor said, "Something complex would be good."

"Do you mean complex by the FAA's description of complex, or do you mean something that's difficult to fly?"

He furrowed his brow. "I can't require you to demonstrate your ability in an aircraft that is above your skill level, but I'd feel better about signing my name to this application if I saw you fly something that falls into both descriptions of complex."

"I've got just the thing," I said. "Do you have a tailwheel endorsement, Doc?"

He hesitantly said, "I do."

"Good. So, does that mean you're okay issuing me a temporary certificate so I can demonstrate my ability in a two-seat taildragger?"

I could see his mental listing of two-seat taildraggers running through his mind, and finally, he said, "Sure. I'm good with that."

I turned to Disco and let the unspoken question float between us. He grinned and gave me the thumbs-up.

I said, "Have your nurse cancel your appointments for the next two hours, and we'll knock this out."

He checked his watch and pulled a sheet of paper from beneath his desk phone. He studied the paper, then slid it back under the phone. "I've got two and a half hours before my next appointment. Can you arrange for the airplane in that time?"

I nodded and stood. Disco couldn't stop giggling beneath his breath, and I couldn't wait to get to the airport.

The flight surgeon followed us through the security gate at the airport, and we pulled up beside our main hangar.

Disco jumped out of the car and waited for the doctor to do the same. When he had, Disco said, "I'll need to move a couple of airplanes out of the way to get to the taildragger. Give me a few minutes."

The doctor and I leaned against the hood of his Mercedes while Disco made a show of pulling out the amphibious Caravan, then the Citation jet, and then the helicopter.

The doctor eyed every flying machine with fascination. "Are all of these yours?"

"All of these are *ours*," I said. But when Disco tugged the P-51 Mustang from the darkened interior of the hangar, I pointed at the old girl with pride overflowing. "That one is *mine*."

The doctor pushed off from the fender of his Mercedes and slowly approached the Mustang, his mouth agape. "You've got to be messing with me. That's the taildragger you're talking about?"

"The very one," I said. "You told me you'd like to see me fly something complex. Can you think of anything that fits that description more accurately?"

He couldn't take his eyes from the gleaming skin of the sixty-year-old airplane that shined like it had come off the production line the day before. He stammered. "I, uh . . . But I'm not, uh . . . I mean, I can't land that thing if you . . ." He motioned toward my prosthetic.

I threw an arm around him. "Don't worry, Doc. I promise to put you back on the ground with your hair on fire and a permanent grin on your face."

The pre-flight inspection took ten minutes, and the doctor never got more than one pace away from me. He touched every piece I touched, and his fascination with the warbird seemed to grow every time his fingertips brushed her skin.

"Well, Doc, if she'll start, I think she'll fly. What do you think?"

He didn't—or couldn't—speak.

I climbed into the rear seat—the same seat Dr. Richter had taken the first time I ever saw the Mustang—and Disco helped the flight surgeon into the front. I went through the pre-start checklist while Disco briefed the procedures for removing the harness and opening the canopy in the event of an emergency.

"You're sitting on the parachute," Disco said, "but Chase has a track record of staying with an airplane until every piece stops moving, even if she's coming apart around him. Do you have any questions?"

I glanced up to see the doctor shaking his head. His grin was almost visible through the back of his head.

Disco slapped him on the shoulder. "Have fun, Doc. You're a braver man than me."

With that, Disco leapt from the wing and gave me a sharp salute. I returned the respect and started the propeller spinning through its enormous arc. Five blades passed the windshield, and the twelve-cylinder, supercharged Merlin engine took her first breath of the day. The propeller became a blur, and the rumble of the engine filled our chests with the anticipation of what was to come.

Without hundreds of pounds of thirty-cal, linked rounds in the wings, and the burden of external fuel tanks hanging beneath the hardpoints, *Penny's Secret* leapt off the deck as if she loathed the ground and ignored gravity.

I held the nose low and the wings level as the machine accelerated only feet above the runway. When the airport fence disappeared beneath the nose, I put the stick in my lap and pinned the doctor's head to the seat. The excess energy I'd allowed the plane to amass over the runway bled off as I traded airspeed for altitude. At two thousand feet, I rolled the wings level, but with the wrong side of the airplane facing the earth. Cumberland Island passed beneath us at two hundred fifty miles per hour.

"Are you okay up there, Doc?"

His answer came by way of the laughter of a child, and I took that as an affirmative.

I rolled back over until the wheels were once again beneath us, and we climbed over the coast. "Have you ever done an Immelmann?"

"Not yet!"

I chuckled. "Does that mean you've not *done* one yet, or you're not *ready* to do one yet?"

"Oh, I'm ready," he said.

"When the nose comes up, hold your breath and tighten your stomach muscles as tight as you can. That'll keep you from blacking out."

I flew two clearing turns to make sure there was no one in our way, then I lowered the nose and eased the throttle forward. The speed came up nicely, and once again, I put the stick in my lap, sending the propeller skyward. The doctor groaned and grunted against the g-forces pushing him into his seat. As the airspeed fell, I kept pulling, forcing the nose through vertical and back in the direction we'd come. As the horizon approached, I snap-rolled to the left, freezing the nose on the horizon.

"How was that?" I asked.

He let out a long breath. "Incredible."

"How do you feel about a Split S? That's essentially the opposite of the Immelmann."

"Oh, I know what it is, but I've never done one."

"You're about to," I said. "But this time, you're not going to be a passenger. Take the controls."

I felt the shake of the stick as he grasped it up front and the shudder in the pedals as his feet landed on the forward set.

"Shake it around a little. Other than flying it into the ocean, there's nothing you can do to hurt it."

He made some gentle maneuvers, then pulled aggressively through a series of increasingly tighter turns.

"Nice, Doc. Now, let her settle in about two hundred, and put the nose on the horizon."

He did as I instructed.

I said, "I'll stay on the controls with you for this one, but I'll only take them if you try to kill us. Okay?"

"Okay."

"Now, pull the nose up about fifteen degrees and the throttle back to just above idle. Keep the wings level, and watch the airspeed indicator. When it falls through one-fifty, roll us left until we're inverted, then put the stick in your lap. Got it?"

"Oh, yeah," he said, and again, he did exactly as I instructed.

We rolled over, and he pulled the nose through the horizon, straight down, until we were in a beautiful dive right toward the blue Atlantic.

"Keep pulling," I said. "And slowly add throttle until we're in straight-and-level flight again."

He did, and we completed an almost perfect Split S.

I spent the remaining hour of our flight with my hands in my lap as the flight surgeon earned his first sixty minutes at the controls of a Mustang.

Back at the airport, he followed me through the landing with his hands and feet on the controls.

Instead of stopping on the runway, I added power and put us back in the sky. "She's all yours this time. Fly the numbers just like I did. She's a handful if you let her get too slow."

He took the controls and flew a long pattern, rolling out perfectly aligned with the runway on a four-mile final approach leg. As we descended on final, the airspeed bled off, and our sink rate became a little uncomfortable.

"Keep your speed up. You do not want to get behind the power curve in this airplane."

He lowered the nose and added enough power to arrest our descent and build our speed.

"Good. I've got your landing gear, flaps, and prop. Just fly the airplane. The gear will pitch the nose down, but the flaps will bring it back up. Be patient, but stay ahead of the airplane."

It wasn't pretty, but he eventually put three wheels on the concrete.

I said, "I have the controls."

We climbed back off the airport, and I surrendered the plane back to him. "You've got it all this time. I'll stay out of your way until I get scared."

He flew the same pattern as before and wrestled with the airplane all the way to the ground.

Just before touchdown, I said, "I have the controls." I lowered the nose to keep the tailwheel from striking first and brought the machine to rest at midfield. "She's all yours again, Doc. You'll want to do some S-turns as we taxi back to the hangar. That big engine is hard to see through."

With another ten thousand landings, I thought the doctor might learn to work with the Mustang instead of against her.

We shut down on the ramp outside the hangar and slid open the canopy.

I climbed from my seat and helped him from his harness. "So, what do you think about the Mustang?"

"She's absolutely breathtaking, and that prosthetic of yours is a nonissue, so you can consider your Statement of Demonstrated Ability as good as gold."

Chapter 11
I Tried to Warn You

With the formalities around my medical fitness to fly fulfilled, I felt at least a little closer to whole again. Flying has always been one of the few elements of my life that crossed the great divide between my professional responsibilities and my personal time. As I sat down for dinner beside Penny, I wondered if she would ever truly feel whole again. In my mind and heart, I viewed her as my anchor to sanity and normalcy, but I wanted her to understand the part of me that longed to step inside the fire.

The formal dining room at Bonaventure was, by far, the least occupied room in the house. For reasons I can't explain, the harvest table in the kitchen had been the heart of the house since long before my great-uncle, Judge Bernard Henry Huntsinger, claimed his great reward for a life well lived and bequeathed the property to me. Trying to predict how many people would arrive at that table for any given meal would be a figure no Vegas handicapper would dare try to guess.

That evening, eleven of us surrounded the table that had been built for sixteen, and we made the space appear far smaller than it was. Perhaps Mongo's presence played the greatest role in the optical illusion. Seeing him with his demure Russian friend, Irina, made my heart happy. They'd fallen together at the same instant her daughter, Tatiana, and Mongo fell in love. Tatiana—affectionately called Little Anya—had been a rising star in the Bolshoi before she and her mother, Irina, had become Americans. It had been Big Anya who facilitated the move, and the teenaged ballerina immediately wrapped our giant solidly around her little finger.

Skipper sat as close to Tony—the newest potential member of our team—as possible without her being in his lap. I liked seeing the two of them together. The analyst spent far too much time with her head stuck inside stacks of data and computer screens. She, like the rest of us, needed a life outside the realm of evil into which we were all too often thrust.

Tina Ramirez poured a second glass of wine for Hunter and reminded him, "If you're driving, this is your last glass."

"Who arranged all of this?" I asked as I slid my chair beneath the table.

Penny said, "We have Skipper to thank for this little get-together."

I raised my glass. "Here's to Skipper for always knowing exactly what we need before we need it."

She blushed. "Cut it out. It's just dinner, and there are too many of us to show up at some unsuspecting restaurant. I'm a terrible cook, so I ordered catering from the bed and breakfast."

The catering service included a pair of apron-clad servers to deliver and clear plate after plate of one of the best meals of my life. Throughout most of the meal, I forgot the ten-pound machine attached just below my right knee, and I felt, for the first time since the accident, like I was still a full partner of the team and family we'd become.

"I wish Clark and Maebelle were here." No sooner had Skipper spoken the words than the tone of the alarm system announced a vehicle coming up the drive.

"Be careful what you wish for," I said. "It looks like that one just came true."

Skipper's eyes widened, and she grabbed one of the server's wrists. "Please tell me you have enough food for two more."

"Relax, darlin'. We've got enough food for ten more."

Clark, Maebelle, and Charlie, the black lab, came bounding through the door, and I placed a finger to my lips. Everyone froze, and we could hear their footsteps—especially Charlie's—as they searched the house for us.

From the kitchen, Clark called, "Hello? Is anyone here?"

Charlie's nose gave us away. He galloped through the dining room door and issued a resounding bark. Soon thereafter, our family was complete, wine flowed, forks clanged against china, and we ate for over an hour.

When the meal was almost complete, the two servers delivered bowls of bread pudding that tasted like gooey gobs of Heaven in our mouths. Port and coffee accompanied the dessert, and soon, everyone—including Charlie—was headed for a food coma.

I said, "Cigars and brandy in the gazebo, anyone?"

Thirteen people and one spoiled black lab accepted the offer, and we headed for the kitchen door.

Clark lit up and inspected his Cuban. "No brandy for me, thanks, but this is one fine cigar."

I exhaled a plume of rich, aromatic smoke. "You couldn't be more correct."

He motioned toward the shop with the butt of his cigar. "A little birdie told me you were already hard at work on this narco-sub gig."

I nodded and stuck the cigar back into my mouth. "You'll have to talk to Earl and Mongo about that."

Earl wrapped a stumpy index finger around her cigar and pulled it from her lips. "You might say we're still in the research-

and-development stage. We've got the first EMP generator torn apart, and I fabricated the bottom half of the shell out of stainless steel."

"That sounds like a start," Clark said. "How long will it take to have it ready for testing in the water?"

Earl cocked her head to Mongo, and he said, "I think it'll take at least two more days before we're ready to splash the first one. It's a lot more complicated than I expected. The biggest problem is powering the thing. It's designed to run on two hundred twenty AC volts, but we can't drag an extension cord down with us."

Clark inspected his cigar. "That sounds like a no-go. What's the plan?"

Mongo spat a tiny piece of tobacco from his tongue. "I'll convert it to DC and power it with capacitors. We only need an instantaneous pulse. After it works one time, we're good."

Clark shrugged. "You're talking over my head, but if you say you can make it work, I trust you. What do you need from me?"

Earl jumped in. "We need you to stay out of our way, Pretty Boy."

Clark threw up his hands in surrender. "It's all yours. I just want the big picture."

Mongo reclaimed the floor. "The big picture is that we'll have a unit ready for sea trials in two days."

Earl held up a finger. "I almost forgot . . . While we're talking about the big picture, Kenny wanted me to pass some good news on to Chase."

I perked up. "I love good news from Cajun Kenny. Let's hear it."

"He wanted me to tell you that he'll have a crew ready to start building your boathouse on Monday. All the permits are approved, and he just needs your go-ahead and a check for materials."

"That *is* good news. Can I send the check with you?"

She grinned. "Sure you can, but that fine man won't be thinking about money tonight when I crawl into his bed smelling like Cuban cigar smoke, brandy, and all this sexiness."

I covered my ears again. "Earl! I told you to stop that. My poor ears are starting to bleed."

"I just love you to pieces, Stud Muffin. Kenny said ten grand will get him started."

Penny leapt to her feet. "I've got it, Chase. Just sit and enjoy yourself. I'll be right back."

She returned in five minutes with a banded stack of bills, then laid it in Earl's lap. "That's twenty thousand. Let us know when he needs more. Why didn't you bring him with you tonight?"

"That man needs his rest. I've got something special planned for him. Oh, and that reminds me. Do you think Chase would mind if I borrowed a set of jumper cables and that big torque wrench?"

Penny covered her ears.

"I tried to warn you," I said. "But you wouldn't listen."

With cigars reduced to ashes, the team adjourned to the ops center.

Clark slapped my hand as I reached for the elevator call button, and he shoved me toward the stairs. "Elevators are for men who *can't* take the steps. You're not one of those men."

His tough love had gotten me through some of the most challenging moments of my life, and that night was no exception. I climbed the two flights of stairs with him only inches behind me, threatening everything from kicks to stabs if I slowed down.

Once ensconced inside the secure ops center, Skipper briefed Clark on our plan. He listened and asked a few questions along the way. When she finished the briefing, he scratched his chin.

"I have one more question. How are you going to know when to start listening for the beacon?"

"I've been working on that, and to be honest, it's a little frustrating. The rainforest canopy prevents reliable satellite imagery, so we can't watch them send it down the river without a team on the ground to either wait and watch or set up some covert cameras. Without some insider information, we're playing a huge guessing game."

Disco rarely spoke during mission planning, but I was pleased to see him jump into the fray. He cleared his throat. "Uh, I've got an idea working here, but I haven't thought it through. How fast are these minisubs?"

Skipper scanned the room until her eyes landed on Mongo.

He said, "Fully loaded, these things can only make twelve to fifteen knots, tops."

Disco nodded. "And are we planning to stage out of the Caymans?"

This time, eyes fell on me.

"I don't know," I said. "If we're right about the surface-support vessel picking up the sub off the Yucatan, I think Cancun might be a better plan. That shortens the run from well over three hundred miles to seventy or so."

Clark bounced a pencil off the table. "That's certainly less opportunity for something to go wrong unless the Mexican military decides they want our patrol boat. We can put up a pretty good fight, but that's the ultimate example of being outnumbered."

Tony said, "I know I'm not really part of the team yet, but I've got an idea. There's a place called Isla Mujeres . . ."

Skipper shot a finger toward Tony. "What do you know about an island of women?"

He held up both hands. "Hey, I was single and . . ."

As much as I wanted to watch Tony continue to crawfish, I tossed him a line. "Isla Mujeres is a great idea, and they've got a nice little protected harbor and a decent airport."

"Decent enough for a Citation jet?" Disco asked.

"I'd have to do some checking, but I think so."

Disco said, "In that case, my idea is even better than I originally thought. I know this is going to sound crazy, but hear me out."

I slapped the table. "That's our favorite kind of plan."

He said, "There's a good airport in Barranquilla called Ernesto Cortissoz International. I've been in there a couple of times. I could take another guy, or maybe two, into Cortissoz in the Citation. We could hike up the river and report when they launch a sub. Then, we could beat feet back to the airport and head for Isla Mujeres. My geography isn't the best, but that's got to be around a thousand miles. We can make that in two and a half hours—a lot faster than the narco-sub."

Hunter pulled a piece of gum from his pocket, stuck it into his mouth, and tossed the wrapper at me. "How do you and that foot feel about a little hike in the jungle?"

Suddenly, the phantom pains were back as if Hunter had summoned them from the depths of Hell, and the jokes started to sting a little. Instead of answering, I bowed my head and concentrated on in-through-the-nose and out-through-the-mouth, coupled with my silent mantra—*The pain isn't real . . . The pain isn't real.*

As if he could see into my soul, Hunter sighed and turned to Tony. "How about you, kid? How are you in the jungle?"

Tony didn't miss a beat. "I'm almost as good in the jungle as I am in the water. Remember that time I kicked your ass, swam the width of the river underwater, and still got the girl?"

Hunter scoffed. "How are those ribs I pummeled while you thought you were kicking my ass?"

Tony pulled up his shirt. "Still bruised a little, but if I were your age, I'm sure it would take me weeks to get over the pain."

Hunter's eyes glazed over and darted around the room. "Okay, who's officially in charge?"

I pointed to Mongo, who was pointing at Clark, who was pointing back at the giant.

Hunter said, "Good. That's two votes for Mongo and one for Clark. Go ahead and approve Disco's jungle idea. I'm taking the kid and turning him into a man . . . if he can keep up."

Mongo and Clark locked eyes and nodded in unison. Following a man as big as Mongo was easy, but living up to his even larger expectations was a different matter. Perhaps the trait that made him the ultimate leader was the demands he placed on himself.

Mongo scribbled a line of notes and looked up. "Earl and I will have the EMP generator ready for sea trials tomorrow night."

"Tomorrow night?" I asked. "I thought you said it would take at least two more days."

He pushed his notebook away and leaned back. "That was before I knew Disco was going to take Hunter and Tony to play jungle rat. There's a lot of water work to do before we can deploy, so I'm not willing to be the reason it costs us another day." He turned to Earl. "We'll get it done, right?"

She grimaced. "We can try, but there's a lot we don't know. Until we get the thing in the water, everything's still theoretical."

Mongo snapped his fingers. "That's exactly why we'll put something in the water in thirty-six hours. It won't be pretty or final, but it'll be a working prototype."

Everyone turned back to me, and I held up a hand. "Don't look at me. I'm a rear echelon troop on this gig. I can watch and listen from here in the ops center, but Mongo's the commander in the field."

Mongo stuffed his notebook beneath his arm. "Yep, but we're not in the field yet. We're still in planning and R and D. That means you're still the boss until we go wheels-up."

Chapter 12
Wind Against Tide

Dawn broke over Bonaventure to find Hunter, Tony, Mongo, and Earl hard at work in the shop. Even the bag of sausage biscuits and tray of coffee I delivered couldn't draw them from their toil.

"That thing is starting to look like a submarine," I said.

Mongo looked up but didn't take his hands from inside the machine. "Yeah, it's coming along, but I'm still working on a plan to power it and keep the weight down."

I leaned in and examined the device. "Take me through it if you have time."

"Sure. Just give me a minute. I'm working on a blind connection, and I'm afraid if I let go of it, I'll never find it again."

I unwrapped a biscuit and stuck it in his mouth. He took a size-appropriate bite, and I laid the other half on the worktable.

An audible click sounded from deep inside the pile of components, and Mongo sighed. "Finally." He snatched the remaining biscuit and devoured it as if he hadn't eaten in days. Wiping the crumbs from his mouth, he began the tour. "We started by dismantling a complete EMP generator and rebuilding it in a configuration that would fit inside our pod. That's what we're calling Earl's shell—a pod. I have it reassembled and operational, but we have to power it. The problem is, this thing is a power hog. If I pack enough batteries inside the pod to generate enough pulse to accomplish our mission, it'll add a hundred pounds to the package, and we'll never be able to get it neutrally buoyant. It'll sink like a rock. If we increase the volume of the pod to accommodate the extra weight, it'll be too big to drag through the water. You remember Archimedes' principle, right?"

I said, "Sure. An object is buoyed upward by a force equal to the weight of the liquid it displaces."

"Very good. Our problem—well, one of our problems—is the fact that this thing weighs three hundred thirty pounds, but it only displaces four point five cubic feet of water. That's two hundred eighty-eight pounds of salt water. Earl is fabricating an extension to increase the displacement."

"That sounds easy enough," I said. "But what's your plan for power?"

Mongo looked over my shoulder at the fast-food bag behind me. "Are there any more of those biscuits? Those are pretty good."

I handed him the bag, and he unwrapped another. With crumbs falling from his face, he said, "I've been thinking about a stack of capacitors and one battery to keep them charged. I think I can do that and keep the weight of the power system under sixty pounds."

"Sixty pounds doesn't sound like much," I said. "But that thing is going to be a monster to drag through the water. I'm not sure the diver propulsion vehicles can pull it fast enough to catch the sub. Maybe it needs a dedicated DPV of its own."

Mongo dropped his biscuit and spun back to face his project. "A DPV of its own . . . That's brilliant, Chase."

I stood in silent awe as the wheels spun inside his enormous brain.

He yelled, "Hunter! Get over here."

My partner scampered from the stool where he'd been holding metal plates in place for Earl to weld. "Yeah, what is it?"

"Two things. First, Chase brought biscuits and coffee. Second, I need a DPV."

Hunter pulled a pair of biscuits from the bag and tossed them to Earl and Tony. "I'll be right back."

As Hunter left the shop in high gear, I said, "Tell me what's going on inside that big brain of yours."

Mongo said, "The DPVs have batteries . . . Big batteries. I can build an umbilical that acts as both a tow cable and a power line."

"Do you mean you can power the EMP generator with the DPV? Is the battery big enough?"

"Yes to the first, and no to the second."

"What?"

"Yes, I can power the EMP generator from the DPV, but no, the battery isn't big enough. That's okay, though. It doesn't have to be. It just has to be big enough to keep the capacitors charged and provide that little extra the capacitors can't do."

"I'm following you," I said. "And I like it."

Mongo fabricated a four-wire umbilical around a section of 3/8th stainless-steel cable. He held up the cable like a proud father holding up his newborn. "All we need now is a pair of waterproof connections, and we're golden."

Hunter returned with a black, torpedo-shaped diver propulsion vehicle cradled in his arms. "Here you go. One DPV, just for you."

He hefted the device into Mongo's waiting arms, and seconds later, the giant had the DPV clamped to a worktable. He pulled panels from the device and soon had its guts exposed to the world. I watched with the fascination of a curious child, and I wanted to ask a thousand questions, but I feared Mongo would shortly have me dismantled and my guts exposed, as well. So, I remained a silent, fascinated observer.

Tony spoke up for the first time. "What we need is one of those SEAL delivery vehicles."

"Yeah, that would be great," I said. "There's just one problem. Those things are twenty-two feet long and weigh thirty thousand pounds."

Tony scoffed. "No way. Are they really that big?"

"Oh, yeah. They're huge. We could put one in the Mark V patrol boat, but our crane couldn't lift it off the deck."

The former rescue swimmer threw up his hands. "Okay, so maybe we don't need a SEAL Delivery Vehicle. It's a shame they don't have a smaller version."

Mongo tapped on the DPV. "They do, kid. They're called diver propulsion vehicles, and we own a dozen of them."

"Why can't we strap a dozen of them together and use them like an SDV?"

Mongo turned from his work. "You've still got that military mindset, kid. Out here in the real world, we use just enough to get the job done. Overkill is for the amateurs and government operations. We're clean, efficient, and quiet."

Hunter broke into a fit of uproarious laughter. When he finally caught his breath, he said, "We just got home from a mission where we flew the biggest airplane the U.S. owns into a tiny country in Western Africa and blew up a ship. Then we waterboarded a French national until he gave up the mastermind behind an international terror ring to steal five billion dollars from the American taxpayers. None of that was clean, efficient, or remotely quiet."

Mongo shrugged. "Yeah, well, other than that, we're pretty quiet."

Tony waved a finger around the shop. "You people. You're insane, and I love every one of you already. What can I do to help?"

Earl said, "You can stop talking and just look pretty. You're obviously good at that."

I said, "You'd better be careful, Earl. Penny lets you get away with calling me Stud Muffin, but Skipper may kill you in your sleep if you mess with her man."

Tony said, "I'm not her man. I mean . . . not really."

I laughed. "You just keep on believing that, but she's got her claws so deep in you that you'd bleed to death if you pulled away."

He rolled his eyes. "Whatever. She's too good for me."

"Oh, you're definitely right about that," I said. "And don't you forget it. She's too good for anybody, but from where I sit, it looks like you're the lucky winner. And she's got half a dozen big brothers who'll tear you apart if you ever do to her what she thought you did last time."

"But I didn't do anything. It was all a big misunderstanding."

"We all know that now, and now you know what'll happen if you ever do what she thought you did."

"I read you loud and clear. If she wants to try again, I'm all in. I'm not afraid of Hunter. He's old and soft, but the rest of you guys scare me a little."

Hunter strolled to the toolbox, slid open a drawer, and withdrew a screwdriver that must've been two feet long. He turned and eyed Tony. "Yep, this looks like the right tool to adjust your screwed-up sense of who to be afraid of."

I said, "Save it until we get home from the mission. We're going to need the kid at least until I can get back in the game."

Hunter bounced the oversized screwdriver off his palm. "Did you hear that, kid? Chase gave you a temporary stay of execution, so watch your step."

Tony stepped toward Hunter and threw an arm around his shoulder. "Don't worry, old man. I won't let anybody hurt you until Chase is back in shape to babysit you."

I knocked on the pod. "I've obviously disrupted important work. I'll go make sure the patrol boat is ready to go for tomorrow's sea trials. Let me know if you need anything."

Earl said, "That's one of the things I love about you, Stud Muffin. You know just when you've worn out your welcome."

* * *

Our Mark V patrol boat was eighty-two feet and fifty-seven tons of unmistakable nautical superiority. With Earl's rebuilt and highly modified diesels, she boasted just over five thousand horsepower capable of pushing the massive weapon across flat water in excess of fifty knots. Decked out with her full complement of weaponry, and manned by my team of warriors, the Mark V was a force to be reckoned with anywhere on the planet.

The engines took their first breaths in weeks as if they'd been run every day. Their thudding pulse echoed through my chest as the suite of electronics came to life. My goal when I stepped aboard was simply to make sure the boat was seaworthy for the following day's testing of Earl and Mongo's pet project, but everything about the boat said she wanted to go play.

With all systems checks complete, I tossed off the lines and backed the massive weapon away from the Bonaventure floating dock. In a display of terrible seamanship, I failed to check the tide, wind, and sea state before roaring off across Cumberland Sound. My poor planning was rewarded with an incoming tide against an outgoing wind, turning the Saint Marys Pass into a churning torrent of deadly walls of water. Aboard a lesser boat, a wise seaman would come about and return to the dock, but I wasn't aboard a lesser boat. I was aboard one of the world's most capable combat waterborne vessels, and on top of that, I've never claimed wisdom.

Instead of coming about and running for the safety of the dock, I leaned in and shoved the throttles to their stops.

What happened next was a fool's reward. The bow rose, blinding me to the cold North Atlantic ahead, but only seconds later, the bow plummeted, submarining and sending a wall of foamy water across the pilothouse. The massive boat became a rodeo bull, bucking and leaping as water sprayed in every direction. The wipers fought a losing battle against the flood of seawater cascading across the glass. The windshield could stop a fifty-caliber round, so the wall of water offered little threat.

The carnival ride was over in sixty seconds, and the Mark V and I found ourselves unleashed on the relatively calm Atlantic. Her speed was impressive, but the smooth, comfortable ride, courtesy of the pneumatic shock absorbers built into the seating, was one of the thousands of tiny elements that combined to make the patrol boat an irreplaceable piece of hardware. We spent half an hour patrolling the east coast of Georgia until I decided it was time to face the roiling waters of the pass one more time.

Getting back into Cumberland Sound was no more challenging than escaping her had been, leaving me grateful for the strength of the Mark V. Pulling the throttles back, I enjoyed a leisurely ride across the Sound and into the North River. A glance over my shoulder at the billowing waters of the pass showed me how treacherous the course had been, but the strength and adversity of the Mark V had weathered the torrent as if it were little more than gently rolling waves.

Maybe my injury—the loss of my foot—was simply wind against tide, and maybe what remained of my body and soul was just as strong—just as capable as the Mark V. Unlike a weaker man, I would lean in and face the waves, their fury, and their might. Perhaps I would stumble. Perhaps I would fall. But unlike those who lack the will and fortitude to return to their feet and continue the fight, I would stand again and again, refusing to be crushed, refusing to be halted, for the welcoming, peaceful waters beyond the battle called to me like the siren's song, promising what waited on the other side was worth everything I would lose in the fight.

Chapter 13
Sea Trials – Day 1

I'll never be the smartest guy in the room, even if I'm the only guy in the room, but I was smart enough to know I offered nothing but disruption anytime I walked into the shop with meaningful work going on. That knowledge kept me on the back gallery at Bonaventure, even though the light streaming from the windows in the workshop beckoned for me to come and disrupt.

My watch told me ten p.m. had come and gone, and the empty tumbler resting on the table to my right said it was time for another pour. Mongo's promise to have the EMP generator ready for sea trials had been overly ambitious, and everyone who heard the vow knew it. My team was made up of unequaled professionals who held themselves to standards that would terrify the people who consider themselves to be "normal." Mongo would rather work himself to death in that shop than admit he missed a self-imposed deadline.

One of the hallmarks of tier-one tactical operators is their insatiable need to torture each other. Only slightly less powerful than that need is our refusal to let our brothers suffer alone and unnecessarily. My team and I were no exception to these rules. With adherence to those unwritten rules being paramount, I set out on a one-man mission of sabotage. Technically, it wasn't really a one-man endeavor. I took four ounces of Gentleman Jack and seven ice cubes with me to the brown and tan VW Microbus sleeping peacefully in the drive. It took Jack and me fifteen minutes to disconnect the battery, and another five to stroll down the path to the shop.

Once inside the heavy metal doors, I was astonished to see how far the project had come . . . and how oddly its creators were behaving. Hanging from a pair of chains beneath the overhead crane was a gleaming, cigar-shaped metal tube, but that wasn't the most fascinating sight inside the shop. Mongo, the giant, stood erect and proud about ten feet in front of the tip of the torpedo, and resting on his shoulders was the greasy, sweaty, two-hundred-pound metal fabricator extraordinaire, Earl. She sat perched on his shoulders as if she'd been born in exactly that position. She sighted down the length of her creation with one eye squeezed tightly closed.

I said, "I'm not sure what kind of cheerleading practice I've interrupted here, but that thing looks a lot different than it did twelve hours ago."

Mongo shot me a look as if everything was completely normal. "We've made some good progress, but we still have a couple of hours left to go."

"Yeah, that's sort of why I'm here," I said. "I hate to put a damper on things, but I need your help."

Mongo leaned down toward a worktable, and Earl climbed from his shoulders. Then, he hefted her to the floor with barely a sound. I silently wondered how much weight he could throw around if the moment demanded it.

With Earl safely on the ground, he wiped his hands on his pants and said, "Sure, what do you need?"

"I'm pretty sure I left the hangar door open at the airport this afternoon, and the battery is dead in the Microbus. I need someone to give me a push to get it started."

Mongo motioned toward the tumbler in my hand. "Maybe somebody other than you and Jack should do the driving when we get the bus started."

I gave him a wink. "You know, that's a great observation. Why don't we shut this down for the night and jump back on it first thing tomorrow?"

Mongo checked his watch. "I really wanted to finish up tonight, but if you're sure you left the door open on the hangar, we need to take care of that. What do you think, Earl?"

She ran her hands through her spikey hair and wiped her brow. "I'm beat, so I think Chase's idea sounds good to me."

Mongo pressed the button on the crane's remote control, and the EMP generator slowly descended from its lofty suspension and came to rest on a cradle below.

I slid a hand across the surface of the device as it came to a stop in its bed. "Hey, that's not stainless steel."

Earl gave the torpedo a tap. "Nope. We abandoned the stainless and went with aluminum instead. It cut the weight in half and got us to right where we need to be for neutral buoyancy."

"Don't we sacrifice some durability, though?" I asked.

"We do, but this is a single-use weapon. It's not like it has to survive a thousand dives. If it does its job, it'll only get wet once in actual use. Besides, this one is just a prototype. There'll be plenty of modifications before we get to the final iteration."

"Mongo's been teaching you big words again, hasn't he, Old Girl?"

She threw a rubber mallet at me, and I caught it like Thor catches his hammer. And I didn't spill a drop of my trusty old friend, Jack.

We locked up the shop and headed for the tree-lined drive where the sabotaged Microbus waited.

When we arrived, Earl said, "Maybe I ought to take a look under the hood before we just assume it's a dead battery."

I panicked. "Uh . . . no! I mean, I'm sure it's the battery. I should've changed it months ago. I just need Mongo to give me a shove, and I can pop the clutch."

Earl held up a hand. "How about you just stay out of the way, and I'll do the clutch-popping. We wouldn't want you to drop that cocktail."

"Good thinking," I said.

She climbed in behind the wheel and slid the seat all the way forward. "Okay, big man. Give me a shove."

Mongo leaned a shoulder into the back of the Microbus, and it started rolling down the drive. With his heels digging into the crushed shell surface, he and the bus picked up speed.

Mongo gave one final shove and yelled, "Okay, Earl. Pop it!"

She did, and the old bus came to life.

As she and Mongo headed back toward the front steps of the house, I pulled my phone from my pocket and held it to my ear, pretending to answer a call that hadn't really come. Seconds later, I shoved the phone back into my pocket. "That was Disco. He remembered the hangar door and took care of it, so I guess all of this was for naught."

Mongo checked his watch and gave me a glare. "That's a pretty elaborate ruse to get me and Earl out of the shop. Don't you think?"

I raised my glass. "Hey, it worked, didn't it? I'll see you two in the morning. The boat is ready when you are."

He rolled his eyes. "There's two things you should know. Number one, you're terrible at faking a phone call. And two, you never forget to secure the hangar. Good night, Chase."

* * *

Fourteen hours later, Mongo lugged the aluminum tube onto the floating dock beside the Mark V, and Hunter maneuvered the onboard crane to lift the torpedo aboard. Tony had the three diver propulsion vehicles pre-positioned aboard the patrol boat, so we were almost ready to start the day's excitement.

Hunter asked, "What are we going to chase?"

I scratched my head. "That's a good question, but let's see how unruly that thing is before we add another variable to the equation."

"Suits me. Besides, I've got to babysit the kid until I know he's smart enough not to drown himself . . . or me."

Tony waggled a finger toward Hunter. "I learned something about you, old man. You're drown-proof. I think God must've given you a set of gills instead of lungs. I've never seen anybody who can stay underwater and fight longer than you."

"I guess that's why they call me Aqua-man," he said.

I shook my head. "Nobody calls you Aquaman, but I can think of a few other names starting with A that are fitting."

With all the required gear aboard, Hunter and Tony slid into their dry suits and inspected their rebreathers.

With the dive gear checked, Tony sat on the gunwale and studied the boat. "How did you guys get ahold of a Mark V?"

"It's good to have friends in low places," I said.

He grinned like an excited child. "How fast will it go?"

I motioned toward the pilothouse. "We'll cast off, and you can see for yourself."

Before Tony could assume command of the vessel, Penny leapt from the dock and across the starboard-side gunwale. "Oh no, you don't. I'm driving."

Tony looked up at me as if someone had stolen his favorite toy.

I shrugged. "What can I say? During peacetime, Penny is the captain."

"Darned right, I am," she said. "And don't you forget it. Where are we headed?"

Hunter said, "Let's run down to the Amelia River behind Fort Clinch. There's a nice sandy bottom down there. If this thing gets away from us, I'd rather pick it up out of the nice, clean sand than the mud and muck up here."

I'll never know how or where Penny learned her boat-handling skills, but she was a master at the helm. She could make boats do things they were never designed to do, and she made it look easy. If I wasn't afraid of her catching a bullet to the skull, I'd love to have her deploy with the team to catch the narco-sub.

She backed the Mark V off the dock and spun her around with a delicate touch none of the rest of us possessed. Tony stood just to Penny's left as she maneuvered the massive craft through the switchback turns in the North River.

When the river gave way and opened up into the Cumberland Sound, Penny turned north, and Hunter frowned. "Doesn't she know where the Amelia River is?"

I nodded. "She knows, but she wants to let Tony have a little fun."

Just as I expected, Penny pulled the throttles to neutral and stepped away from the helm. "She's all yours, Tony. Just don't hit the Earth or anything attached to it."

The former Coastie stepped to the helm and examined the controls. A minute later, he pressed the throttles forward, and the vessel responded like a sports car. He put the boat through her paces and laughed every time he made a turn.

After fifteen minutes of playtime, Penny shouldered him from the helm. "I have the controls."

He obediently stepped aside and surrendered the boat into Penny's more-than-capable hands. She made a long sweeping turn to the south and pointed the bow toward the mouth of the Amelia River. A pair of shrimp boats chugged their way toward the pass and open water at ten knots, so Penny gave them a wide berth to their stern.

It was impossible for the Mark V to go anywhere without becoming the center of attention, and that day was no exception. The crews of the shrimp boats lifted binoculars to their eyes and examined the massive black leviathan. Penny glanced over her shoulder at me as if asking permission to give them a show. I couldn't resist approving her request.

She set the throttles and trim tabs so the bow would stand up twenty feet into the air, and then she spun the wheel hard over to port and buried the starboard throttle. This sent the eighty-foot vessel spinning like a tornado and throwing a wall of water fifty feet into the air. The boat and all aboard were invisible from the shrimpers' perspective. After four complete revolutions, she cranked the wheel back to starboard and opened the port-side throttle. The boat rolled out of its spin and picked up speed. Once clear of the massive wakes she'd generated in the spinning turn, Penny spun the wheel until the bow pointed back into the center of her torrent. As the bow rose over the first massive wake, she shoved the throttles to their stops, and the enormous engines roared. The stern rose as the bow fell and became a submarine. The front third of the vessel vanished beneath the waves, sending two walls of water through the air. With masterful control, Penny spun the ship like a Jet Ski and stopped it on a dime. The shrimpers cheered, and a few of them even pulled off their shirts and swung them over their heads. Penny climbed from the cockpit and onto the foredeck. She pulled off her hat, letting her lion's mane explode from underneath. Discovering the skipper was a woman only served to magnify the cheers from the shrimpers.

With the show complete, Penny stuck us into the Amelia River and came to a stop a mile into the waterway. "Will this do?"

Hunter said, "I'll tell you in a minute." He gave Tony a slug to the shoulder. "Go get me a handful of bottom."

Tony didn't hesitate. He shoved his feet into a pair of fins, threw on a mask, and stepped over the side. When he resurfaced, he extended his hand and deposited a fistful of clean brown sand into Hunter's waiting palm.

"This'll do just fine."

I helped Tony back aboard and into his rebreather while Mongo helped Hunter don his gear.

Tony and Hunter stood facing each other and inspecting each other's gear.

"You are rebreather qualified, right?" Hunter asked.

Tony held up his mouthpiece. "I breathe through this, right?"

"Only if you want to stay alive. How about the DPV? How much experience do you have behind one?"

Tony turned serious. "I've only played with one for a couple of days, but I've never been through the course."

Hunter shook his head. "You probably should've mentioned that when we started planning this little mission. Come on. I'll give you the crash course."

Hunter slipped over the side and into the water. Tony followed. Mongo lowered the first diver propulsion vehicle into Hunter's hands, and then the second to Tony.

Hunter spun toward the Coastie. "Clip this carabiner to your belt so you don't lose this five-thousand-dollar DPV. Your controls are under your right thumb. Hold the handles like a steering wheel, and turn the direction you want to go. That's all there is to it. Give it a try."

Tony stuck his mouthpiece where it belonged and descended a few feet beneath the surface. Hunter remained on the surface but rolled his face forward into the water so he could watch his student. I followed Hunter's head movements for several minutes before he sank, no doubt, on a teaching mission.

A few minutes later, both men surfaced, and Hunter gave the closest thing to praise Tony was going to hear. "Not bad, kid. But this is clear, calm water with no current."

Mongo leaned over the rail. "Are you ready for the device?"

Hunter raised the okay signal, and Mongo set the crane into action. With the torpedo suspended just above the deck, Mongo connected the tether and umbilical to the third DPV. With everything connected as designed, he hoisted the rig across the gunwale and let it come to rest in the water between Tony and Hunter.

Hunter inspected the connections and threw an arm across the EMP generator. "This thing's floating pretty high in the water. It's definitely positive."

Mongo leaned down. "There's a small valve on the belly. Give it a squeeze to let enough water into the ballast to get it neutrally buoyant. If you overflood it, there's a pair of switches just beside the valve. They open a container of pressurized air to blow the water ballasts."

Hunter messed with the controls until the torpedo submerged just below the surface. "All right, kid, here's how this is going to work. You hold your DPV with your right hand and the drone rig with your left. I'll station on the port side and hold the rig with my right. We have to manage all three machines as if they're one. Don't run off, and don't slow down. If you're going to make a turn, get my attention and signal with your head. Got it?"

"I got it," Tony said. "What's our goal?"

Hunter said, "Our first goal is to learn to move in unison without killing each other. I've never done anything like this, so it's going to be a huge learning curve. Let's descend to the bottom right here and then try to move south in a straight line."

Tony nodded, and they descended out of sight. I didn't like it. I wanted to be on the bottom with them. I should've been down there learning with my partner instead of waiting on the boat like a one-footed, useless observer.

Fewer than five minutes later, the dive team resurfaced, shaking their heads.

Hunter spat out his mouthpiece. "Are you all right, kid?"

Tony shucked off his mask and took a long breath. "Yeah, I'm okay, but that sucked."

"What happened?" Mongo asked.

Ignoring the question, Hunter clipped the tethers to the boat and climbed aboard. He turned and offered Tony a hand as he climbed back into the boat.

"What's wrong?" Mongo growled.

Hunter said, "It's chaos. Your missile does fine at two knots, but any faster than that, it turns into a bucking bronco. It's impossible to control."

Mongo asked, "Is it the DPV or the generator that's out of control?"

"Maybe both," Tony said. "It's just like Hunter said. The whole thing tried to beat us to death."

"I need to see it happen," Mongo said.

Hunter pulled off his rebreather. "I'm not doing that again without a full facemask and comms."

"Agreed," Tony said.

I pulled a pair of full facemasks from the locker and handed them to the divers. They soon had the rebreathers configured so they could not only talk to each other, but also feed video and audio back to the boat.

Back into the water they went, and I brought up the multi-function display with a split-screen view showing both camera feeds from the facemasks.

We watched in silence as Hunter and Tony timidly started another attempt. The DPVs accelerated slowly, and the torpedo followed obediently until Hunter said, "Okay, let's bump it up to four knots."

They increased their speed, and the tail of the torpedo whipped like an errant banner in the wind.

Mongo watched closely and groaned as the scene played out. "It needs stabilizing fins like fletching on an arrow."

"I agree," Earl said. "Let's get them back on board."

Chapter 14
Game On

We hoisted the equipment back on board and helped Hunter and Tony out of their gear.

Hunter wiped his face. "Bucking bronco is a pretty good description, don't you think?"

Mongo groaned. "Yeah, I'd say that covers it. We're going to weld some stabilizing fins onto the shell and see if that helps rein it in."

"It sure can't make it any worse," Tony said as he peeled off his dry suit and inspected his leg. A massive bruise had formed on the outside of his left leg.

"What happened?" Earl asked.

Tony pointed at the torpedo. "Your pet attacked me, but it was my fault. I wasn't expecting it to get violent. I got careless and got bitten."

Mongo leaned down and inspected the bruise. "That's nasty. Do you think we should have it X-rayed?"

Tony shook him off. "No. Nothing's broken. It just gave me a good wallop. I won't let it happen again."

Back at the dock, Earl said, "It's easier to bring the welder and fins to the boat than to haul this thing back to the shop. I'll be right back."

She returned minutes later and backed her truck to the edge of the floating dock. Earl pulled cables from the welder in her truck and climbed back aboard with three flat pieces of aluminum tucked beneath her arm. "Where do you want 'em, Mongo?"

He took the fins from her and positioned them against the aluminum skin of the torpedo. He silently studied the problem. "Let's try them right here."

He held the first plate in place while Earl tacked it to the torpedo. They placed two more, and Earl welded them solidly in place.

Mongo leaned back and took a look at their handiwork. "If we could build a swivel into the umbilical, we could set the fins to cause a spiral like throwing a football. That would stabilize it, for sure, but a swivel with an electrical connection is a complex piece of work."

"Maybe this will take care of it," Earl said.

Hunter checked his watch. "If we're going to splash this thing again today, we need to do it now. The tide will start receding in another half hour. That'll turn the visibility to garbage."

Penny took us back across the Sound in record time, and we had the team back in the water with fifteen minutes to spare.

We watched and held our breath as the second attempt filled the screen aboard the boat. The torpedo trailed better than before, but the nose still danced in violent arcs.

Tony's tinny voice came from the speaker beside the display. "I've got an idea. Let's shorten the tether. That'll give it less room to jump around."

Hunter said, "Is that possible, Mongo?"

He leaned forward and pressed the talk button. "Sure. Tie the tow cable in a sheepshank, and wind the electrical umbilical around the DPV handles."

Tony skillfully whipped the tow cable into a sheepshank while Hunter stowed the electrical lines.

"That cut's out about three feet," Tony said. "Let's try it again."

They started slowly, and everything looked like it was going to work perfectly until they hit five knots. At that magical threshold, the nose of the torpedo rose, sending the nose of the DPV downward and toward the sand. Hunter and Tony tried to overcome the downward force by steering their DPV's nose up. The maneuver started a porpoise effect with two men and one torpedo chasing three DPVs that refused to behave.

After ten more minutes of wrestling with the equipment, Hunter said, "I'm calling it. The tide is starting out, and we don't want to get sucked into the ocean. We're coming up."

They surfaced with the equipment about a thousand feet away, and Penny idled toward them. When the divers and equipment were back aboard, Penny said, "The tide is running out at just over two knots."

Hunter let out a whistle. "That's enough to turn our little rodeo into a trip to the emergency room. We'll have to try again tomorrow."

I helped Tony out of his dry suit and inspected his bruise. "It's getting bigger. Are you sure we shouldn't have them shoot an X-ray just to be sure?"

"It's not broken," he repeated. "I know how a broken leg feels, and this is just a nasty bruise."

"It's *your* leg," I said. "But you're too important to lose on this one."

"If it'll make you feel better, I'll go get an X-ray, but I'm confident it's just bruised."

I shrugged. "Whatever you want."

He gave the EMP generator a kick. "I want that thing to behave. I'm starting to think that SEAL Delivery Vehicle is the only answer, no matter how big it is."

Mongo said, "You may be right, and that gives me an idea."

Back at the dock, we unloaded the Mark V and relocated the torpedo and all three DPVs into the shop on Mongo's directions.

While Mongo and Earl labored away in the workshop, the rest of us migrated to the gazebo.

Hunter tapped Tony's boot with his own. "You did good in the water today, kid. You've got a long way to go to be as good as Chase, but I'm not afraid to dive with you."

Tony put on the half smile that proved he was Clark's brother. Only genetics could create a crooked grin like that. "Thanks, Hunter. You're not so bad yourself. It's obvious you've spent a lot of time in the water."

Hunter ignored the compliment. "Have you been to the combat diver course in Key West?"

Tony nodded. "My brother got me a slot. It was the toughest school I've ever been to, but I learned a ton."

"It shows," Hunter said. "What are you afraid of?"

Tony frowned. "Afraid of? What do you mean?"

"Everybody's afraid of something. Mine is snakes. I hate snakes."

Tony inspected the ceiling of the gazebo. "I guess I'm afraid of getting old."

Hunter scoffed. "Getting dead is the only way to keep from getting old. You don't want that, do you?"

Tony considered the question. "No, I don't want to be dead, but I ain't afraid of dying. I've got things right with the Lord, so I figure He'll take pretty good care of me when I quit breathing here on Earth."

Hunter smiled. "I'm glad to hear that, kid. Singer's our de facto chaplain, but we're all believers."

Tony stared out over the North River as a pair of pelicans dived on baitfish in the shallows. "How could anybody look at a place this pretty and not be a believer?"

"I don't know, kid. I just don't know."

We sat in silence for a few minutes, watching the late afternoon sky turn from blue to orange.

Hunter said, "I'm going to get a shower and hit the sack. I figure Mongo will have some new prototype ready to kick our butts, bright and early. Besides, I promised Tina we'd have dinner—just the two of us."

Skipper came down the gallery steps and across the yard toward the gazebo. "How was it?"

I reached for Penny's hand and stood. "Tony can tell you all about it, and he can show you his boo-boo."

I led Penny up the steps and into the kitchen. I guess it was curiosity, or perhaps voyeurism, that made me stand by the window overlooking the backyard. I motioned toward the gazebo. "Look."

Penny leaned over the counter and peered through the window to see Skipper sitting on Tony's lap. "That's sweet," she said just before hitting me with the dish towel. "Now, get away from that window and leave them alone, you dirty old man."

"I was just . . ."

She thumped my knuckles with a wooden spoon. "You were just spying is what you were doing. And you try to convince me you're not a spy. Ha!"

I sat down beside my wife at the table and slid my hand into hers. "I've got some concerns about the two of them."

Penny sat back. "What kinds of concerns?"

"If we put Tony on the team and take him into the field with us, I'm afraid Skipper will get distracted when we need her to focus on the mission."

She pulled her hand from mine and squeezed my arm. "Take it from me . . . It's hard to sit in that ops center up there and know my man is getting shot at or stabbed or run over, but Skipper's not like me. You've said it yourself. She's all business when a mission kicks off. I think she can compartmentalize. As you say . . . she's the best analyst you've ever seen."

"You're probably right. I'll have to wait and see. Lucky for us, this mission isn't particularly dangerous. We shouldn't encounter any bad guys if we do it right. We'll just nab their submarine, hand it over to the authorities, and come back home. Nothing to it."

She giggled. "Oh, yeah . . . nothing to it. You're too much, Chase Fulton."

She gave me a wonderfully warm kiss that made me forget everything outside that kitchen, then she whispered, "It's hard for you, isn't it?"

"What's hard for me?"

"Not being in the water with Hunter."

I sighed. "Yeah, it's hard, but I've got faith in Tony."

"I'm not talking about Tony. I'm talking about you. Are you handling it okay?"

I knocked on the wooden table. "I'm doing the best I can, but you're right. It's hard. I took the boat out by myself yesterday and had an epiphany."

"Oh?"

"I'm going to beat this. Whatever it takes, I'm going to come back stronger. I'm not the first person to get a metal foot. I mean, there are people out there running marathons and climbing mountains with prosthetics. If they can do it, I can, too."

She laid her face against my shoulder. "That's the man I love. I knew he was still in there."

* * *

Day two of sea trials began with an unveiling. Mongo had a canvas tarp draped over whatever he'd cobbled together the night before. He pointed toward the covered surprise. "I can't take all the credit for this one. It was Tony's idea. He kept saying we needed a SEAL Delivery Vehicle. He was wrong about that, but he wasn't wrong about the concept. Here's my cut-down version of the SEAL Delivery Vehicle."

He yanked the tarp away, revealing three diver propulsion vehicles attached to a stainless-steel framework connecting them together to form one large platform, with a cradle for the EMP generator built beneath the platform.

Hunter and Tony immediately knelt beside the creation and studied every inch of it. "How do we steer it?" Hunter asked.

Mongo pointed toward a single stick situated at the rear of the device. "Just like you steer an airplane. That stick controls an elevator and a rudder up front. It's going to be highly responsive."

Tony said, "Amazing. You built this in one night?"

Mongo said, "Oh, no. I didn't build it. I just designed it. Earl built it."

She took a bow. "That's right. I built it. And if you two yahoos wreck it, there's gonna be hell to pay."

That got a hearty round of laughter, but I knew Earl wasn't joking.

Hunter said, "Let's get this thing in the water and see if she'll fly."

We loaded up in the Mark V and headed for Amelia Island. The anticipation was palpable, and my disappointment that I'd have to watch from the boat stung me to my spine.

Penny brought us to a stop at the same place we'd worked the day before, and Mongo hoisted his creation into the water.

He said, "There's a pair of bladders left and right. If I've done the math correctly, the sled is slightly negative and should sink slowly. The bladders are to offset the weight. They should be more than enough to make it float. The valve is just to the right of the control stick. The round button inflates, and the square button deflates. I made them shaped instead of colored because I assume the real mission will happen in the dark. Any questions?"

"Only one," Hunter said. "When are you going to shut up and cut this thing loose?"

"When are you going to stop asking stupid questions and get in the water?" Mongo returned.

A minute later, Tony and Hunter were suited up and in the water. Hunter hit the button to inflate the bladders, and Mongo opened the hook, releasing the contraption from the crane. The sled floated with the bladders full of air. Even with the platform of the sled on the surface, the DPVs were submerged, and Hunter gave the controls a nudge to power away from the boat.

After a couple minutes of adapting to the controls, Hunter palmed the square button, emptying the bladders and descending below the surface. I turned to the screen to see Tony and Hunter flying the sled through the water as if they'd done it for years. They took turns at the controls until they'd both mastered the sled.

Hunter flew the device to the sandy bottom and piled half a dozen rocks into a line. His electronically modulated voice came through the speaker. "Let's see if we can land this thing precisely on these rocks."

Tony nodded and slid behind the controls. He flew the sled away from the rocks, leaving Hunter to watch from the riverbed. A few seconds later, he came back into view and stopped the sled with the EMP generator resting gently on top of Hunter's pile of rocks.

They traded places and repeated the game until both could land on target, with or without the other attached to the sled.

They flew the sled back to the surface and pulled off their facemasks.

Hunter said, "Mongo, you're a genius. This thing is perfect."

"Not so quick," Mongo said. "You may be able to land it on a pile of rocks, but we need you to be able to land it on a submerged, running submarine. And here comes your training dummy, now . . ."

Clark was motoring across the Sound in *Aegis*'s dinghy. The bow was high, and the engine sounded as if it were struggling. Clark came alongside the Mark V and let the starboard tube of the RHIB come to rest against the rail.

Hunter pulled his facemask back into position and stuck his head underwater. When he emerged, he said, "Ah! That looks like fun."

"What is it?" I asked with an obvious lack of patience.

"It's a mock-up of the narco-sub," Hunter said. "It isn't powered, so we'll have to tow it behind the RHIB, but it'll give us a chance to master landing on a moving target."

"Let the games begin," I said.

Clark motored away to the south, and Hunter and Tony gave chase. The game proved significantly more challenging than landing on a pile of rocks, but after an hour of practice, both Tony and Hunter could easily land the sled squarely on the mock-up of the sub.

With everyone and everything back aboard the Mark V, Penny took us home, and the energy in the eyes of everyone on the team made it clear that practice was over, and it was game on.

Chapter 15
Which Way is Up?

Back at the dock, Mongo and Earl tugged, pushed, shook, and rattled every inch of their underwater flying sled.

I asked, "Well? What's the verdict, doctors?"

"She's steady as a rock," Earl declared. "But that's only half the battle."

"What do you mean, half the battle?"

She planted a knee on the deck of the Mark V and turned to face me. "Surely you don't want us to end up like the dog who finally caught the UPS truck. Just because we can catch one of those submarines doesn't mean we've accomplished anything. According to what Mongo says, after we catch it, we have to zap it, get it to the surface, and get it into the right hands. All we've proven so far is that we can catch it."

I leaned against the gunwale. "I guess I got caught up in the excitement of the chase."

"That's all right, Baby Boy. We've got everything under control. You just stick to doing what you do best—smiling and looking pretty."

"Yep, that's my forte."

She reached out and tapped my prosthetic with a screwdriver. "Don't get too cocky. You still ain't as pretty as Clark, but that skinny Penny's got her all the man she can handle. I'm sure of that. Oh, and if that foot of yours needs a tune-up, you just let Momma know."

"I'll keep that in mind," I said as I took a step away. "So, what's next?"

Mongo fielded that one. "Next, we throw a bunch of electronics in that dummy Clark's pulling around and see if this thing can turn them into pudding."

"Speak of the devil," I said as Clark motored up to the dock.

He shut down the RHIB's engine and tossed a line around a cleat. "This is the wrong boat for pulling that drone of yours. It's all it can do to make fifteen knots, and it's putting a lot of strain on this little thing."

Mongo eyed the RHIB and its tagalong. "We can tow it with the Mark V as long as Penny doesn't do any more showboating."

My wife landed her hands on her hips. "It wasn't showboating. It was a demonstration of capabilities."

Mongo chuckled. "Let's do a little less demonstrating and a little more testing."

Hunter and Tony disconnected the drone from the RHIB and tied it to the stern of the patrol boat.

"What are we going to use to simulate the electronics in the narco-sub?" I asked.

Mongo said, "I've got that under control. Based on what we learned from the two subs we captured, we know the system is twenty-eight-volt DC circuitry. Earl and I rigged up a simple circuit we suspect is a little more robust than what the subs carry, so if we can fry this one, the electronics of the sub don't stand a chance."

Mongo unbolted and opened a waterproof hatch on the drone and activated the circuit inside. With the hatch once again secured, he gave the towed drone a shove with a foot.

Hunter said, "Are we going to fire this thing off this time?"

"That's the plan," Mongo said.

"Is there any chance of it hurting me or the kid when we set it off?"

"There's no threat to either of you unless you're wearing a pacemaker. All you have to do is land this sled on top of the sub and hit the plunger. The electromagnetic pulse will last about a tenth of a second, and the sub will be a fifteen-thousand-pound baby doll in our hands."

Tony twisted his upper body out of his dry suit and took a seat on the edge of the sled. "What about the DPVs? Won't the EMP melt their circuitry when we fire it off down there?"

"That's a great question," Mongo said. "I built a shield three hundred fifteen degrees around the generator. That should allow the pulse only to travel through a forty-five-degree opening in the bottom of the shield. As long as you and Hunter stick this thing to the top of the sub and keep it right side up, it should be a piece of cake."

Tony slid a hand across one of the DPVs mounted to the sled. "And we're going to be doing this in the open ocean and probably at night, right?"

Mongo said, "It'll definitely happen in the open ocean, but we're just guessing at nighttime. If I were running the drug-sub, I wouldn't want it on the surface during daylight. If they're smart enough to build these things and put them into operation, surely they're smart enough to keep them submerged when the sun is out."

Without a word, Tony stood and tied the sleeves of his dry suit around his waist. I watched him walk across the dock and claim a seat beside Hunter on *Aegis*'s starboard hull.

Hunter examined the look on Tony's face. "What's wrong, kid? You're not getting cold feet already, are you?"

"No, sir. It's just that I don't know how we're going to find this thing in the dark, in the middle of a billion miles of ocean."

"I told you to quit calling me sir, and you're sweating the small stuff." Hunter motioned toward Mongo. "Those big-brained people over there will put us right on top of this thing. All we have to do is land it and push the button."

Tony said, "As long as you say we're good, we're good."

Hunter inspected a fingernail. "Well, kid . . . I say we're good. Let's go kill Mongo's circuit."

Tony hopped to his feet. "Yes, sir."

Hunter froze. "What did I tell you about that *sir* business? If you do it again, I'm cutting a hole in your dry suit."

We mounted the Mark V and motored away from the dock.

I tapped Mongo with the boat pole. "What do you think about trying this one up here in the North River? We don't need the sandy bottom anymore, and the poor visibility up here will simulate darkness underwater."

Mongo stared down at Hunter. "What do you think? Do you want to add another element?"

Hunter zipped up his dry suit. "Sure. Me and the kid could pull this one off in a tub of chocolate pudding."

Tony followed suit by securing his dry suit and donning his rebreather. Penny brought us to a stop at the south end of a quiet stretch of river a mile north of what used to be the paper plant. The water was dark but still at slack tide. Soon, the mighty Atlantic would once again lean toward the western shore of Europe in its predictable cycle that hadn't changed in thousands of years.

"Let's run this one like the real thing," Mongo ordered. "Hunter, Tony, mount up."

They stepped from the deck of the Mark V onto the sled and knelt in place.

Mongo leaned toward the pilothouse. "Give us five knots upstream."

Penny followed the order and cracked the throttles. With the patrol boat idling along and the towed drone invisible somewhere astern, Mongo activated the crane, slowly lifting the sled from the deck. With a gentle swing of the arm, he moved the load over the starboard rail. As he lowered the device toward the water, it twisted with its nose pointing downriver.

Hunter ordered, "Hang a foot in the water, kid. We've got to get this thing turned around."

Tony stuck a finned foot in the water, and the sled turned, orienting itself perfectly with the course of the patrol boat.

"Bombs away!" Mongo opened the clamp, releasing the apparatus and our two divers into the murky black water of the North River.

The visibility seemed to be less than six feet, according to the screen where the divers' camera feeds were being displayed.

Tony's voice was the first to crackle through the speaker. "Yes, it's different in the dark."

Hunter replied, "Relax, kid. Mongo thought of everything. Turn that knob in front of your left hand."

Instantly, the screen filled with light emitted from the nose of the sled.

I gave Mongo a slap on the back. "Nice touch."

"I knew Hunter was afraid of the dark, so I wired up a nightlight for him."

I pressed the mic button on the panel. "Okay, guys. It's time to go hunting. Find me a narco-sub, and kill it dead."

"They don't call me Hunter for nothing."

It took just over three minutes for Hunter and Tony to find the drone and land their sled right on top of it. "We're in position and ready to fire the pulse," came Hunter's no-nonsense transmission.

Mongo nodded, and I gave the order. "Fire at will."

Several seconds passed, and Tony said, "Aren't you going to hit the plunger?"

Hunter said, "Nope. You do it. That way, if it kills us both, I can spend all eternity blaming you."

Tony chuckled. "We've all got to go sometime." He held his gloved hand over the plunger and wiggled his fingers until Hunter ran out of patience and slapped his hand down on top of Tony's. The instant the plunger fell, the screen went dark.

I grabbed Mongo's arm. "What happened?"

"I don't know yet." He scanned the boat's instrumentation. "Everything else is working, right?"

Penny scanned the panels. "Yes, all systems are go. It's not the boat. It's the transmitters from their facemasks. We're not receiving their signal."

"All stop!" I ordered, and Penny pulled the transmissions out of gear. I landed a palm on the push-to-talk button. "Hunter, Tony, how do you read?"

Nothing.

I yelled, "Haul in the drone!"

Mongo winched the cable, drawing the drone toward the boat. As we drifted to a stop, the drone and the sled surfaced ten feet behind the boat, but neither diver was anywhere to be seen.

Clark scanned the water behind us. "Hunter! Tony!"

An instant later, he threw open the dive locker and pulled a mask, snorkel, torch, and fins from inside. He was over the gunwale and in the water before I could stop him.

Penny hit the side-scan sonar, hoping to spot them on the screen, but the returns showed nothing. Everyone moved to the stern of the boat and peered helplessly into the black water.

Following Clark's lead, I pulled a mask, snorkel, light, and one fin from the locker. It took only seconds to disconnect my prosthetic. With one fin, I rolled over the gunwale and splashed into the cold, dark water.

Swimming with one fin is hard enough, but doing so while everybody on the boat yelled for me to get out of the water made it even more challenging. Everybody on the boat was safe, but my partner and Clark's brother were somewhere beneath the black veil of brackish water, and nothing would keep me from finding them.

The search was all but futile. Even with the powerful torches, Clark and I could only see a few feet into the murk. I tried diving several times, hoping to catch a glimpse of one of them, but it was wasted effort.

As panic approached, relief came in the form of Stone W. Hunter spitting, gagging, and cursing. "Well, that sucked!"

I spun in the water to see both Tony and Hunter hanging onto each other on the surface about twenty feet away. I kicked frantically with my single fin. If mermaids could do it, why couldn't I?

"What are you doing in the water?" Hunter scolded.

As I labored to close the distance, the moment turned from stern to comical.

Hunter said, "You ain't got but one leg, Lieutenant Chase."

"Oh, you're funny. I risked my life to come find you, and you're making jokes."

He was far from finished. "I don't know what you were going to do with one fin. I guess you'd be pretty good at swimming in circles."

"I'm going to drown you when I get to you."

He splashed water toward me and laughed. "I would say the shoe's on the other foot now, but you've only got one foot."

Penny idled the Mark V to pick us up. Mongo leaned over the rail and scooped me up as if I were a child's toy, then he gently sat me down on the deck.

Penny tossed me a towel. "That wasn't very smart, Chase. What were you going to do out there?"

I wrapped the towel around my shoulders. "I don't know, but one thing's for certain . . . I wasn't going to stand on the deck of a boat and *hope* my teammates were alive."

She lifted the towel and dried my hair, then kissed my forehead. "I'm sorry. I shouldn't have fussed. I was just worried."

"It's okay to worry, but expecting me to stay in the boat in that situation is always going to result in disappointment. I may be one-legged, but I'm not out of the game when people I love are missing underwater."

She wrapped her arms around me. "I'm sorry."

"Don't be sorry. Just get us home. You know how Clark is. He'll be whining like a baby girl because he's cold."

Five minutes later, all the hardware was back aboard the boat, and we pulled into the Bonaventure dock.

"What happened out there?" Clark was the first to ask.

Hunter said, "Mongo's pulse generator worked, but his shielding did not. As soon as Tony hit that button, that's the night the lights went out in Georgia. Everything went dark, and the comms in our facemasks got torched . . . like literally torched. My mask was full of smoke and the smell of burnt everything."

"Mine was the same," Tony said. "Our torches wouldn't work, and we were tethered to that sled. It took a couple of minutes to get our bearings and cut away. I don't know about Mr. Hunter, but I didn't know which way was up. All I knew for sure was that I had to get my dive buddy to the surface."

Hunter said, "I'll give the kid credit for one thing. Once he got his hands on me, there was no way he was going to let me go. He takes that rescue-swimmer stuff pretty seriously. Oh, and in the interest of absolute honesty, I didn't know which way was up, either."

Mongo looked like the weight of the world had just crashed down on him.

Hunter said, "Buck up, Mongo. It wasn't your fault. Besides, we're fine. It just shook us up a little."

The giant shook his head. "It *was* my fault, and I'm sorry. I thought I had everything figured out, right down to the mark. I still don't know what went wrong."

"You'll figure it out," Hunter said. "I've got faith in you. But if you wouldn't mind, could you build a remote switch for the next one? I don't ever want to be that close to an EMP again."

Chapter 16
On the Disco Round

Hot showers and cold sandwiches punctuated our afternoon with everyone gathered on the back gallery overlooking the North River and our armada. In one of those rare moments when no one had anything to say, it was safe to declare everyone tired, some of us waterlogged, and one of us absolutely downtrodden.

I laid a hand on Mongo's tree limb of a forearm. "It wasn't your fault, big man."

He pulled his arm away and cleared his throat. "I've got something to say, so listen up. I screwed up, and I almost got some of my brothers hurt. I'm not making excuses, mind you. I'm just telling you how it happened."

A round of dismissiveness rose from the crowd, but Mongo held up a hand. "Stop it. I know we're all on the same team and all that, but when one of us screws up, he has to be man enough to own up to it. I screwed up. I was tired. I was pushing myself too hard. I built a shield to protect us and our equipment from the EMP generator, and I built it only slightly stronger than the required pulse to shut down the circuitry of the narco-subs. What I didn't take into consideration was the fact that we have a generator capable of producing far more power than necessary to take out the sub."

Hunter said, "Take it easy, Mongo. We all—"

Mongo held up an island-sized palm. "No, Hunter. Let me finish. I set a personal deadline that was unrealistic and caused me to work when I should've been sleeping. It won't happen again, and I'm sorry."

Hunter reclaimed the floor. "We're the kind of people who push ourselves far beyond the point when most normal people would've given up. Sometimes we get hurt or hurt somebody when we do that, but we can't stop doing it just because somebody might get hurt. We're tier-one operators. We're not normal people. We're the abnormal freaks the rest of the normal people rely on to keep them safe. As far as I'm concerned, you can blow me off a homemade EMP generator sled a thousand times if it saves one innocent life. How 'bout you, Tony? How do you feel about it?" Hunter slugged the rescue swimmer.

"We're not hurt," Tony said. "It was shallow water, and it was just a few melted circuits. I'm with Mister Hunter."

Hunter leaned back, placed the sole of his boot against Tony's shoulder, and shoved him off the gallery, sending him tumbling down the steps. "I told him a thousand times to quit calling me *mister* and *sir*. The kid's gotta learn."

Tony picked himself up, dusted off, and started again. "Forgive me. I misspoke. What I meant to say was, I'm with that jackass, Hunter."

That got the laugh it deserved . . . even from Mongo.

Amused but determined to keep us on track, Clark said, "Okay, that's enough. What's the plan to move ahead?"

Mongo said, "I plan to sleep tonight and tear into the sled tomorrow morning. I have a theory that our pulse generator did such a good job that it even melted itself. I don't know that yet, but I'd put money on it. I do have a question, though. How far do you want me to dial it back? I can cut the pulse in half and still accomplish the mission if the generator is sitting on top of the sub. The power requirement goes up with the square of the distance in meters that we move the generator away from the target."

Clark said, "I don't know what that means, going up with the square of the distance or whatever, but if you can make the thing a remote trigger, I say keep it turned up as high as it'll go. Honestly, we don't care about the sled after we hit the sub with the EMP."

"A remote trigger is easy," Mongo said. "Honestly, I should've thought of that the first time. We'll build another one, but I need forty-eight hours this time. Is everybody okay with that?"

Clark answered for the rest of us. "Yes, take all the time you need. It's not like they're going to stop sending these things anytime soon."

Tony raised a finger.

Clark said, "Spit it out."

"I know I'm still on probation or whatever, but I have a question. How do these subs get back to Colombia after they get emptied in South Florida?"

Mongo spoke up. "We don't know, but the prevailing theory is that they can make it home on a single charge since they're empty and light. The second theory is that they get stuffed full of cash and then set sail back south with an intercept boat picking them up for a tow and recharge, just like they do on the northbound leg."

Tony considered Mongo's answer. "Again, I know I'm the new guy and I should probably shut up and do what I'm told, but if these things are emitting a signal from some sort of transmitter, why don't we listen for that signal in the Everglades and grab one of these things before it gets unloaded?"

Mongo said, "That'd be a great idea if that's how they worked, but the only time they activate their locator transmitter is when they're at sea and in need of a tow and a charge."

We sat listening to the sounds of the marsh until the cooling air after sundown sent us scampering inside. When I made it to my feet and regained my balance, Disco caught my arm.

"I'm fine," I said. "I got it."

"I wasn't catching you. I need to talk with you. Can I have a minute?"

I stepped aside and let the rest of the gang past me.

"Sure, Disco. What is it?"

He looked down at my foot and then across the yard. "If you feel like it, let's go to the gazebo."

I grabbed the handrail and started down the steps. We settled into a pair of Adirondack chairs, and I asked, "Is everything all right?"

He stared between his feet, and I was instantly terrified.

Is Disco leaving the team? Have we pushed him too far? Is an island of misfit toys too much for our chief pilot?

"Yeah, everything is okay, except I don't feel like I'm pulling my weight. Everybody else on the team can do it all—or at least they can do multiple things. Hunter's unstoppable in the water, but he's equally skilled on land, and God forbid somebody start a fight with him. That's not going to end well."

"Where's this going, Disco?"

He shrugged. "It doesn't end with Hunter. I mean, look at all the stuff Mongo can do in addition to ripping down telephone poles. He can design and build an EMP generator."

"We've all got our skill sets," I said. "That's what makes us valuable to the team."

"That's exactly my point. Everybody's got their skill sets, except for me. All I can do is fly, and that's not exactly a rare skill around here. You and Clark can do anything I can do in the cockpit."

"That's not true. You've got skills in the front seat that Clark and I will never have."

"Okay, let's say that's true. That's still the only skill set I have. I've been thinking a lot about the jungle recon mission. I'm going to fly Hunter and Tony to Colombia and wait for them at the airport while they disappear into the jungle to track a narco-sub floating down the river. You're paying me a huge salary to be a high-speed bus driver."

"Let's not beat around the bush, Disco. What do you want?"

He played with a cigar ash with the toe of his boot. "I want to feel like I'm doing my part. I know I'm not twenty-one and bulletproof anymore, so I can't go off to Ranger school, but I'm in good shape for an almost forty-five-year-old guy, and I'm willing to learn."

I leaned back and propped my prosthetic up on the cannon cradle. "Are you asking to go to The Ranch? Because if that's what you want, I can't recommend it. It doesn't matter how fit you are, that place will kill anybody over thirty. You don't know what you're asking."

"No, I don't want to go to The Ranch. I'm too old for that. But I'm not too old to go to Hunter's version of The Ranch, Singer's shooting school, your boat operator course, and Clark's Krav Maga academy. There's a lot of great experience right here around me, and I'm not being used to my full potential. Teach me to fight and shoot and dive and run boats. I'm tired of feeling like a liability."

"You're far from a liability. We don't carry dead weight around with us. You're a valuable, respected, and trusted member of the team. We're thrilled you're here. You free up a knuckle dragger to kick in doors and pull triggers every time you get in the cockpit. If you weren't here, one of us would have to be up there doing the driving."

He nodded. "I get that, but when the turbines aren't spinning, I'm not much help. I want to change that."

I grinned. "You don't know what you're asking for, my friend. Learning to shoot and run boats is fun, but learning to fight sucks. So does water operations with Hunter. Just ask Tony. He's half your age, and Hunter is killing him in the water. He won't be any easier on you."

"I wouldn't ask him to treat me any differently. I believe in what we're doing, and I'm not afraid. When I get pushed too hard, I'll do what Clark recommends and 'embrace the suck.'"

I sat silently for a moment, staring across the cannon. "Is this about my leg?"

"What? No. What are you talking about?"

"Do you think I'm not coming back? Do you think you need to step up because I'm on the sideline?"

His gaze hit the ground again. "I won't lie, Chase. That's part of what made me bring this up. Tony's on board now, and I'm sure he's capable, but with you on the disabled list for a while, that leaves some pretty big holes in the team. I can't fill those holes, but I can stick my thumb in the dyke and slow the leaks down until you're back at full strength. But that's not the only reason . . . I meant what I said about not feeling like I'm pulling my weight. I want to do more and learn more. Teaching me will only serve to strengthen us as a team. I'll never be the tip of the spear like the rest of you guys, but even a dull sword hurts when you get hit with it, and I'm okay being a dull sword because that's a lot better than no sword at all."

I stood from my chair and stuck out my hand. He shook it, and I said, "As soon as this mission is over, you can consider yourself the first official student enrolled in the Bonaventure Academy of Pain. I'll tell Singer to pray for you."

Chapter 17
An Unexpected Helping Hand

Two days later, Mongo came through the kitchen door, wiping his hands on a shop towel and wearing a look of satisfaction. Clark, Hunter, and I looked up from the table.

I said, "That's the look of a man who beat a deadline."

Mongo checked his watch. "Yeah, I guess I did."

"Tell us about it," Hunter said. "Did you figure out how to zap the sub without zapping us?"

He let out a chuckle. "I think so, but per Chase's requirement, I built a remote activation switch and a few extra bells and whistles. Do you want to see it?"

Hunter was the first to his feet. "If I can pry him away from Skipper, I'll get the kid."

"Did you send Earl home?" I asked.

Mongo said, "She's been gone since about four o'clock. All the fabrication was done by then. I just had some electrical work and finishing touches to take care of."

"I don't know how you do it," I said. "That big brain of yours is going to explode one day."

"I wouldn't worry about that, but I *could* use a day off. There's a couple of ladies I haven't seen in a couple of weeks, and I miss them."

I grimaced. "Yeah, there's something I've been meaning to tell you about Irina and Tatiana."

Mongo raised his eyebrows in concerned anticipation. "What about them?"

"If you went to Athens tonight, you wouldn't find them there. I'm afraid they're gone."

"Gone? What do you mean, gone?"

Before I could take the ruse any further, Penny came through the kitchen door with Irina and Tatiana in trail. The teenaged ballerina raced across the kitchen and leapt into Mongo's outstretched arms. The contrast of his bulk against her tiny dancer's frame made the scene even more dramatic than the joy on his face.

Tatiana's accented, excited English filled the kitchen. "It is so long to see you, and I have wonderful news . . . Well, is expected news, but is still wonderful for me."

Mongo cast his gaze between Tatiana and her mother.

Irina stepped toward the two and smiled the way only a beautiful Russian woman can. She laid her head against his chest and breathed, "*Ya skuchayu po tebe.*"

He leaned down and kissed her on her forehead. "I missed you, too. And also our little ballerina."

Irina ran her hand through Tatiana's hair. "Tell to him news."

She rolled her eyes. "Mother, ugh. It is not so difficult. You should say, 'Tell him the news,' not 'Tell to him news.' We are American now, and English is our language."

Irina blushed. "I will learn. This to you I make as promise."

The eye rolling continued, as did Tatiana's excitement. "I auditioned for the Atlanta Ballet Company, and I was brilliant."

Mongo beamed. "Of course you were, and now they want you in the company."

"Yes, of course. I am the only Bolshoi-trained ballerina in the company. I am, naturally, the best dancer."

Irina gasped. "*Ne bud' vysokomernym*, Tatiana."

The girl shook her head. "It is not arrogance, mother. It is only truth. *The* truth. I worked very hard to become great dancer."

Irina beamed. "I know this, and you will be most beautiful ballerina in all of company, even if is not Bolshoi, but only American company."

Seeing Irina, Tatiana, and Mongo together left me wondering if my injury earned on a mountain top in Afghanistan, that left me incapable of fathering children, had robbed me of a joy I could never know. My life was being shaped, one injury at a time, by forces beyond my control and in ways I would've never believed possible a decade earlier. Perhaps a man is what he holds most dear in his heart and not the sum of his physical parts. God knows I was quickly running out of parts.

Mongo pulled me aside. "Thanks for bringing them here. It means a lot to me. I know I have responsibilities to the team, but I love those girls, and I think maybe they need me. It has to be tough. Athens isn't exactly Moscow."

I gave my friend and the smartest man I know a slap on the shoulder. "I don't know if they need you, but it's obvious they love you just as much as you love them."

He cast a look over his shoulder and couldn't suppress the smile the displaced mother and daughter brought to his face.

I said, "I've got an idea. Why don't you three take *Aegis* for the night? The weather is nice, and it's almost a full moon. You can anchor out and have some quiet alone time."

"Thanks. I think they'd like that. We'll be back."

I waved him off. "Come back when you're ready to come back. We're still several days away from being operational, and even then, it's the Hunter and Tony jungle show. Who knows how long we'll have to wait before they launch another sub from Barranquilla. You've got plenty of time to relax and enjoy your time together."

Skipper yelled down the stairs minutes after Mongo and his Russian contingent left through the kitchen door. "Uh, Chase. Somebody's moving *Aegis*."

I peered out the window to see the gleaming white catamaran motoring down the narrow river, and I called back up the stairs. "How did you know the boat was moving?"

Skipper bounded down the few remaining steps. "Nothing happens on this property that isn't monitored from the ops center."

"Sometimes it frightens me to think about what you're capable of doing up there in that room."

She gave me her best witch's cackle. "I'll get you, my pretty . . . And your little boat, too."

"I'll get you a new broom to ride to work. Don't worry about the boat. Mongo has it out for the night. I had Disco fly over and pick up Irina and Tatiana."

"Hmm, that's odd. You doing something nice for someone. I think I'll have to write this one down. How come you never let me take the boat out for the night?"

"You can have it anytime you want. Just don't sink it or break it."

"I'll keep that in mind," she said. "I guess you're in charge again since Mongo's gone to play house."

"I don't know. Why do you ask?"

She pulled a note from her pocket. "I just got off the phone with some guys from Justice. Hang on a second." She ran a finger down the page in her hand. "A dude named Michael Conroy is the special agent in charge of support for this mission. Oh, and get this. They've given the op a code name. It's Operation Dragon Snare. Isn't that ridiculous?"

"It is pretty bad," I said. "What was the discussion with Conroy about? Surely it was more than just naming the op."

"I'm not so sure you're going to like what he had to say, but I'm not sure we can do anything about it."

"Let's hear it."

She scanned through her notes and looked up. "He says he has men in the field in Colombia who can let us know when the next narco-sub sets sail."

"We've already decided Hunter and Tony will do the recon. I don't like relying on an outside source for critical intel."

"I know, and I told him that, but he was insistent."

I considered her careful choice of words. "Insistent, huh?"

"Oh, yeah. It was like he was personally invested in this thing."

"Do you know if this is the only case he's working right now?"

"I have no way to know, but he made it sound like there was nothing more important."

"I don't like it," I said. "Where's Clark?"

She spun in a circle and glanced down the hall. "I don't know. He was just here. How does he slip away like that?"

"I stopped trying to figure that out years ago. When you find him, bring him to the library. Something about this Conroy guy smells rotten."

She scampered off down the hall, and I headed for my favorite room of the house. After the fire, the library was one of the rooms built back as close to the original as possible. The contractor hadn't missed a single detail, right down to the wavy glass in the windows, giving the room an old feel in a new house. The leather wingbacks, fireplace, and mountains of bookcases framed the space as an office for an old Southern judge, just as my great-uncle Barnard Henry Huntsinger had been. I wondered what wisdom and knowledge were lost as the arsonist's fire raged about its horrible work. Thousands of books—many of them first editions of historical significance—perished in the orange, lashing flames, and the desk where the Judge had sat to smoke his pipe and ponder the mysteries of the law was reduced to ashes, never to be equaled by a modern craftsman. I scoured the Southeast in search of a suitable replacement and finally settled on a beautifully ornate desk that had belonged to a long line of ship's captains in old Charleston. Apparently, the last of the captains had left his home and furnishings to descendants who lacked the sophistication or respect to treasure the collection. The desk alone held two hundred years of sweat, knowledge, and toil of men of the sea whose lives, like mine, were a study in duplicity. When ashore, the old captains wrung their hands considering how the cruel world away from the bounding main was torturing his crew. How many hours had bearded men with salt water in their veins plotted, planned, and pondered upon and above the mahogany creation? Its softly rounded corners of age being rubbed, and scars from the teeth of hounds at their masters' feet, gave the old desk a personality and warmth a modern replica could never possess. Would I leave the world someday with my corners worn smooth, and scars low and long, from the fangs of beasts who tried but couldn't pull me down? Would I meet the Judge on the other side, where he is no longer old and his hands no longer twisted and hard? Will we walk together beside Heaven's river with my father and mother and sister who were torn from the world's cruelty too young? Will I leave behind the aged desk and the steel and stone of a hand and foot that were never mine, but only brief, crude replacements for God's work of flesh and bone?

"Chase? Hello? Chase!"

I shook myself from my stupor to see Clark settling into a wingback. "Sorry, I was just thinking."

"That was some heavy thinking, brother. Are you all right?"

I pulled two bottles of water from the cooler in the corner and tossed one to him. "I'm fine. I was just thinking about what comes next."

He twisted off the plastic cap and downed half the bottle. "I'll tell you what comes next. We figure out a way to get the Conroy character off our playground."

I drank a normal-human-sized drink of water, unlike my Neanderthal handler. "I was actually thinking a little beyond that, but thanks for reeling me in. First, where's Skipper, and second, what do you think Conroy is up to?"

He leaned forward and sighted down the hallway. "Who knows? She said something too fast and too high-pitched for what's left of my ears to understand. It sounded something like, 'A baby bear, and I'm starting to care.'"

"What?"

He shrugged. "I told you I don't know, but I think she's coming down the stairs now."

He was at least partially correct. Skipper bounded from the bottom step and across the foyer to the library door. She plopped down beside Clark. "What did I miss?"

The look on my face must've been horrendous.

She leaned forward and squinted. "Are you okay, Chase?"

I waved a hand. "I'm fine, but Clark said you said something about a baby bear and starting to care."

She screwed up her face. "All I said to Clark was, 'Chase wants to see us in the library. I'll be right there. I've got to grab something from upstairs.' And from that, he got care bears?"

He finished off his bottle of water. "Hey, don't look at me. You'll see how the world sounds after you've sent a couple million rounds downrange and had a few dozen grenades cook off ten feet away. Trust me, care bears will be the least of your worries. Now, let's get to work. Tell us about Conroy."

She held up three sets of papers, each stapled together, and tossed one onto the desk and the other into Clark's lap. "This is Conroy's down-and-dirty dossier. He's got the typical fed bloodline. Poli-sci undergrad from Notre Dame. Didn't have the grades to get into law school at South Bend, so he ended up at Northwestern Pritzker School of Law. Did well enough to graduate, but failed the bar twice. Ta-da! Welcome to government service. He started out at Alcohol, Tobacco, and Firearms, but got hurt at the Academy. After some shuffling by an uncle who was a federal judge in some court of appeals somewhere, our boy Conroy ended up in an admin role at Drug Enforcement and somehow got himself a badge and a gun. As far as I can tell, he's never done anything meaningful except get himself promoted to a bigger office and a fancier title. He's the reason the government spends nine thousand dollars for toilet seats."

I finished my water and made a three-point shot into the can across the room. "Okay, so big deal. Conroy is a bureaucrat with too much body fat and not enough spine. If those were disqualifiers for government service, Washington would be a ghost town."

Skipper continued. "Agreed, but this guy is something special. It seems he's built his career finagling his way into sideline roles on big-ticket operations and padding his résumé riding the coattails of people who actually catch the bad guys."

"So, what is his official role in this operation?" I asked.

"I can't figure that out, but he keeps calling himself 'the special agent in charge,' and then barely above a whisper, he uses the word *support*. I think he got wind of this thing and decided it would be the next feather in his cap."

"Do we need this guy?" I asked.

The answer came in stereo. "No!"

I followed that one up with, "What does he want from us?"

Skipper said, "That's the beauty of his little scheme. He's playing it like he's here to help us."

"That brings us back to my first question to which the answer was clearly, no, we don't need him. How much did you release to him?"

"Just a few crumbs, but what really rang his bell was when I told him we were dispatching a pair of scouts to watch for a narco-sub to hit the open water in Colombia. That's when the bureaucratic BS started floating to the surface. He insisted that he had a team of embedded agents who could provide the intel we needed and save the federal government hundreds of thousands of dollars it would cost for us to fly, equip, train, deploy, support, and recover a pair of scouts. He blathered on about good stewardship of the taxpayers' money."

"What did you tell him?" Clark asked.

"I told him we would have minimal expense associated with the scouting element of the overall mission. Our only expense would be jet fuel, and we wouldn't pass that little cost on to the federal government."

"He had to love that," I said.

She huffed. "No, he hated it. He started quoting codified law about providing favors to the federal government in return for consideration on future projects and how contractors like us are the number one legislative complaint in recent years."

Clark pulled out his pocketknife and pretended the gleaming blade was a toothpick. "Yep, *we're* the problem in this country. It just takes a lawyer with a six-figure salary and without a bar card to explain it to us. When was the last time we sent the feds a bill? And an even better question is, when was the last time we bid on a federal contract?"

I leaned back and propped up one foot and one robot on the corner of the desk. "So, are we looking at some sinister intent with this guy or just another in a long line of self-aggrandizement by a mid-level government cake-eater?"

Skipper said, "I have my opinion, but I want to hear Clark's first."

Having apparently excavated whatever had become wedged behind his cuspid, my handler said, "I see a harmless bureaucrat who should probably be in the unemployment line, but after what we know now, I don't smell anything sinister. That doesn't mean I wouldn't like to throat-punch this Conroy dude, but to me, he's a non-issue."

I turned to Skipper. "And your assessment?"

"I cautiously share Clark's thoughts. There's something about how forceful he was when he insisted his team in the field would spot for us. It leaves me a little leery."

I pretended to flip through his dossier while I was thinking. When I finally formulated a plan, I said, "Here's an idea. Take him up on it. Let his team watch for the boat and send the intel up the chain."

Skipper said, "I don't think—"

I held up a finger. "Let me finish. Give the guy exactly what he wants, and thank him for explaining the complex scenario to us. Let him task the operators in the field or whatever blows his skirt up, and we'll do exactly what we've been planning all along. The feds don't need to know we have a pilot and two operators in the jungle. Hunter could sneak into the DEA operators' tent, give them a pedicure, and sneak back out before they ever knew he was there. He'll keep Tony in the shadows and watch the watchers. I trust intel we gather, and we can simply ignore what the feds try to feed us."

Chapter 18
All the King's Horses

Clark folded the three-page dossier of Special Agent in Charge Michael Conroy into a sleek paper airplane and made a beautiful landing on the aircraft carrier deck that was my desk. Skipper skipped folding her copy into an airplane and instead slid it across the desk toward me. I stuck all three copies into the shredder that cost almost as much as the desk. It chewed up the sheets, cutting them in seven directions and rendering them impossible to reconstruct . . . even with all the king's horses and all the king's men.

I said, "I guess we should brief the rest of the team. Where are they?"

Skipper said, "Hunter, Tony, and Disco are watching reruns of *Baa Baa Black Sheep*, and Mongo's having date night with two Russian girls on your boat."

"You make that sound dirty," I said. "One of the Russian girls is only thirteen or so."

Skipper palmed her forehead. "No, *I* didn't make that sound dirty. *You* did. And I think she's more like fifteen."

"Whatever," I said. "Go get the boys, and tell them we need to talk."

Skipper rose from her chair to play fetch.

"Wait a minute," I said. "Oh, never mind. We'll go to them."

In the home theater consuming the northern end of the first floor, we found our three missing operators doing exactly what Skipper said they were doing.

The Black Sheep of Marine Corps Squadron VMF-214 were slicing and dicing a flight of Japanese Zeros over the Solomon Islands. Greg "Pappy" Boyington was trailing black smoke from his F4U Corsair, but he was still in the fight.

Skipper snatched the remote control from the arm of Hunter's chair and paused the show to the jeers and ire of the room's inhabitants. "Relax, boys. I just paused it. You can pick up where you left off as soon as the briefing is done."

Tony threw up his hands. "But Sugar Monkey, Pappy's been shot, and we don't know if he's going to make it back."

Skipper turned nine shades of red and growled under her breath. "Don't call me that around these guys. You don't know how they are."

Hunter cackled. "Sugar Monkey? That's hilarious, and it's way better than a boring nickname like Skipper."

She pointed a finger at Hunter. "Don't you dare, or I'll tell Tina about Cindy at the post office."

And then Hunter blushed. "Hey, can I help it if the clerk at the post office has great taste in men? No, I cannot. She knows a quality specimen of a man when she sees one."

Tony couldn't resist jumping into the fray. "Is Cindy the one with those blue eyes and those—"

Skipper cut him off. "Watch it, big boy! You're already in enough trouble for the Sugar Monkey thing. I don't think you want to start compounding offenses, now, do you?"

Hunter leaned over and whispered, "Yep, Cindy's the one."

"Thought so," Tony whispered back.

Clark took command of the room. "All right, listen up. It's getting close to game time."

The tomfoolery ended, and the Black Sheep were forgotten.

"Disco, Hunter, Tony . . . You're wheels-up day after tomorrow for Barranquilla, but you're going to have some company."

"Company?" Hunter said. "What kind of company?"

Clark scowled. "The sooner you shut up and let me finish, the sooner you can find out if Pappy makes it back to Vella la Cava."

"Sorry, boss."

"Don't be sorry. Just listen. There's a soft admin puke in DC who likes to make his stripes on the backs of those of us who actually do the work. He insists on having what he calls 'his team' conduct the recon for us and feed us intel up through the chain. For a thousand reasons, we plan to ignore his intel and rely on Hunter and Tony to feed us the real picture down there. The downside is making sure you spot the sub without the DEA boys spotting you."

Hunter raised a hand. "Can I talk now?"

Clark sighed. "What is it?"

"Why do we have to make sure guys on our team don't see us? Wouldn't it make more sense to work together?"

Clark said, "It would if it weren't for the swamp dweller in DC. I don't trust him. He's never been an operator. He got a medical out of the ATF Academy and ended up at Justice in the admin chain at DEA."

"Gotcha," Hunter said. "Now it all makes sense. Are we going to be wired for sight and sound, and am I leaving our driver at the car or taking him with us upriver?"

Clark turned to Skipper and me, and I fielded the questions. "Yes. You're wearing bodycams and sat-coms so I can see and hear what's going on from the ops center. I may be out of the fight for this one, but that doesn't mean I can't sit in the press box and watch the game."

"What about Disco?" Hunter asked.

I said, "Oh, yeah. Sorry. I forgot your question was a two-parter. Whether or not you take Disco or leave him with the airplane is up to you. If we think there's little chance of contact on the river, I can't think of a reason not to take him along for the experience."

Hunter turned to our pilot. "Do you want to go up the river with us or hang out in the air-conditioned hotel room while the kid and I have all the fun?"

Disco chewed on his bottom lip for a moment. "I want to go with you."

Hunter threw up his hands. "Me and two new guys in the jungle, hiding from the DEA, and snooping on the world's heaviest drug trafficker. What could possibly go wrong?"

"My sentiments exactly," I said. "As soon as the narco-sub hits open water, you three will boogie your butts to Isla Mujeres and suit up for a little offshore diving. Singer and Mongo will meet you there with the Mark V. Clark, are you going?"

"That's up to Mongo. If he wants an extra trigger puller, I'm game. But I don't think you'll need me."

I gave our analyst a glance. "Have you got anything else, Sugar Monkey?"

She raised an eyebrow. "Oh, is that how it's going to be? Keep at it, big boy. If you think learning to walk on one fake foot is tough, just keep calling me that name and see how you like having a matching pair."

I took a step away from her. "At least I don't flirt with Cindy at the post office like Hunter does."

Hunter yanked the remote from Skipper's hand. "You two leave me out of this. I'm minding my own business and watching *Black Sheep*."

Tony spun in his chair. "I know I'm the new guy, but where's the sniper?"

I said, "Singer is at the monastery with his brother in South Carolina."

His eyes turned to saucers. "Our sniper lives in a monastery?"

It was too good to pass up, so I took full advantage of the opportunity. "Well, yes. Don't all snipers live in monasteries?"

Tony shook his head. "This operation gets weirder by the minute. I think I'm going to stop asking questions."

Clark made no effort to let Tony off the monastery hook. "Okay, that's it for this evening. Go back to watching the Marines kick the stuffing out of the Japanese."

Back in the hallway, I took Clark's elbow. "Should we start working on getting Tony a slot at The Ranch?"

"I'm going to separate myself from that decision since he's my brother. You're the team lead, so it's your call, but if you want my advice . . . You *do* want my advice, right?"

"Always."

"I thought so," he said. "If I were making the decision, I'd wait until Hunter puts him in the jungle. He's already proven himself in the water, but we need to know what kind of operator he'll make when his feet are dry. And don't forget, he's a Coastie. Who knows if he can even spell *gun*, let alone point the bang-bang end toward the bad guys."

"That's why I always want to hear your advice. Because you say things like 'bang-bang end.'"

"I'm just full of sage wisdom. After all, there are three kinds of people on Earth: those who can count and those who cannot."

I ignored whatever that was supposed to be and changed the subject. "I'm going to do something you're not going to like."

He stepped away. "That's nothing new. What's on your mind?"

"I can't get this Conroy character out of my head. I need to know more about him than what Skipper dug up."

He lowered his chin. "What are you doing, Chase?"

"If I tell you, you'll order me not to, and I don't want to have to disobey a direct order."

He reached for his collar and patted the material of his shirt. "I'm not wearing any rank insignia. What makes you think I can give out orders?"

"In that case," I said, "I'm going to call a guy at the Justice Department and ask him about Conroy."

Clark narrowed his gaze. "What guy at Justice? You sound like you've got a back door inside."

"Not exactly a back door. It's more like a doorbell. But I think this guy will answer when I ring."

"Let's hear it," he said.

"The guy who's running Anya on the undercover op is a supervisory special agent named White. I think it's Raymond White. If he did his homework—and a career agent at that level doesn't let the dog eat his homework—he knows who I am."

Clark moaned and grabbed my shirt with both hands. "You're right. I don't approve, but I'm not going to order you to stand down. You're a big boy, and you have to live with your choices. But you'd better heed my advice on this one . . . Are you listening?"

I pulled away. "I'm listening."

He laid a finger in the middle of my chest. "Make the call from the ops center on speaker with Penny Fulton, your beautiful wife, sitting right beside you to keep your head on straight."

"It's not about Anya," I said. "I just want to use that connection to open a line of communication."

His finger became a fist. "Stay on the reservation, Kemosabe. If you don't, I'll lend Penny my knife so she can chop off the appendage of her choice. And she can keep the knife."

I looked at Skipper, who was putting on a rare demonstration of her ability to listen without speaking. She held up both hands. "Oh, no! Don't drag me into this. You're on your own. I'll give you his phone number, but that's the end of my involvement. And I'm with Clark. You're not getting the number until Penny approves—preferably in writing."

I motioned to the door behind Skipper, and she stepped aside. I tapped on the door to Penny's office and waited with my heart in my throat.

Her subdued voice came through the door. "It's open."

I turned the knob and stuck my head and shoulders inside. "We need to talk with you about something."

Clark stuck a finger between a pair of my ribs. "No, sir! That's the wrong pronoun, Boy Wonder. *We* don't need to talk to Penny. *You* need to talk to her."

Penny's curiosity was obviously piqued. "What is it? Is everything all right?"

"Everything is fine," I said. "We've got a situation with a guy who works in the admin stack at Drug Enforcement. He has an outside connection to our mission, and I've got a bad feeling about him."

"Okay. What does any of that have to do with me?"

I inhaled a long breath and slowly let it out. "I know Skipper told you that Anya is working with the Justice Department on an undercover operation."

"Yeah, she told me about that."

"Well, we . . ."

Another jab between the ribs.

"Okay. I'm going to call the agent in charge of that operation and get the skinny on the guy at Drug Enforcement. I think it would make you feel more comfortable if you were in on the conversation."

She furrowed her brow. "Why would I want to be in on a conversation with some stuffed shirt at the Justice Department? You're not calling *her*, are you?"

"No, I'm not calling Anya. I'm only calling Special Agent Ray White."

She bounced a pencil against her desk. "Chase, I live in L.A. half the time, and you're off saving the world the other half. We're grown-ups. Call whoever you need. I've got work to do. I trust you. Now, close the door." Penny snapped her fingers. "Oh, wait! There's one more thing."

"What is it?"

She smiled. "Tell the little boys across the hall that's the episode where Pappy has to bail out over the ocean, and he gets rescued by a submarine crew."

Chapter 19
I Know You

Expecting a federal civil servant to answer his office telephone after five o'clock was the first misplaced belief of the evening. The second was my ridiculous belief that I could fall asleep that night.

I lay awake beside the woman who loved me more than anyone else ever could, and I thought about Anya. I even tried counting sheep, but they always morphed into the tall, lean figure with golden hair cascading across the bullet-scarred shoulder of Anastasia Burinkova.

What makes her so impossibly captivating?

No one would deny her physical beauty, but the woman lying beside me and breathing softly in sleep's perfect embrace outshined the Russian in every category. Perhaps it was the lioness behind her smoky blue eyes who wouldn't be ignored—the lioness who moved in silence, stalked with singular intent, and struck with unequaled precision. Perhaps the soul of the huntress that was forged and hardened and polished to a razor's edge made her the siren who would not be dismissed, the treasure that could never be possessed.

The sleep that should've been mine became, instead, the torment of a seemingly endless night and left me questioning if I had been honest with myself in my decision to invite Supervisory Special Agent Ray White into my life. Did I truly need the information he would share about Conroy, or was there a blackened corner of my mind that needed to hear the voice of the man who'd temporarily ensnared the former Russian assassin? Perhaps I would have the answer if the sun would ever creep across the horizon and reward my hours spent in silent, darkened, awakened misery with the dawning of a new day. Perhaps I would never know.

When morning finally came, I kissed Penny's forehead as she slept, and then I slid from the bed as quietly as a one-legged man is capable of doing. I was either quiet enough to keep from waking her or she was kind enough to pretend I hadn't.

There are rooms I always expect to be occupied; churches, grocery stores, and libraries feel awkward and amiss when I'm the first to walk in. The Bonaventure ops center was no different. The soft glow of monitors and screens, and the hum of a thousand things that create noises that are impossible to hear when the room is occupied, sang their dull song.

Clark's warning about making the call alone had lost its teeth when Penny insisted that she had no need to be with me during the exchange, so I planted myself alone in the chair that was rightfully Mongo's and pressed the buttons of the speakerphone.

The pleasant but still slightly sleepy voice of a federal government executive assistant filled the room. "Good morning. SSA White's office."

"Good morning, ma'am. Is Agent White available?"

"Who's calling, please?"

I wasn't prepared for the question, and in haste, I gave the wrong answer. "I'm Supervisory Special Agent Chase Fulton with the Secret Service."

Although I carried the credentials bearing that information, it was a lie—a lie designed to get me out of situations I should never allow myself to be in. I stammered, "Wait . . . Just tell him it's Chase Fulton. I think he knows who I am."

The woman said, "As you wish, Agent Fulton."

"No, ma'am. Just Chase."

"As you wish, Mr. Fulton."

The line went silent, and I could hear my heart pounding in my ears.

Seconds later, a displeased voice boomed through the speakers of the ops center. "White."

I cleared my throat. "Good morning, Agent White. I'm Chase Fulton . . ."

"I know who you are, Mr. Fulton. What I don't know is why you'd be calling me, especially while the steam is still rising from my first cup of coffee."

Undeterred, I said, "I need some information."

"I don't know what kind of information you expect from me, but if you're calling to check on your girlfriend, you're wasting both your time and mine."

"I'm calling to get some information on one of your cake-eaters who is insistent on inserting himself into my operation."

"Your operation? I didn't realize you were running federal government operations these days."

"I didn't say it was a federal government op, Raymond. May I call you Raymond?"

A long pause filled the line, and I thought I detected a hint of his shell breaking.

"You can call me Ray, Chase. Let's hear about this operation of yours."

"It's classified."

He laughed out loud. "Classified? I thought you said it wasn't a government op. How can it be classified?"

I held my ground. "It's classified because my handler and I say it is. If you don't think civilian ops can be classified, maybe you should hop a plane down to Atlanta and try to get the boys over at the Coca-Cola factory to let you have a peek at their secret recipe."

"Point taken. And my coffee is cool enough to drink, so let's stop circling and sniffing. Tell me what you need."

"I need to know about a guy named Michael Conroy over at Drug Enforcement. From what I've been able to gather, he has no field experience, and he's worked his way up the chain to an SSA."

The sound of coffee being sipped rang through the phone. "Ha! These days, they pass out supervisory special agent credentials like prizes from Cracker Jack boxes. I had to earn mine. What about you?"

I said, "I thought we'd stopped circling and sniffing."

Another sip. "Fair enough. Give me his name again."

"Michael Conroy. He seems to think he's running a team in Central America, but you're not going to find any jungle mud on his wingtips."

"Hang on a minute, Chase. I'm going to put you on speaker, but don't make any sounds. Just listen. Got it?"

"I got it."

The phone clicked, and White yelled, "Martha! Get in here."

I listened as White directed a show just for me.

Martha said, "Yes, sir. What do you need?"

"What do you know about a cat named Michael Conroy over at the DEA? I think he's an SSA, but I'm not sure. Definitely an admin guy and not an operator."

She said, "There are two agents over there named Conroy. One is a relatively new guy. Yale Law, grandson of a congressman . . . the whole nine yards."

"That's not the one," White said. "What about the other one?"

"The other one is a snake. When I was with Drug Enforcement, he was a mid-level administrator. He made a habit of claiming credit for everything from a full moon to winning the Super Bowl."

White asked, "Does he run field ops?"

"I doubt it. As far as I know, he's never been anything more than a support administrator. But it's been almost eleven years since I left the DEA to come work for you."

"You don't work *for* me, Martha. You work *with* me."

"Whatever you say, Agent White."

He said, "Okay, one more question. If he is running a team in Central America, would you trust him as a liaison between a civilian and a government op?"

"Agent White, I wouldn't trust him to babysit a pet rat."

"Thank you, Martha. That's what I needed to know."

The door closed, and White said, "Did you get all that, Chase?"

"I did, and I appreciate the dog and pony show."

"Hold on a minute, Chase." He apparently covered the phone with his hand, but I could still hear through the muffled speech. "Yes, Martha? What is it?"

The woman said, "*She* is in the building, sir."

"That's what I need this morning. Keep her outside until I'm off the phone."

She laughed. "Yeah, right. Just how do you suggest I do that?"

"Just do what you can, Martha."

White returned to the conversation. "I've got to go, Chase. Is there anything else you need to know?"

"I think that covers it. I appreciate your time, and I'm sorry your coffee got cold."

"Don't worry about my coffee, Supervisory Special Agent Fulton. I'm in a federal government office building in downtown DC. If there's anything we have no shortage of, it's coffee."

"I can think of at least one other commodity you have in abundance up there."

"Yeah, well, that particular commodity is about to hit the fan, so I've got to run. Before I go, though, I will tell you one more thing."

"What's that?"

"She's fine. She's a pain in my ass, but she's safe and making friends."

I let his reassurance pour over me. "Don't let her seduce you, Ray."

"I'm relatively immune to those things, Chase. I'm not as young as you, and I'm smart enough to know how a bad decision smells. But she's got her hooks pretty deep in one of my young agents."

"I guess that makes me feel sorry for the guy and envious at the same time."

"Don't be jealous, Chase. The young agent isn't a guy. It's Special Agent Gwynn Davis. Take care of yourself. It's nice to finally put a voice with a dossier. Next time you're in DC . . ."

"I try to avoid that place, but next time you're in Saint Marys, Georgia . . ."

"Goodbye, Chase."

I sat in the relative silence of the ops center and let my chin fall to my chest. I'd successfully extracted the information I needed from a man who I believed was a gunfighter like me. Elusive sleep came as my mind ceased its torture of my body, and I drifted off, reassured by the knowledge that Anya was, at least, alive and safe.

Chapter 20
Lessons from a Water Bottle

The warning tone indicating someone would soon come through the door jarred me from my sleep at the conference table. I stretched and yawned as Skipper stepped inside her lair.

"Oh, hey," she said. "Good morning. I didn't expect to find anyone in here this early. Is everything okay?"

I reached down to scratch an ankle that no longer existed. "Good morning. Everything's okay. I've been—"

"You've been on the phone with Special Agent White at Justice, haven't you?" I nodded, and she said, "I thought Clark told you not to make the call without Penny."

"I talked with Penny about it. She's got more important things to do than worry about me talking to a fed."

She laid a stack of files, a laptop, and a cup of coffee on the console. "I don't think it has anything to do with talking to a fed. I think it's more about Anya."

"Again, Penny has more important things to worry about. Anya is not a threat."

She huffed. "You clearly know absolutely nothing about women, but what did White have to say?"

I wiped the sleep from my eyes. "You're exactly right about that. I'll never understand women."

"Some things are meant to be mysterious, and we're one of those things."

"Truer words have never been spoken. So, back to business. White doesn't know Conroy, but his secretary apparently does."

"Executive assistant. They're not called secretaries anymore."

"Whatever she is, she says he's a snake and a glory grabber who can't be trusted."

"I guess that means Clark's instincts were right again."

"They usually are," I said.

"So, what's the plan?"

"I'm going to discuss it with Clark and Mongo, but my recommendation is to let him *think* he's running the intel side, and we'll proceed as if we've never heard of him. We'll still put Hunter and Tony on the ground."

She took a sip of coffee. "I think that's a good plan. We don't care who gets credit for the win as long as the good guys get a check in the W column."

"I'd like your opinion on something," I said.

She raised an eyebrow. "You may want to wait until I've reached the bottom of this cup. I'm not sure how many valuable opinions I have right now."

"This one shouldn't be too taxing. What do you think about sending Disco up the river with Hunter in Colombia?"

"Instead of Tony?"

"No, in addition to Tony."

She pondered the question and took another sip. "As long as Hunter's okay with it, I don't think there's any reason not to take him. The experience will be good for him."

"That's my thought, as well. I'll get out of your hair and let you go to work. Is anybody else up?"

"I don't know who's up other than Tony and Hunter. They're on the back gallery having coffee and Spy Craft One Oh One."

My fake foot and I chose the stairs and made our way to the kitchen to find exactly what Skipper described: Hunter and Tony were kneeling at the open kitchen door with picks hanging from the lock.

I poured a cup and watched. "I'll have another key made for you if you've lost yours. You don't have to break in."

Hunter looked up. "Can you believe a grown man doesn't know how to pick a lock?"

"It looks like you're changing that."

"I'm trying, but my student isn't exactly a prodigy."

"It'll come," I said. "It just takes time and practice. What's next on the agenda?"

"I thought we'd do a little hand to hand and maybe some rifle work this afternoon. Are we still on schedule for deployment tomorrow?"

I checked my watch. "Yes. Twenty-four hours from now, the two of you and Disco will be southbound for Barranquilla."

Hunter laid a hand over one of Tony's. "Gentle pressure on the tensioner. Don't bind the pins. Just relax and envision the mechanism. Pick each pin individually. Don't rush."

He stood and took a seat at the kitchen table. "Did you learn any more about Conroy?"

"I did. He's a snake, so we're going to ignore him. Try not to get tangled up with the DEA on the river. We're going to let Conroy believe we're leaving the recon to *his* team."

Tony shouted, "Yes! I did it!"

Hunter reached for the door and relocked the bolt. "That's good, kid. Now, close your eyes and do it blind. Ninety percent of the lock-picking you'll do will be in the dark, so learn to do it entirely by feel, and you'll be ahead of the game right from the start."

* * *

Just before two o'clock, while I was practicing stairs with my robo-foot, *Aegis* rounded the bend of the North River with Tatiana at the wheel and Mongo standing closely behind her. My training turned into watching as the giant patiently taught a five-foot-tall ballerina the fine art of docking a fifty-foot catamaran. After three aborted attempts, Tatiana finally managed to land the boat against the dock without breaking off any of the big parts.

Mongo stepped down to the dock. After securing the boat, he reached up and hefted Tatiana from the deck. Instead of accepting Mongo's offer to help her down, Irina sat on the deck with her feet hanging over the edge, and Mongo stepped between her dangling feet. I couldn't hear their conversation, but the kiss they shared said they'd thoroughly enjoyed their time aboard *Aegis*.

It took forty-five minutes to bring Mongo up to speed on everything he'd missed in the previous twenty-four hours.

"So much for trusting the feds," he said.

"We don't need them, but they're an extra hurdle we'll have to dodge in the jungle."

With the briefing complete and decisions made, Mongo said, "We still have to test the new sled at least once before we deploy."

Back into the water we went with Mongo's new-and-improved weapon. Hunter and Tony flew the first run by hand and backed off for the pulse. Everything worked exactly as we'd hoped, and we ran a second attempt, completely remote. Hunter and Tony stayed in the water to recover the sled if it went rogue. Thankfully, the remote test was a success, and we lifted everyone and everything from the cold North River.

Mongo said, "It looks like the hardware is ready to go. How does everybody feel?"

Tony enthusiastically answered, "Ready to go to work."

Hunter laughed. "You'll grow out of that, kid. When we leave home, people tend to shoot at us and take turns trying to blow us up."

"Sounds like a party to me."

Hunter motioned up the slope. "There's a pretty girl in that house who'd disagree."

"Yeah, you're probably right about that, but I'm still looking forward to going downrange with you guys."

Hunter propped up against the gunwale of the Mark V. "Let's have a talk, kid."

Tony pulled a towel from the stack and dried his hair. "Sure. What do you want to talk about?"

Hunter gave me the eye, so I took a seat.

"Listen up, kid. I know you spent five years of your life jumping out of helicopters into twenty-foot seas to pull boaters out of crap they shouldn't have ever put themselves into in the first place. I'm sure you worked your way through being scared of the ocean, and you're all hero to the core, but what we do ain't what you did. As a general rule, we don't rescue people. We kill people and break things, and that's a nasty business. The people we kill almost always try to kill us first. Our job is to not let them. And the things we break usually try to break us first. This isn't the kind of job where we jump in the water, send a frostbitten fisherman up to a chopper in a basket, and then fly home. I'm not making light of what you did. It was noble and heroic and all that front-page, make-your-momma-proud stuff. But if you get your picture in the paper while you're working with us, there's a better-than-good chance one of us will shoot you in the face."

He paused for a drink and then tossed the bottle to Tony, who caught it, twisted off the lid, and wiped the rim.

Hunter said, "Freeze."

Tony froze as if terrified.

"That's the difference between what you were and what we are," Hunter said. "Sooner or later, you and I are going to bleed together in some godforsaken, mud-covered corner of the world. One or both of us may never make it out of that hole, but I can look you dead in the eye and swear to you that not a single man on this team would hesitate to reach inside your chest and clamp off a bleeder with one hand while sending lead downrange with the other. That's what you can expect from us, and we have to know you'd do exactly the same for us. What we do is life and death every time we leave home, and if you ever forget that, one of those bastards shooting back at us will remind you. So, next time one of your brothers on this team throws you a bottle of water, don't let me catch you wiping off the lip . . . because that's not the brother we need."

Tony stared at the deck of the boat as Hunter's words washed over him. After a long moment, he looked up. "It's easy to look around at the airplanes and boats and houses and envy the world you guys live in. I guess I needed the gut check. I'm sorry I didn't show it the respect it deserves."

I held up a hand, and Tony landed the water bottle in my palm. Without a wipe, I finished off the contents. "Don't be sorry. Just don't do anything in the field that'll get any of us hurt. This mission shouldn't include any bullets in the air, but we can't afford to forget who we're messing with. Macario Mateo is a serious player with a hundred-million-dollar-per-month export business. He's not going to sit quietly while we tear apart his distribution channel. If we get caught, it's going to get ugly in a hurry. Hunter's going to shoot with you this afternoon, and if he's not happy with what he sees, you'll be riding the bench on this one. This is a pass-or-fail team. Notice I didn't say pass-or-fail man. I said team. We fail together, or we succeed together. No exceptions. Welcome aboard. Now, let's go to work."

Chapter 21
Day One

I stood on the ramp at what had once been the Saint Marys Airport and watched the Citation climb out and turn south with Disco, Hunter, and Tony headed for the Colombian jungle. Over the previous months, the airport had become a chunk of low-country dirt, grass, concrete, and hangars no longer owned by the city but deeded to Clark and me as indivisible halves.

I loved owning an airport for the sake of privacy. Some of the things my team and I did would attract too much unwanted attention and leave me trying to explain why six men in tactical gear swarmed from a helicopter in the middle of the night. The element of a private airport I didn't like was the absence of other pilots coming and going to care for their beloved flying machines and telling semi-true stories. Life at an airport is similar to life in a marina. The characters are the same. The lies are the same. The only difference is the medium on which the machines float. Sacrificing such pleasantries was but one of the necessary evils of my line of work. Watching half of my team disappear into the southern sky was the most recent sacrifice. I envied not only the sleep they would enjoy on the flight, but also the time spent moving silently through the jungle in pursuit of our prey while dodging the watchers who could be the end of our operation before it began. I wanted to be on that airplane. I needed to be in that jungle.

* * *

Six hours later, the ops center had been transformed into a command post being manned without interruption. As long as operatives were in the field and at danger's fingertips, someone would be on duty in the darkened room, only a radio or sat-phone call away.

The first call came on my watch, leaving the sour taste of envy stinging in my mouth.

Being the phase-one operational commander, it was Hunter's voice on the line. "We're safe on deck in Barranquilla, and we'll be operational inside an hour."

"Any problems so far?" I asked.

"None. Believe it or not, Disco didn't get us lost this time."

"That's an excellent start. Do you still feel good about Tony?"

"He'll be fine if I can teach him to move without making noise. He's heavy-footed like someone else I know."

I stared down at my robot. "I have only half as many feet as everyone else, so maybe I'll be quieter when I'm back in the field."

He laughed. "We could float you in a balloon, and you'd still be noisy. We're cramming some calories down our gullets now, but we'll be in the thick long before sundown."

"Do you need anything from me?" I asked.

"Just answer when we call."

"We will. Don't worry about that. How about Disco?"

"I'm taking him into the bush with us. If babysitting both of them turns into a circus, I'll send Disco back to the airport, but I think he'll be fine."

"Just don't let the Drug Enforcement guys roll you up."

"We won't. Don't worry about that. I'll let you know when we dive in."

I made the log entry showing the jungle team's boots on the ground, and day one was officially underway. With every second that passed, I wanted to be back in the saddle even more. My brain went as far as wondering what the team was having to eat before vanishing beneath the jungle canopy.

A tone I didn't recognize sounded from somewhere within the impressive suite of electronics in Skipper's lair. I scanned every console and screen, hoping to identify the tone and respond appropriately, but my search was wasted. The sound erupted again, and I did the only rational thing I could do at the moment: I opened the secured door, leaned out, and yelled down the stairs. "Skipper!"

The tone continued from behind me, but the sound that interested me was the patter of bare feet on the steps. "I'm coming!"

Skipper topped the stairs, and I pointed into the ops center. "It's making a noise."

She pushed past me. "Yeah, that's what happens when the team on the ground opens the satellite channel. Why didn't you activate the monitors?"

I followed her into the room. "I told you all I know about this situation when I said, 'It's making a noise.'"

Shaking her head, Skipper typed a string of commands into her computer, and the large monitor came to life. A shaky scene of Central American jungle came into focus. She said, "Comms established and secure. How do you hear?"

Hunter's voice sounded through the four speakers near the ceiling. "Loud and clear."

"We have you the same, and video is stable. Give me a three count."

Hunter stuck his fingers in front of the camera strapped to his chest and raised three fingers, one at a time. "One . . . Two . . . Three."

Skipper stroked a few keys. "Audio and video are synced."

I'd been through this exercise many times, but only from the field—never inside the ops center. I watched Skipper with singular focus, but her hands moved too quickly for me to keep up.

"I'm never going to get this end of things."

Skipper huffed. "No kidding. Even Clark is better in here than you. This isn't your world, to say the least. I could really use Penny's help if she's not covered up."

"I'll go ask her," I said, thankful to have an excuse to leave the room.

I found my wife in her office with her feet on the desk, reclining in the oversized chair and eyes closed. Slipping into the chair across from her, I watched her in silence for a moment. Seeing her completely relaxed and content did my heart good. I crossed my legs, and my robot rattled, drawing Penny from her zone.

She smiled and met my eyes, careful not to look at the fake foot. "Hey. How long have you been there?"

"I just sat down. Were you napping?"

She pulled her feet from the desk. "No, I was picturing a scene that's giving me trouble. I can write it, but I can't imagine how the director is going to bring it alive. Now that I've seen the process, it's changed the way I write. It's sort of like an architect designing something that can't be built. If my scenes can't be filmed, I have no choice but to rewrite them. That's where I'm at with this one."

"It sounds like you're busy, then."

She shook her head. "No, not really. It's just rewrites and a little editing at this point."

I caught myself looking toward the ceiling, and she chuckled.

"Skipper kicked you out of the ops center, didn't she?"

"A little," I admitted.

"And she sent you down here to recruit me, didn't she?"

"A little."

She closed the file on her computer and pushed herself from the chair. "I'll be happy to help." She crossed the room, closed the door, and sat down on the floor at my feet . . . foot. She pushed up the leg of my cargo pants and ran her finger down the titanium and carbon-fiber creation attached to my stump. The look in her eyes was pain, but not her own. "Does it hurt?"

I sighed. "Sometimes."

She unlaced my boot and pulled it from my prosthetic, then had the last reaction I could've expected: she giggled.

"What's funny?"

She wrapped both hands around the robotic thing that resembled a foot. "Now I understand why there have been half the number of socks in the laundry. I guess you don't need a sock for this foot, huh?"

I chuckled. "No, but sometimes I still pull two from the drawer."

"Old habits."

I brushed my hand through her hair. "Thank you."

She cocked her head and looked up with the most beautifully curious smile I'd ever seen. "Why are you thanking me?"

I laid my hand on top of hers that was resting on my metallic ankle. "For looking at it."

She swallowed hard. "If I could trade with you, I would gladly give you my right foot, and I'd wear the prosthetic. I can write without a foot, but what you do—what you are—doesn't happen on a keyboard."

"I could never ask that of you."

She rested her chin atop my hand. "That's love."

I nodded, trying to keep the glisten in my eye from becoming a tear. "That's exactly why I'm thanking you."

She stood, leaned down to kiss me, and whispered, "How can a prosthetic foot still smell bad?"

I loved her ability to turn moments funny when they shouldn't have been. "I think we can blame the boot for that one."

"I guess so. Come on, let's go check on Skipper. Are the guys on the ground yet?"

"They are. I had everything under control up there until I had to actually do something." I slipped my boot back onto my foot and tied the knot. "Race you to the stairs."

She slipped through the door. "Race you to the top."

She won, but not by much, and we found Skipper right where she was most at home.

Penny stepped behind her, glancing over her shoulder. "Chase said you kicked him out."

Without looking up, Skipper said, "Chase kicked himself out, and that's an accomplishment for a guy with one foot. He's terrible up here. Can you help?"

"Sure, I'm putting the finishing touches on the screenplay, so I've got plenty of time. Which shift will be mine?"

Skipper checked her watch. "I'll stay on until eight a.m. if you could pull four hours until around noon."

"That doesn't leave much time for you to rest."

Our analyst extraordinaire motioned toward the screen. "It'll be dark soon, and they'll camp for the night. I can catch some z's right here until they're on the move again. I'll be fine."

"Okay, I'll see you at eight in the morning. Do you need anything tonight?"

"Maybe some popcorn. We're out in the cupboard up here."

I leapt from my chair. "Finally! Something I'm qualified to do."

When I made it back to Bonaventure's third floor, Penny was missing, and the screen in front of Skipper had turned dim as the sun was setting. She wore a single-sided headphone and microphone combination. I stuffed the box of microwave popcorn in the cupboard and studied the picture on the screen.

Hunter moved slowly forward, carefully placing his boot on each stride.

Skipper said, "Roger. Do they appear to be armed?" Silence filled the air until she said, "Roger. Keep the channel open."

She leaned toward the screen with unparalleled focus, and I slid into the chair beside her and whispered, "Can you put him on speaker?"

She held her finger to her lips and activated the speakers overhead. I watched the scene play out on the screen. Hunter carried his suppressed MP5 at the low ready as he leaned against a mahogany tree. His position temporarily blinded the camera, leaving the screen full of the rough bark of the tree and bouncing in time with Hunter's heart. The picture gyrated and seemed to float from behind the tree. He'd obviously removed the body camera from his chest and lodged it into a crease in the mahogany bark. Two men came into crisp focus in a rough-looking boat with an outboard. The man in the bow stepped from the boat and landed in the soft mud of the bank. He scampered up the slope directly toward the camera with his hands reaching for his belt.

Hunter stepped into the frame and locked onto the approaching man. I could suddenly feel the beating of my own heart and taste the adrenaline. My team had been in the jungle for less than an hour, and they'd already found a potential fight.

Chapter 22
A Lot to Learn

As the man stepped ever closer, the look on his face showed discomfort, but not hostile intent. He kicked his toes into the soil of the slope and unzipped his pants. As the man deposited the last three cervezas he'd drank onto the leaf-covered ground at his feet, Hunter stepped from behind the cover of the tree.

Skipper pressed the transmit mute switch and whispered, "What's he doing?"

"Don't worry," I said. "There's no better time to surprise a potential opponent than when he has his hands full . . . so to speak."

In passable Spanish, my partner said, "Hola. ¿Cómo estás?"

The man jerked, and the spigot was cut off. His hand flew to his scabbard, and he drew a knife. I focused on the glistening blade, but I was certain I wasn't the only one. Without a doubt, Hunter couldn't take his eyes from the weapon, either.

A rustling sound came, and Hunter patted the air behind him, giving the signal to wait. Our pilot or the rescue swimmer had, no doubt, drawn his weapon to join the coming fight, but Hunter kept his composure.

The interaction began in tense Spanish that I hoped Hunter could understand. The man holding the knife stood with his pants still inconveniently open and his feet spread awkwardly. "Who are you?"

Hunter spoke with calm confidence. "My name is Stone, and I want to buy your boat."

The look on the man's face morphed from surprised fear into confusion. "Buy our boat?"

Skipper spun toward me. "I didn't know Hunter spoke Spanish."

I shrugged. "I suspect there's a lot of things we don't know about Hunter, but he's doing fine for now."

The man lowered the knife a few inches, and what light remained danced across the blade as his hand shook.

"Whatever that guy is," I said, "he's not a fighter. He's too scared to zip his pants, let alone win a knife fight against Hunter."

"Yes, I want to buy your boat. How much?"

The man eyed Hunter cautiously, then sent a glance over his shoulder. "Hey, this guy wants to buy our boat. What should I tell him?"

A sound from the surface of the water returned, "What guy?"

"This guy," the man said.

Although out of frame, the man was obviously climbing from the boat to create a better angle.

Hunter took a step forward, and the man flinched, then raised his knife back into the original threatening position.

Hunter kept moving in. "Relax. I'm not going to hurt you. I just want to buy your boat."

"This is a very strange request. Who are you?"

Hunter took another step, placing himself well within the knife's range. "If I were going to kill you, I would've already done it. I just want your boat, and I'm willing to pay for it."

"Hey," the man yelled to his friend. "How much do you want for the boat?"

The second man stepped into the picture. "It's a very nice boat. It is very valuable."

Hunter sighed. "There are a thousand more just like it between here and the ocean. I'm going to buy one of them. If you want my money, tell me how much for the boat."

My partner was obviously approaching the limit of his Spanish vocabulary, but he was doing well enough to get his point across.

"U.S. dollars or pesos?" the second man asked.

Hunter reached into his pocket and withdrew a roll of cash. "Dollars, amigo. How much?"

The grin of the second man showed an absence of at least three teeth with the remaining few clearly on their last legs. He withdrew his knife and stepped beside his friend. "Why don't we just kill you and take all of your money and keep our boat?"

Hunter shook his head. "You don't want to try that. It won't end well for you. I don't want trouble. I only want your boat."

The man laughed. "There are two of us, and we are armed. You are alone."

Hunter said, "This is a bad idea, guys. I'll give you more than enough money to go back to Barranquilla and buy any boat you want. Just don't do anything crazy, okay?"

The man's smile vanished, and he took a step forward. "Give us your money, and we will let you live, okay?"

Hunter drew in a long breath, held it for a few seconds, then let it out. With his hands raised to shoulder height in surrender, he took a half step backward. "Don't turn this day into your last. I'll find another boat. Just walk away, okay?"

Instead of turning back for his boat, the man lunged forward, thrusting the knife toward Hunter's chest. Hunter easily sidestepped the attack by the untrained fighter and shoved him into the tree. The second guy followed the first and jabbed at the air with his blade. Hunter stepped inside the attack, captured the man's wrist, and spun to face the first attacker.

The guy bounced from the tree, shook off the blow, and lunged back down the slope toward my partner and the other guy. Hunter threw an elbow strike to the face of the man whose hand, wrist, and knife were still well controlled. The strike sent him stumbling backward down the slope, forcing Hunter to release his wrist.

The downhill attack from the guy by the tree came faster and harder than Hunter had anticipated, but he still managed to brush off the blade as it passed his shoulder. Undeterred, the two men regrouped and charged back up the slope toward Hunter, who was waiting patiently for their arrival. The attackers had apparently combined each of their small brains into one big one and moved in with an aggressive, coordinated strike. One man raised his knife well above his head and drew the blade downward toward Hunter's head while the second man charged toward his stomach.

A smile overtook my face as Hunter strengthened his stance to defend against the two-pronged attack that we'd practiced thousands of times with Clark directing the show. Hunter would let the men come and then dive between them, allowing the overhead attack to land high on the lower man's back like a *Three Stooges* skit, but inexperience and anxiety foiled Hunter's plan.

A pair of spitting hisses of nine-millimeter rounds leaving the suppressed muzzle of an MP5 cut through the air. The first attacker's face imploded, and the back of his skull filled the air in a pink mist. The second attacker, diving forward, caught the round at his collarbone, and the lead projectile tumbled through his chest and abdomen, lodging someplace deep inside of him.

Hunter spun, fury raging in his face. "Dammit! What were you thinking?"

Tony's voice filled the speakers. "They were a second away from carving you in two. I saved your life."

"No, they weren't. They were absolutely no threat. The whole thing would've been over in three seconds, and we would've had their boat." Through gritted teeth, Hunter growled and punched the mahogany tree, knocking the body camera from the bark and sending it to the ground with the face of the first man centered in the frame and a nine-millimeter hole just above his right eyebrow. Still fuming, Hunter ordered, "Get these bodies in the river while I mod the boat."

Tony's and Disco's boots came into focus on the darkened earth, and soon, the body of the head-shot fisherman disappeared down the slope. Sounds of splashing and pounding poured from the speakers, and my mind churned as I tried to figure out what the pounding sound could be.

Disco lifted the body camera, peered into its fisheye lens, and wiped it with the sleeve of his shirt. He stuck the Velcro backing to his vest. When he turned back toward the river, the camera focused on Hunter chopping triangular chunks from the gunwale of the wooden boat.

With the two bodies sinking in the murky water, Hunter said, "Get the cowling off the engine, crush it, and bury it as far away from the river as you can get without losing sight of me."

Tony followed Hunter's order, and Disco joined my partner hacking away at the boat.

"What exactly are we doing?" Disco asked.

Without stopping his chopping, Hunter said, "We're modifying the boat so whoever sees it won't connect us with the disappearance of two local fishermen. Why the hell did you let that kid shoot those guys?"

Disco shook his head. "It happened so fast, it was over before I realized what was happening. When I saw them split their attack high and low, I knew you had them, but only because Clark has put me through that drill a dozen times. There was no way for

Tony to know. I'm sure, to him, it looked like they were seconds away from killing you."

Hunter took a long breath and settled to one knee beside the boat. "Smear some mud into the notches. We don't want the white interior of the wood showing. I want the cuts to appear old."

Disco scooped a handful of mud from the riverbank and rubbed it into the notches, leaving the damage appearing as if it had been done decades earlier.

The sound of approaching footsteps came, and Disco turned to see Tony descending the slope.

Hunter asked, "Did you get it buried?"

Without a word, Tony nodded, and Hunter stuck his knife into the wooden deck of the boat. "I know you haven't been through the same training as the rest of us, but taking a life is always the last resort. When we get home, I'll put you through some drills so you'll understand the dynamics of close-quarters battle. Until then, don't shoot anybody else unless they're holding a gun to my head. Got it?"

Tony nodded. "Yeah, I got it. I was so sure you were a second away from your last breath . . ."

"It's over, and now you know. Get everything out of this boat that could identify it as belonging to the dead guys."

Tony stepped into the small boat and prowled through everything on board. He came up with a leather wallet. "What should I do with this?"

Hunter stopped his chopping and mudding. "Throw it to me." He caught the wallet and opened the flap. After studying the contents, he shoved a handful of rocks into the wallet and tossed it toward the center of the river.

"What just happened?" Tony asked.

Hunter pulled his knife from the deck. "I memorized the guy's name and address so we can take care of his widow and orphans, then I sank the wallet. The only thing worse than getting caught on this mission would be getting caught with a dead man's wallet."

Tony went back to work and mumbled, "I've got a lot to learn."

Chapter 23
Second Worst

With the boat sufficiently modified, Hunter stepped across the gunwale and onto the deck. Disco followed, and Tony shoved the bow off the mud as he stepped inside.

Hunter said, "Hey, Coast Guard. What's your plan if the engine doesn't start?"

Tony looked up. "What do you mean?"

Hunter shook his head. "Never push a boat off the bank until the engine starts. If it doesn't start, I'm pretty sure I know which creek we'd be up without a paddle."

Tony grabbed a line from the deck, tied a lasso, and roped the stump of a tree on the bank. He secured the line to a cleat on the bow. "We're not victims now."

Hunter gave the starter rope a pull, and the engine fired on the first attempt. A puff of white smoke rose from the exhaust, and Tony whipped the slack in the line, lifting the lasso from the stump and coiling the rope.

Hunter almost laughed. "You may not know when to shoot or shove off, but I've got to hand it to you. You can rodeo."

"Just wait 'til you see me ride a bull," Tony said.

Hunter pulled the engine into gear and added just enough throttle to point the boat upstream and creep along the steep incline to the north. "I don't think they ride bulls down here. I think they dress up in funny-looking outfits and stick swords in their back."

Tony said, "In that case, just wait 'til you see me in a cape."

They motored up the river for a few minutes until Hunter slapped at his chest and spun the boat around.

Tony scanned the area. "What's happening?"

"I left my body camera back there, stuck to a tree. We've got to go back."

Disco pulled the camera from his vest and tossed it toward Hunter. The image on the screen tumbled and spun as the camera flew through the air.

Hunter plucked it from flight and stuck it onto his chest. "I guess we'd better check in."

Skipper flipped the mute switch. "No need to check in. We watched the whole thing."

Hunter adjusted his earpiece. "Roger. Did you see the shots?"

"We did," Skipper said.

Hunter asked, "Who is we?"

"It's just Chase and me."

Hunter said, "Good. The two corpses are on me. I should've done a better job prepping the new kid."

"It happens," I said. "Is everybody okay?"

"Except for the two bodies bouncing along the bottom of the river behind us, we're all good."

"How about fuel?" I asked.

He reached down and shook the plastic fuel tank. "This one's full, and there's two more tanks behind me." He twisted and lifted the edge of each tank. "They're full, as well."

I said, "I guess first contact screwed up the original plan, huh?"

Hunter said, "It always does. We could've camped out for weeks waiting to see a sub go by, but having a boat changes the timeline, for sure."

"It also changes your vulnerability," I said.

"That's precisely why this just became a night op. It's too risky to move during the day."

"Do you have enough batteries for your night-vision equipment?"

"No, but we've got a nice moon as long as the cloud cover stays away. I figure we can make forty miles between sunset and sunrise, so we should be somewhere near Magangué on the third night."

"I like it," I said. "That definitely speeds things up. I'll brief Clark and Mongo. Do you have an egress plan yet?"

The question sent Tony's and Disco's eyes toward Hunter, who said, "We'll burn that bridge when we come to it. Maybe we can catch a ride on a submarine."

I checked my watch. "Kill the video feed for now. It's too dark for us to see anything, and we need to save the batteries. Check in at the top and bottom of every hour with a position report and sitrep."

"You got it. Anything else?"

Skipper's eyes darted around the room. "Yeah, two more things. First, give me the guy's name and address, and I'll take care of his family."

Hunter recited the information and said, "Both guys looked alike, so they're probably brothers, if that helps."

"I'll do some digging," she said.

Hunter asked, "What's the other thing?"

"Don't kill Tony in his sleep."

Hunter huffed. "Don't worry. He's not getting any sleep tonight."

The screen went dark, and she turned to me. "How bad is Tony's screw-up?"

"I'm not going to sugarcoat it. It's the second-worst thing that can happen on a mission."

"What's the first?"

"Being the one who got shot."

She made the log entries, and Mongo came through the door. He pulled his oversized, custom-made chair from its parking spot and rolled to the table. "How's it going so far?"

I grimaced. "Good and bad."

"Let's hear the good first. Bad can always wait. I've got some bad news of my own, but you go first."

He had my attention, and everything inside of me wanted to hear his bad news before delivering mine, but technically, this was his operation, so I fell in line. "Hunter took both Disco and Tony downrange. They encountered a pair of fishermen along the river and tried to buy their boat. Long story short, the fishermen caught a couple of nine-millimeters in a skirmish."

He squeezed his eyelids closed. "Who was the shooter?"

"Tony."

"I was afraid it was too early to put him in the field. Any friendly casualties?" I shook my head, and he said, "Good. Let's hear the good news."

I briefed him about the acquisition of the boat and how it would speed up the timeline.

He listened carefully before saying, "That's solid. You've got them reporting every thirty, right?"

Skipper said, "Yes, at the top and bottom of every hour. Their plan is to move at night and hide when the sun comes up."

Mongo drummed his fingers on the table. "I just got off the phone with Singer. He's on his way home."

"He's coming home?" I asked. "I thought he was staying with his brother at the monastery until we were ready to fly."

"That *was* the plan," he said, "but his brother apparently killed himself this afternoon."

Skipper gasped. "What?"

The big man hung his head. "Yeah. Singer said his brother started talking right after lunch."

I raised an eyebrow. "Talking? I thought he didn't talk."

"Apparently, he'd been silent as long as he could. Singer said it'd been over twenty-five years since he'd said a word. Anyway, he talked about everything he remembered before the incident."

"What incident?" Skipper asked.

I turned to her. "Don't you know the story about how Singer's brother ended up in the monastery?"

"I know there was some kind of trouble with their parents and that they went to live with a preacher, but that's all I know."

I said, "Apparently, Singer's father was violent and unpredictable when he drank, which was too often. Singer says his dad attacked his mother one night while he and his brother were watching. Singer grabbed a shotgun from behind a chair and took care of his dad."

She covered her mouth. "Took care of? Do you mean, like, he killed him?"

"Yes, he shot his father to protect his mother, but it was too late. She was already dead from the beating and choking. A preacher took Singer and his brother in, but his brother stopped talking. The preacher and his wife didn't know what to do with a nine-year-old boy who refused to speak, so they tried every doctor they could find. They finally left him with the monks, and that's where he'd been ever since."

A tear left Skipper's eye. "That's horrible. I had no idea."

Mongo cleared his throat. "Yes, horrible is the only appropriate word for it. Singer said his brother hugged him, told him he was sorry that he couldn't protect him, and went to the bathroom. He never came out. Singer checked on him and found him in a puddle of blood with both wrists open."

The lump in my throat felt like a baseball as I sat brokenhearted for the best sniper I've ever known, the most devout man of God anyone has ever known, and my friend. "Is he coming here?"

Mongo said, "I don't know. He said he was coming home. I assumed that meant here. I'd say there's a pretty good chance he'll go straight to the church."

I felt like I'd been kicked in the gut. "What time do you expect him?"

"He was about an hour south of Savannah when I talked with him, and that was thirty minutes ago."

I stood from my chair and turned to Skipper. "When Hunter checks in, try not to let him know. He's got his hands full down there, and I don't want to drop this on him in the middle of the operation. I'm going to the church to meet Singer."

Mongo pushed himself from his chair. "I'm coming with you."

Chapter 24
Gravy by Association

Singer's church was a twelve-decade-old, white-frame structure with a steeple that bore the scars of those years. Nobody could remember if the spire was original, but if it was, only God Himself could've sustained it against the hurricanes, lightning strikes, and drunken teenagers hell-bent on scaling the monolith that rose at least two dozen feet higher than any other manmade structure in old Saint Marys.

The headlights of Singer's Suburban pierced the darkness beneath the live oak overhanging the gravel parking lot. Our sniper pulled to a stop a few feet from where Mongo and I stood and stepped from his truck. The face that carried a perpetual smile had been replaced by a blank canvas bearing no emotion. No one spoke, but the broken man before us motioned up the root-buckled sidewalk and toward the side door of God's house.

Inside the office lined with volumes of text and thousands of years of history told through the eyes of the faithful, the three of us settled into comfortable chairs, and Singer closed his eyes. Perhaps it was based in respect, or maybe my lack of knowing what else to do, but I joined my friend in the darkness behind my eyelids.

Prayers are the most intimate things humans do—not the ones we say before cutting into our first bite of dinner or the ones some self-righteous deacon belts out to dismiss the Sunday morning service, but the ones in which we whisper directly into God's ear when no one else can hear. Although I've heard Singer pray on more occasions than I can remember, the soft, measured breaths he took in and allowed to escape that evening were the most fervent communion with God I've ever heard.

When his moments alone with his god were finished, he spoke softly. "I'm sorry to bring this into your lives during a mission."

"Never apologize for something like this," I said. "It's the world that owes you an apology. We can't take away the pain, but we're here for whatever you need."

He reached across the table and laid his hand on my forearm. "That's what family does."

I nodded and longed for some morsel of wisdom I could share to put his broken heart back together, but nothing came.

Mongo, the intellectual among us, poured out a piece of himself I never knew existed. He said, "I won't pretend to know your pain, but I'll share mine with you in the hope that broken hearts understand each other."

Singer looked up, and Mongo spoke barely above a whisper. "The day I turned twenty-one, I was on a field-training exercise with the Eighty-Second at Fort Bragg. Five other Green Berets and I were playing opposing force, sabotaging the communication system of some field artillery unit, when a chaplain came stomping through the woods, yelling, 'Sergeant Malloy! Where are you?' I thought it was a trap, so I dug into a muddy creek bank and waited for him to leave. He was persistent and kept yelling. Finally, he yelled, 'Marvin! It's Captain Lamont, the chaplain. I need to talk with you about your sister.'"

He paused long enough to gather his thoughts as Singer and I listened intently.

"That got me out of the creek, and I was on an airplane an hour later in a clean uniform and with all the emergency leave I needed. When I got home, my baby sister was in intensive care with hoses and wires sticking out of every inch of her body."

A tear left his eye, but he made no effort to wipe it away. "My only sister, who I loved more than anybody on Earth, died of an overdose of amphetamines and alcohol while I held her hand. There hasn't been a second of my life since that day when I haven't thought about my sister and hate myself for letting her suffer in silence. I had no idea she was hurting so badly. No one knew. Weeks later, we learned from her diary that she'd gotten pregnant and had an abortion because she was afraid our parents would throw her out of the house if they found out about the baby. I couldn't save her because I didn't know she was dying inside, and I have to carry that weight around with me every day. It wasn't my fault, but maybe I could've prevented it if I'd given her the chance to open up to me. I was a soldier serving his country instead of a man serving his family. That's why I love you guys so much. You're my family now, and we're yours. We love you by choice, and there's nothing we wouldn't do to help you carry your load."

Singer stared between Mongo and me as if boring a hole through the wall behind us. "He and I were the last of us, and now, it's just me. Maybe that's how it should be. Maybe the evil that ran in my daddy's veins will die when I lie down, and that will make the world a better place."

Just months away from earning my master's degree in psychology, I should've had something comforting to offer, but I was left stricken mute and hurting for my friend and brother.

Mongo said enough for all of us. "Sometimes, it's just pain that will never make sense, but you don't have to bear it alone."

Singer let his face fall into his hands with his elbows propped on the table. "I have to bury my brother, but I won't let you and the team down. I'll deploy when you need me."

I finally found my words, and the same words fell from Mongo's lips simultaneously. "We can do this one without you, Singer. Take all the time you need."

The sniper stared first into Mongo's eyes, then mine. "I've let my brothers down for the last time. It's my job to watch over you and not let anyone or anything get to you. With the team, I do that through the lens of my scope. With my brother, I tried to do it through the eyes of a boy who was forced to become a man before his time, and I failed. I'll not fail you."

Mongo said, "You've never failed any of us, Singer. And we know you never will. It's time for you to take care of yourself until you're ready to put your boots back on. Until then, we'll look after you."

To see a man of such boundless faith and fortitude break beneath the weight of his pain was the most agonizing scene I've ever witnessed. Singer was the best of all of us—the best of every man—and at least in that moment, the little boy who'd been forced to take his own father's life sat before us and cried. And we cried with him.

* * *

The next morning found me at the console in the ops center with Skipper.

"We have to tell them, Chase. It's just not right if we don't."

I said, "If we tell them, there can be no positive outcome. Hunter has his hands full as it is. If we lay this on him, he'll have no choice but to call off the mission and come home."

Skipper rolled her chair in front of mine and stared into my sleep-deprived eyes. "What if it were you down there in that jungle? Would you want to know?"

The clock on the wall chirped its hourly announcement of the passing of sixty more minutes, and Hunter's voice fell from the overhead speakers. "Ops, Hunter. Sitrep."

Skipper handed me a headset and mouthed, "Tell him!"

I pulled on the headset and adjusted the microphone in front of my lips. "Hunter, Ops. Send the sitrep."

"We made forty-one miles overnight, and just before sunrise, we found a nice tributary where we could camouflage the boat and get some rest. I'm on first watch while Disco and Tony get a couple of hours."

I asked, "Any encounters overnight?"

"None, but we spotted a camp that had all the hallmarks of an overnight stop for some feds. There were American beer cans in their burnt-out firepit and a roll of toilet paper by a tree."

I chuckled. "Yeah, I'd say they were some of ours."

"We didn't pick up any human movement in the trees, so at least for now, we're alone."

"How did your students do?"

"I had another come-to-Jesus talk with Tony, and he's going to be all right. Disco's got ice water in his veins. He's doing fine. We'll have him turned into a ninja in a matter of weeks. The jury's still out on Tony, but I'll keep you posted."

Skipper banged her palm against the console. "Tell him!"

She was right. If I'd been in Hunter's shoes, I'd be furious if no one told me about Singer's brother's death, so I said, "I've got some bad news." Hunter didn't respond, so I continued. "Singer's brother killed himself at the monastery yesterday. Slit his wrists."

In his measured, confident tone, my partner said, "How's Singer?"

"He'll be okay in time, but it's tough on him right now."

He asked, "Should we head back for Barranquilla?"

I let the question linger as I studied the only two options I had: calling the team home or asking Hunter to continue the mission. With my decision made, I said, "You can't make it home in time for the funeral. We're burying him tomorrow morning. If I were in your shoes, I'd continue up the river, but the decision is yours."

Without hesitation, he said, "Roger. We're continuing the mission."

His decision wasn't cold. It was practical, and in the field, nothing is more deadly than decisions made from emotion.

The decision was made, and discussing it would be pointless, so I said, "Send situation reports at change of watch for daylight hours."

"Roger. Expect next sitrep in two hours."

The line went dead, and Skipper said, "You did the right thing."

"You're probably right, but it doesn't feel that way."

I left her alone in the ops center and joined the rest of the team for breakfast in the kitchen, where I discovered Singer standing in front of the stove, stirring a massive cast-iron skillet of gravy with a piping-hot pan of homemade biscuits on the counter beside him.

I glared at Clark, then at Singer, and back to Clark. I mouthed, "What's he doing?"

Clark said, "I suggest leaving him alone. He hit me in the head with a wooden spoon when I tried to stop him."

I snuck a hand around the sniper in a wasted effort to nab a biscuit, and I was rewarded with a swat from a gravy-covered spoon to the back of my hand.

I said, "What are you doing? Go sit down. I'll finish this."

He gave me a shove with his hip. "Service is the gift I've been given. Don't rob me of the joy of making the most of my gift."

I threw an arm around his shoulder. "The world would be a better place with a few billion more just like you."

He huffed. "Ha! I don't know about that, but I do know you make terrible gravy, so go sit down. I don't want you screwing up my gravy by association."

Chapter 25
Angles and Dangles

Breakfast was an exercise in abnormal quiet. None of us knew exactly how to interact with Singer, and I suspected his strong façade was a performance for our benefit. Although I doubted his fortitude was sincere, there was nothing fake about Singer's breakfast. His gravy wasn't as good as Maebelle's, but it was undeniably better than mine.

I broke the ice. "What time is the service for your brother tomorrow?"

Singer wiped his mouth and laid down his fork. "I don't know."

"You don't know?"

He shook his head. "No, the monks rarely speak. Not even in times like this. Trappist monks don't take a vow of silence like some other orders, but they prefer silence. Although Tommy wasn't a monk, they accepted him as one of their own and cared for him with the kind of love only God can create. He'll be buried on the grounds of the monastery in a Trappist ceremony that will most likely be silent."

Surprised by the revelation, I said, "We're allowed to attend the service, right?"

"I don't know. I don't even know if I can attend. That will be up to the abbot."

Trying to wrap my head around what he was saying, I said, "Forgive me, but I'm a simple Protestant. I've already learned more about Catholic monks this morning than I ever thought I'd know."

Singer smiled. "There's no need to be forgiven, and you shouldn't apologize for being Protestant. As you know, I'm Baptist, and I know only slightly more than you about the monks. The thing I know without a doubt is that the monks loved and cared for Tommy with unmatched kindness, and he's now in the arms of God, where his pain is washed away and he'll never hurt again. That's what brings me solace." He paused and lifted his fork, raising a bite of biscuit and gravy to his lips. Then he said, "And that allows me to eat breakfast with the people I love most without crying for the loss of my brother."

My belief that Singer was putting on a brave front was instantly replaced by the knowledge that his immeasurable faith in what awaited his brother beyond death's veil was the reason he could smile that morning.

"You're a remarkable man," I said.

He shook his head. "No, Chase. I'm a man of faith and love, and those things are stronger than anything this world can pour out. When they lay Tommy's body in the ground tomorrow, it doesn't matter if I'm there because Tommy certainly won't be there. All we have left of him on this Earth is our memories and his mortal shell."

"That's a beautiful sentiment," I said, "but it's not entirely true."

Singer furrowed his brow.

I continued. "He left behind the sadness that you feel for the loss, and that has to be acknowledged, as well. We know your brother is safe and in the arms of God, but your grief and loss are real. You know I hate the word *closure*, but it's important for you to mourn Tommy's passing."

"I've done that," he said. "You and Mongo were there when it began. I spent most of the night on my knees in the church, and my prayers and mourning were answered with peace. That's one of God's greatest gifts to those of us who love Him. We receive a peace and assurance that nonbelievers can't understand."

I knew at that moment I would never stop learning from Singer, and even more than before, I yearned so badly to share his abundant faith.

* * *

We spent the day preparing the Mark V patrol boat for its journey to Mexico. Earl polished the diesel fuel in the massive tanks and gave the engines a thorough checkup while the rest of us loaded and secured Mongo's EMP sled. Singer worked alongside the team as if nothing was out of the ordinary.

With everything loaded and secure, I said, "It's a long way to Mexico, and there's nothing smooth about the ride. I think we should take her out for angles and dangles."

Earl stuck a finger into my chest. "You listen to me, Stud Muffin. If you break *my* boat, you better hope you die in the crash."

I laughed. "Don't worry, Momma. I don't think I can do anything to *your* boat that she can't handle. I just want to make sure our lashing will keep that sled from becoming a loose cannon. We don't need that thing bouncing around the deck while we're bucking the Gulf Stream."

Mongo watched the exchange and then pulled me aside. "What's angles and dangles?"

I stepped aside and motioned for him to climb aboard. "Come with me, and I'll show you."

As we boarded, Earl lumbered across the gunwale and onto the dock.

"Where are you going, Earl?"

She waved a dismissive hand. "Anywhere but out there to watch you try to kill *my* boat."

"You're not fooling me," I said. "You're going to find your lover boy."

"I wish, but he's down in Jacksonville on a big construction job. He'll be home tonight, though, and you can bet I'll make him glad he's my man when he gets home."

I threw up both hands. "I told you to stop doing that. I don't need that mental picture bouncing around in my brain."

She waddled off the dock, climbed into her dually, and disappeared in a cloud of diesel smoke.

Clark strapped into his seat and patted the empty one beside him. "Come on, Mongo. Strap in. You're going to enjoy this."

Instead of mounting the seat Clark recommended, Mongo skipped one and climbed onto the next seat, giving himself plenty of room for his girth.

I yelled from the pilothouse, "Are you coming, Singer?"

He checked his watch and raised a finger. "Yeah, I'm coming, but give me a couple of minutes."

I warmed up the engines while Singer took a call.

Minutes later, we were all aboard and underway. The tune-up Earl had given the engines was noticeable long before we hit open water. They were more responsive than I ever remembered them being, and they even sounded more powerful.

Just as I'd hoped, the Saint Marys Pass was in turmoil. The outgoing tide against the incoming wind turned the water into a washing machine. I left Cumberland Sound at full throttle and hit the raging water at fifty knots. The bow rose, launching us across the first set of combative waves. The full hull didn't completely leave the water, but we flew enough to rattle our teeth when we touched down. Any rational boat pilot would've pulled the throttles back and kept the heavy machine on the surface, but I didn't qualify as rational.

I did pull the throttles, but only long enough to let the bow pierce the water in front of us. As soon as our nose submarined, I shoved the throttles forward, plowing into the waves and raising the bow toward the sun. We danced across the billowing water, and my passengers rode in relative comfort on their pneumatically cushioned thrones. Behind them, our cargo never offered to move.

I continued out the pass and into the North Atlantic, where Poseidon provided the conditions I'd hoped to see. Eight- to ten-foot swells rolled across the surface creating an aquatic washboard that was perfect for giving our boat and cargo a solid beating. I teased the throttles to find the sweet spot that would launch our tonnage from the surface. It took several minutes, but I finally found it and turned our fifty-ton watercraft into an airborne missile. The landings were violent, but the structure of the solidly built vessel absorbed the shock, taking it in perfect stride.

Our adventure lasted an hour before I brought us back through the still-tumultuous pass between Amelia and Cumberland Island and turned into the docile waters of Cumberland Sound. At dead slow, I set the autopilot and crept across the surface at five knots. My crew unstrapped and set about pulling on everything that could've come loose. Nothing moved, and I declared our vessel seaworthy for the nine-hundred-mile journey that lay ahead.

Back at the Bonaventure dock, Mongo said, "I think I like angles and dangles."

I patted the Mark V's panel. "So does she. By the way, that's an old submariner's term for putting a boat through its paces with the steepest angles she can achieve and watching for things to dangle and fall. Falling objects in a sub are never good, so the skipper always wants to know how his boat will perform under the rigors of combat."

We secured the boat to the dock, and Singer checked his phone. I waited until Clark and Mongo left the dock, and I asked, "It's rare to see you checking your phone so often. Is everything okay?"

"It's fine. I talked to the abbot at the monastery about us attending Tommy's funeral."

"What did he say?"

He re-pocketed his phone. "He said he would discuss it with the monastic community and let me know."

"Monastic community?"

"Yeah, that's what the monks call themselves."

"I've got so much to learn," I said.

He gave me a shove. "We all do."

We walked up the gentle slope of the backyard to the gazebo and slid into a pair of chairs overlooking the river.

Times spent alone with Singer were some of my favorite moments in life. I was concerned about his ability to deal with the loss of his brother but still intrigued by how confident he appeared. "I'm only going to say this once, then I'll leave it alone."

He propped up his feet on the carriage of the cannon. "I know what you're going to say, and I'll take you up on it if I need someone to talk to. Thank you for being that someone for me, Chase. It means more than you know, but what I need more than anything else right now is to be treated as an equal member of the team, just as it was a week ago. Tommy's passing doesn't change the responsibility I have to you and the team."

I threw my prosthetic onto the carriage beside his foot. "Look at that. It's not real. It's a robot. And nobody has treated me the same since it happened. So, I know exactly how you feel. I can't promise we're not going to coddle you for a few days, but if we do, it's out of love and respect."

He stared at my foot. "The big difference between your situation and mine is that nobody can make a prosthetic brother for me. Thankfully, I have the team, and so do you. You can lean on us just the same as I can lean on you. Don't forget that, Chase."

How can a man who just lost his only living relative be so utterly unselfish? How is it possible that he can turn the conversation around to make it about me and my lost foot? How can any man be that good?

He looked out over the river and the marsh grass swaying in the afternoon breeze. "Are you going to brief me on the mission?"

I spent the next ten minutes telling him everything I knew about the Colombian drug lord, the submarines, Mongo's waterproof electromagnetic pulse generator, and our plan to capture one of the subs. He listened intently and even asked a few good questions. The best question was, "When do we leave?"

"Not before we bury your brother."

He met my eyes. "I told you already, Tommy has gone home. There's nothing we can do to or for him now. The burial is simply hiding his mortal shell while it returns to dust. His soul isn't going into the ground."

"Does that mean you don't want to attend the funeral?"

He cast his eyes to the decking of the gazebo. "The weak, earthly part of me wants to be there, but my soul knows it's only ceremonial. Unless you order me to stand down, I'm going with you, and I'm going to provide overwatch the same as I always do so we won't have to bury any more of our brothers anytime soon. Just like I told you at breakfast . . . Don't rob me of the joy of using my gift."

Chapter 26
The Calls Came In

The call came in, and Singer slid his phone from a pocket. He listened intently for several seconds and said, "Thank you."

He returned the phone to its home and chewed on his bottom lip. When he looked up, he said, "The weak, earthly side has won."

* * *

Two hours later, Hunter's reports returned to thirty-minute intervals. The fading light of the jungle filled the ops center screen, and my partner's voice filled the air. "We're moving back to the water. Our fuel supply is adequate, the engine is more efficient than I expected, and we had some visitors this afternoon."

"What kinds of visitors?" I asked.

"Keep your pants on. I'm going to tell you. At about three thirty, five armed men in a heavy boat came down the river, obviously looking for something. They spotted our boat and motored in to inspect it."

"Did you not have it camouflaged?"

He growled. "No, Chase. We left it anchored in the middle of the river with the stereo blasting. Of course we had it camouflaged, but there's only so much hiding you can do with a twenty-foot motorboat on a narrow river."

"Did they see you?"

"No. Thankfully, I was able to keep our Coast Guard gunfighter from mowing them down. He's learning to be quiet, but we've still got a lot of work to do."

"Who do you think they were?"

"Disco has a theory. He thinks they're an advanced party for a sub. It makes sense they'd send a patrol out before sending a shipment downriver. There were no official markings on their boat, and none of them were in uniform, so I can't come up with a better guess than Disco's."

"How about DEA?"

"We've seen a handful of guys who could be agents. They looked American and carried American gear, but we've not had any encounters."

Skipper asked, "What's the plan for tonight?"

"We're going to continue upriver. If Disco is right, we'll probably encounter the sub before sunup. If we do, I plan to get in front of them and run for Barranquilla. If we get trapped behind them, they'll make open water ahead of us, and we'll be behind the power curve."

Skipper turned to me. "Have you got anything else?"

I looked up at the screen, even though Hunter and his team couldn't see me. "Keep your head down and your powder dry. We're going to the funeral in the morning, but we're ready to deploy. As soon as you spot the sub, we'll head for Isla Mujeres in the Mark V and meet you there."

Hunter said, "I wish we could be there. Is Singer doing all right?"

Singer didn't give me time to answer. From his spot at the table, he said, "I'm doing fine, Hunter."

Hunter couldn't hide the surprise in his voice. "I didn't expect you to be there. I'm real sorry . . ."

"Don't be sorry," Singer said. "Just keep doing what you do. I'll see you in Mexico."

My partner stammered. "Uh, are you sure? I mean . . ."

Singer said, "Somebody has to watch over you boys, and I can't bear the thought of anyone other than me being that guy."

Skipper said, "Report every thirty minutes or report contact. If you don't have anything else, ops out."

"Hunter's out."

The line went silent, but the image on the screen continued.

Skipper said, "We're keeping open video when there's enough light and open audio anytime there's contact. So far, that's working pretty well. The solar array is keeping the batteries charged, even beneath the jungle canopy, so I'm happy about that."

I spent the rest of the evening refueling the Mark V and loading weapons and ammo. By nine o'clock, we were deployment-ready, and everyone was ready for some sleep.

* * *

We took off in the Caravan at eight the following morning and headed north toward Moncks Corner, South Carolina. I flew a low pass over the Cooper River abeam the monastery to look for floating debris, shallow water, or anything else that might render our amphibious Caravan incapable of taking off again. Convinced the river was free of hazards, I flew the approach from the southeast and touched down a thousand feet from the Abbey.

Six monks in black robes stood on the riverbank, watching our every move. The looks on their faces turned to concern as I pointed the bows of the pontoons directly toward them and added power.

I called over my shoulder, "Hey, Singer. You might want to let these guys know who we are. I don't want them to call down fire and brimstone on us . . . or whatever monks do to intruders."

After opening the hatch, he climbed down to the starboard pontoon, gave them a wave, and tossed the anchor line ashore. Although they didn't return the wave, two of the monks lifted the anchor and carried it farther ashore. Five minutes later, I was on the grounds of a monastery for the first time in my life. I don't know what I expected, but what I found wasn't it.

Their gardens were beautifully manicured, and the grounds were spotless. The simple structures shone in the bright, midmorning sun, and the smell of incense burning filled the air.

The six monks wordlessly surrounded Singer and walked in lockstep away from the river. Clark, Mongo, Penny, and I followed the procession deeper into the property. We came to a clearing, where two dozen marble headstones stood, brilliantly white against the lush surroundings. An open grave waited a few feet from the last headstone in the row. Two of the monks who'd escorted Singer to the site turned and motioned for us to stand near the tree line. We followed his unspoken instruction, and they continued to the grave.

A man I assumed to be the abbot walked down a well-worn path with his robe flowing as if he were floating just above the ground. He stood on the opposite side of the grave and bowed his head. Out of respect, I knew I should've bowed, as well, but my curiosity wouldn't allow it. I couldn't take my eyes off the scene.

The abbot raised a hand, and the six monks were joined by at least two dozen more, dressed identically in black robes. Behind the congregation of monks came six more carrying a simple wooden casket with no decoration or adornment. They placed the casket on three lengths of rope and stepped back as the abbot laid a hand on the casket and lowered his head a second time.

As if they'd practiced the ceremony countless times, the six monks lifted an end of each rope and sidestepped in perfect unison over the open grave. They lowered the casket into the grave with measured precision and pulled the ropes from beneath.

The abbot approached Singer, and they walked arm in arm to the side of the grave and stood in silence for a long moment. The abbot then took Singer by the shoulders and turned him around to face the gathered brothers. Two of the six who'd carried the casket stepped beside Singer and locked arms behind him, scooping him up as if cradling a baby. They carried Singer to us and stood him up two feet in front of us. The abbot led me to Singer's side, then he did the same with Clark. How he chose the two of us, I'll never know, but he took my right arm and Clark's left and interlocked them behind Singer. With a gentle push against our shoulders, he encouraged us to walk away with our arms around Singer.

We continued walking until we were back at the riverside. I had so many questions, but that wasn't the time. Clark retrieved the anchor, and we climbed aboard the Caravan, where we found two large casks of beer and four baskets of bread.

Airborne and cruising back toward Saint Marys, I couldn't hold my questions any longer. "Are you okay, Singer?"

"I am. Thank all of you for coming with me. It means more than I can tell you."

I said, "This may not be the best time, but can you explain any of that to us?"

Singer almost chuckled. "I was hoping one of you could explain it to me. I've never been to a funeral at a Trappist monastery. The symbolism seems simple enough. The abbot allowed me to see my brother's casket in the grave, and he had two of his brothers deliver me into your hands. That's what I took from it."

Penny said, "Regardless of what it was supposed to mean, it was beautiful and powerful."

Singer said, "That, it was."

Clark asked, "What's with the beer and bread?"

Singer said, "I know the answer to that one. The monks don't own anything, but they make beer and bread to raise money to support the monastery. Even a simple life like theirs requires financial support. The beer and bread are gifts from them to us as their way of saying they're sorry for our loss."

Clark said, "Maybe the world needs more monks. They seem to have things figured out."

We landed back at Saint Marys, and I checked my phone while Clark and Mongo put the Caravan back in the hangar. The missed-call notification from Skipper sent my thumb flying to the recall button.

"Where are you?" she said.

"We're at the airport, and we'll be back at the house in ten minutes. What's going on?"

"The call came in. Hunter made contact with the sub, and she's underway."

"Did they get out in front of it?"

She said, "No, they're trapped north of it, but they're working the problem."

We secured the hangar and made it back to the ops center in less than my predicted ten minutes. "Get him on the line," I ordered as we burst through the doors.

"I'm already here," came Hunter's voice through the speakers.

"Catch us up," I said.

"We made camp about an hour before sunrise a mile from Magangué. Tony had first watch while Disco and I caught some sleep. Just after sunrise, Disco kicked my boot and pointed toward the river. Our vantage point wasn't the greatest, but we repositioned and got a better look. Skipper should have the video."

She nodded. "Yeah, I've got it. I'll play it on monitor number two."

The screen came to life, and a pair of wooden boats appeared. The one in front appeared to be towing the trailing boat, but something wasn't exactly right about the second craft.

"What's going on with the trailing boat?" I asked.

Hunter said, "I thought you'd notice that. It's sitting a little high in the water and making way too much wake for a boat that size and shape."

"Is that what I think it is?" I asked.

Hunter said, "If you think it's a narco-sub with the shell of a boat resting on top of it, it is. We camped in a big bend of the river, so I sent Tony across the peninsula with a mask, fins, and a snorkel. He got in the water well ahead of the vessels and did a little underwater recon. The river is too murky to see much, but the port side of the sub now has Tony's fingerprints all over it."

"Well done!"

Hunter said, "Not really. We screwed up and let them get between us and the Citation, so I'm working on a plan now."

"What's in your head?" I asked.

"There's a spot about ten miles downriver where the river slows down and spreads out. It's probably half a mile wide at that point. My plan for the moment is to get as far away from the boats as I can and get ahead of them. I'm not sure we have the fuel to run at top speed all the way back to Barranquilla, but they're only making four or five knots, so if we can get in front of them, staying ahead won't be a problem."

"Do you're thing, but don't get caught. We're hitting the water in two minutes, and we'll see you on the Island of Women."

Chapter 27
Grand Theft Auto

Mongo took me by the elbow. "We need to talk."

I followed him from the ops center and settled in the pair of chairs outside the doors.

He said, "When this mission came down, you said it was mine to run, but you're having trouble stepping aside. I need to know my role."

I sighed. "You're right. I did say that, and then I kept sticking my nose in it. The reason I initially wanted to take myself out of the field operation was my inability to be one hundred percent because of my foot. The planning and pre-deployment were things I could still do."

"It's not your foot that's keeping you out of the fight. It's the other end of your body. You let your brain talk you into being incapable of operating. Maybe you can't dive with Hunter yet, and for the first time ever, we can all outrun you, but none of us can outthink you in the field, Chase. You're our leader, and we'd follow you into any fight you wanted to start. This one is no exception. You proved yesterday during angles and dangles, that nobody can run that boat like you. I'll bet you never thought about your foot one solitary time while we were out there dancing all over the ocean."

"I guess I didn't."

"You're still in charge, Chase, and as long as you're breathing, that's never going to change. Grab your go bag and take us into the fight."

I took the stairs two at a time and found Penny in the kitchen. "I'm going with them. I can still run the boat, and I can—"

"Your go bag is on the back gallery, and *you're* the only one who didn't know you were going. Be careful, come home safe, and catch the bad guys." She kissed me and stuck a brown grocery bag in my hand.

"What's this?"

"Sandwiches I made with the bread from the monks. Call me when you stop for the night. I love you."

I took the bag of sandwiches, kissed my wife, and threw my go bag across my shoulder. Mongo and Singer were waiting aboard the Mark V with the engines warming up.

Mongo asked, "Do you want the first watch at the helm?"

I shook my head. "No, you take it. I'm tearing into this bag of monk bread sandwiches."

Mongo took us off the dock and through the pass into the North Atlantic. The swells weren't as bad as the previous day, and thankfully, we were running parallel to them instead of across them. The ride wasn't pleasant for our guts, but at least we weren't being pounded to death.

The bread was some of the best I'd ever eaten. Although I wasn't much of a beer guy, I was looking forward to getting back home to break into the casks the brothers at the monastery had given us.

The Mark V is an autonomous vessel in open water. The GPS and autopilot made the southbound leg of our journey relatively easy. Other than monitoring the temperatures and checking the cargo every half hour, we were little more than passengers.

Nine hours and over three hundred fifty miles later, we laid in at Boca Chita Harbor behind the lighthouse about fifteen miles northeast of Key Largo. Feeling my way into an unfamiliar harbor in the dark was never something I enjoyed, but our bodies needed rest, and Boca Chita was the perfect place to spend the night without drawing any unwanted attention. An eighty-foot-long, floating weapon of war tends to get more than it wants in busy marinas.

We anchored in twelve feet of water in the middle of the harbor. When we shut down for the night, we were the only boat in the harbor, but if another skipper was brave enough to attempt the entrance in the dark, we didn't want to be in his way along the seawall.

We checked in with the ops center to find Penny at the console. "We're safe at anchor in Boca Chita. The boat performed beautifully, and your sandwiches were a hit. Has there been any word from Hunter's team?"

"I'm glad you're safe and your bellies are full. It seems that Hunter failed at passing the boat towing the sub, but he succeeded in stealing a truck."

"That's my partner," I said.

"I thought you might say something like that. So far, he's taken Skipper's boyfriend all the way to Central America, killed two men, and stolen a boat and a truck. I'm starting to think he's a bad influence."

I said, "Tony volunteered, but you're right, Hunter is a terrible influence. I wouldn't have it any other way, though. Where are they now?"

"They're having cocktails on Isla Mujeres and waiting for you."

"We're at a slight disadvantage. The Mark V can't do five hundred knots like the Citation, but we'll be there before sundown tomorrow."

"I'll pass along your ETA. Do you need anything else from us?"

"Yeah. Send more sandwiches."

"Good night, Chase. Get some rest, and let us know when you're underway again."

Sleep came quickly, and we woke to find the same empty harbor we'd entered eight hours earlier.

Although I trusted the fuel gauges, I dipped each tank to verify the readings. The gauges were spot-on, and we motored out beneath the Boca Chita Lighthouse.

The wind had shifted to the northeast, and that made for a relatively smooth ride down Hawk Channel, just off the Florida Keys. I checked in while Singer took his turn at the controls. The number of boats operating in the channel made it necessary to constantly watch for other traffic. The radar did a nice job, but at forty knots, it didn't take long to close on another vessel.

Skipper answered when I called.

I said, "We're headed southwest in perfect conditions. Will you arrange for some fuel for us on Key West?"

"I'm way ahead of you, Hopalong Cassidy. The Navy is expecting you on Boca Chica."

"From Boca Chita to Boca Chica. I like it. Let them know we'll be there in less than three hours."

"I'm still way ahead of you. I'm tracking you, so I already calculated your ETA and passed it along."

"Have you talked with Tony?"

She said, "I talked to him last night for a few minutes. He's beating himself up about the shooting."

"I know it sounds harsh, but he should be. That was a boneheaded move. As long as he remembers how it feels to screw up, he'll learn something with every new experience. What's your feeling about him sticking around?"

"He's in for the long haul if you decide to keep him. Either way, I'm keeping him. It's nice to have him back."

"We'll talk more about this when we get home, but I'd like to know your thoughts on him staying on the team."

She took a moment before saying, "Now I know how Penny feels when you deploy. It's not a great feeling, but if this is what he wants to do, I'm all in."

"I've got one more question, but you don't have to answer it now. You can chew on it for a while if you want."

"Let's hear it," she said.

"If Clark and I decide not to keep him on the team, are you going to be okay with that? It won't be anything personal. If we don't keep him, it'll be because we think he's not cut out for the job. Hunter's input will weigh heavily on our decision, too. I just want to make sure you're still on board if Tony's not."

"I get it," she said. "I've thought about that, and I can say, without a doubt, my first responsibility is to the team. If anything ever happens to change that, you'll be the first to know."

"Thanks, Skipper. We'll let you know when we make Boca Chica."

"That's not necessary. I'm tracking you, remember? Just let me know if anything goes wrong, and check in when you make it to Isla Mujeres."

"I will."

I climbed from the cabin and into the pilothouse. "Put us in the marina at Boca Chica. The Navy has generously offered us a few hundred gallons of diesel."

Mongo programmed the GPS. "I found a new function of the autopilot." He pointed to the display. "See the word *TAM* in yellow?"

"I see it."

"That means traffic avoidance mode. If the radar or AIS picks up a conflicting return, it'll adjust our course to miss the target by the closest point of approach I program. I have it set for half a mile right now, but at slower speeds, a thousand feet would be plenty."

"I guess we should've read the manual, huh?"

He laughed. "We're not really manual-reading guys."

"No, we're not, my friend. Do you need a break?"

"No, I'm good for now."

Two and a half hours later, we idled into the Navy marina at Boca Chica. We took advantage of their restaurant and bathrooms while a young sailor topped off our tanks. The Mark V's onboard computers did the calculations, but I double-checked the numbers on a napkin. Our fuel burn was slightly higher than expected, but that was likely a function of the work Earl did to tweak the engines for power instead of fuel economy.

The stop took less than half an hour, and we were back on the water. The four-hundred-mile trip from Boca Chica to Isla Mujeres was long and boring, just as open water crossings should be. We considered slipping into Havana to play a little cat and mouse with the Cuban gunboats, but discretion being the better part of valor, we motored on.

"Maybe we can have some fun with them on the way back," I said.

Barely making my prediction, we motored into the marina on Isla Mujeres just as the sun touched the western horizon over mainland Mexico. Hunter, Tony, and Disco met us on the dock.

I checked in with the ops center on the secure satellite uplink in the cabin of the Mark V. "The gang's all here and together again."

That time, it was Clark who answered, "I'm glad you made it. I hope you didn't decide to play 'catch me if you can' with the Cubans."

"That wouldn't have been much of a game. The only thing they have that can catch the Mark V is maybe an old Russian MiG."

He said, "We've had a slight change of plans."

"This doesn't sound good."

"It really doesn't change our role. You're still going to intercept the sub, neutralize it, and turn it over to the proper authorities."

"Let me guess. The 'proper authorities' have changed."

"You're pretty good at this game, Peg Leg. It turns out an old friend of ours is going to take the sub off your hands after you rope it."

I was intrigued. "Oh, really? And who might this old friend of ours be?"

"Remember Captain Stinnett from the research vessel *Lori Danielle*?"

"How could I forget him?" I said. "He saved my life with the recompression chamber in his sick bay during that Panamanian thing we did."

"That's him," Clark said. "There's just one catch."

"I don't like catches."

"This one isn't so bad. It'll just leave you vulnerable for a few minutes. It turns out the crane on Stinnett's boat can't lift the weight of the sub *and* its cargo, so you'll have to hand off the cargo into a net until you get the weight down enough for the crane to bear the weight of the sub."

"Why can't we just chunk it in the ocean?"

"Great minds think alike, but the CIA has other plans for fifteen tons of cocaine."

"I don't want to know."

"Neither do I," he said. "So, here's the plan. Stinnett will loiter at the approximate coordinates we believe the sub will surface. We're still working on that calculation, but Skipper will have it for you by morning. You can rendezvous with the *Lori Danielle* prior to the grab or run out on your own. That's up to you."

I considered the decision. "If the seas are calm, I'd rather hook up before the snatch. That eliminates at least one set of variables. This thing is fluid enough, so anything we can nail down is progress."

He said, "I agree, but you're the onsite commander. I can't make those calls from here."

"Sounds good," I said. "Do you have a rough estimate for the rendezvous with the sub?"

He said, "It looks like around fifty hours from now, but we're still working on currents and tide. Like I said, we'll have a good number for you by morning."

We broke the connection, and I rejoined the rest of the team at the marina restaurant and bar. Hunter stuck a cocktail in my hand, and I held it high. "Here's to Hunter's new favorite hobby . . . Grand theft auto!"

Chapter 28
The New Kid

We took advantage of the downtime and the beautiful island of Isla Mujeres. The people were friendly, the water was potable, and the weather was perfect. After a long night's sleep restoring our bodies to their pre-voyage condition, it was time to have a couple of talks with Hunter and the new kid.

We had breakfast at the restaurant in the hotel, and I asked Tony to take a walk with me. He obliged, and we parked ourselves in a pair of loungers under an umbrella on the beach.

"So, what do you think so far?"

He groaned. "I thought that might be what this walk was about. Have you talked to Hunter yet?"

"Not yet. He's next, but I need to know what you think. His opinion doesn't matter if you've decided this isn't the life for you."

He dug a toe into the sand. "To be honest, I'm in way over my head. I don't know what I'm doing, and so far, I've screwed up everything I touched. I feel, quite literally, like a fish out of water."

I laughed. "I remember that feeling well. I spent eighteen months training for this job and learning from some of the best operators in the business, but when they dumped me in Havana Harbor with orders to kill a Russian assassin, I was terrified. I wasn't ready, but that didn't stop me. Nobody is ready for their first assignment, no matter how much—or how little—training they've had. Hunter's a good teacher and a top-notch operator. If he says you're a keeper, you've got a spot on the team, if you want it."

"Oh, I want it. I want it more than anything in the world. But I don't know if I've got what it takes."

"You need to think about Skipper."

"What do you mean?"

"It's obvious you two are joined at the hip. It's hard on the people we leave behind who love us. She's going to watch and listen to you getting hurt, and maybe even killed one day. You need to think about what that will do to her. You've not been around long enough to know, but she has skills most analysts only wish they had. She's good at her job—maybe the best natural analyst in the world. We get cut, shot, beat up, drowned, and even lose body parts sometimes. It'll happen to you, too. It's part of the game. Just think about it and talk to Clark. He's been in the game longer than any of the rest of us. He has answers I'll never have."

He looked up. "You're not thinking about cutting me before we catch the sub, are you?"

"No. I'm not thinking about cutting you at all. You and Hunter are the only two who can pull off the dive to capture the sub. I'm out of commission when it comes to water ops, and your brother's caught too many bullets and broken bones to go back in the water. That's the prize that awaits all of us if we're lucky to live long enough."

He seemed to ponder what I'd said. "You talk to Hunter, and I'll talk to Clark when we get home. If you'll have me, I'm willing to go through whatever training you put me through."

I slapped him on the back. "Let's go find the rest of the guys before they burn down the hotel."

Skipper was good at everything, especially booking hotel rooms. She had the team in a five-bedroom suite. I didn't know five-bedroom suites existed, but not only did Skipper find one, she put us in it. Tony, being the new guy, got the couch while the rest of us enjoyed the spoils of whatever we were doing.

The morning call came around nine thirty, and we gathered around the speaker.

Skipper said, "All right . . . We have a solid estimate of the rendezvous time and coordinates. Do you have something to write with?"

"Of course we have something to write with," I said as I pilfered through the desk drawer.

"Let me know when you find it."

I shot a look at Tony. "I told you she was good."

With notepad and pen in hand, I said, "Let's have it."

She said, "It'll be tomorrow night between ten thirty and eleven, central time. That'll be zero four thirty to zero five hundred Zulu. You'll rendezvous with Captain Stinnett and the *Lori Danielle* at twenty-one degrees, forty-two minutes north by eighty-five degrees, twenty minutes west at four p.m. tomorrow afternoon. They'll be loitering in the area, and you can hail them on the secure uplink on the Mark V. They're expecting you, but remember, you are stealthy with the radar-absorbing finish on the boat, so they may not see you coming."

I laughed. "Stinnett is a retired spook and still a contractor for the CIA. He'll find a way to see us coming."

She said, "You're probably right. Just don't intentionally try to sneak up on him. You know how he is. He's got an itchy trigger finger. Let's not give him a reason to use those deck guns."

"We won't. Are we supposed to just surrender the sub to him and disappear?"

Clark said, "That's right. This thing is a CIA operation as soon as you hand over the booty. I don't know how the Agency got involved, and I don't care, but our orders are to put the whole mess in Stinnett's lap and walk away."

I said, "What am I missing here? It all feels too neat and tidy. I don't like it."

Clark sighed. "I know what you mean. It doesn't smell right to me, either, but I can't find the holes in the plan. Maybe you can get it out of Stinnett when you hook up with him tomorrow afternoon."

"What about the other boat?" I asked.

Clark said, "What other boat?"

"The boat that's going to be there expecting to charge and tow the sub when it surfaces."

Skipper jumped back in. "We hope you can get to the beacon and disable it before the intercept vessel gets a good position fix."

"You hope? When did we start *hoping* everything was going to work out? Maybe the tooth fairy will swoop down and leave quarters under all our pillows."

Clark said, "The intercept vessel is the wildcard. We don't know what kind of boat it is or what kind of capabilities it will have. That's what makes it so critical that you pick up the beacon first. There's very little chance the other boat can outrun the Mark V unless it's an offshore racing boat."

I grumbled. "That's the piece I was missing. I don't like it. Why don't we stand off and watch? If the vessel is no threat, we track it while it tows and recharges the sub. Then we can grab the sub when it cuts it loose. If the boat is capable of putting up a fight, Stinnett can keep it busy by playing a nice, friendly game of 'don't make me shoot' while we grab the sub."

"You're the on-site commander, Chase. If that's the call you make, that's how we'll play it. The only problem I have with forced contact is the fact that somebody will have a lot of questions to answer if you or Stinnett gets into a gunfight at sea with a civilian vessel."

Skipper said, "There's one more thing to consider. If you wait to grab the sub when the tow vessel cuts it loose, it'll be fully charged, and it could dive back to cruising depth before you can get to it."

"I still don't like it," I said. "This is a detail we should've worked out before now."

Skipper said, "There's one more thing you should know."

"Oh, goody . . . something else. Let's have it."

"We heard from our favorite Washington bureaucrat Special Agent Michael Conroy."

"And what did he have to say?"

"He gave us a solid report," she said. "On top of that, he told us that his guys encountered a three-man team of possible hostiles on the river. They even got a picture."

Hunter leaned in. "Our picture? No way."

"Pull out your phone and stand by."

Hunter slipped his phone from his pocket, and it vibrated seconds later. He stared down at the screen in disbelief before tossing the phone to Tony, who caught it and shook his head.

"That's us, all right," Hunter said, "but thankfully, it's our backs, and it looks like it was taken through night vision."

I palmed my forehead. "Great! Now a lowlife DEA cake-eater in DC has pictures of part of our team."

"It's just our backs," Tony said. "You can't make out any of us from that picture."

I said, "No, not from *that* picture, but how many more does he have?"

I sat back in my chair and tried to make sense of everything I'd just learned.

Clark said, "It's not too late to scrap the mission. We can walk away and hand it to another team. We have the EMP sled, the beacon receiver, and we can identify the subs coming out of the mouth of the river in Barranquilla. The hard parts are done. Chase, if you don't feel good about it, call it off."

I stared at the insides of my eyelids for a long time. "Not yet. We'll hook up with Captain Stinnett, and I'll get the details out of him. If he doesn't want to play ball, I'll call it off and we'll come home. If the tow vessel is a Mexican gunboat, I'm not going to mix it up with him out here. We don't need an international incident, especially with our pictures floating around DC."

I turned my attention from the phone to the room. "Somebody plot those coordinates and tell me how long it'll take us to get there."

Mongo pulled a chart from his pack and soon had a solution. "It's ninety miles. We can be there in less than two hours."

I said, "Find out where Stinnett is."

Skipper answered instantly. "He's on-site now."

I picked up the phone. "Tell him we'll be there in two hours."

We were packed and aboard the Mark V in fifteen minutes. I took the helm so I could think without being interrupted. The ocean, for once, seemed to be on my side. With very little wind, the sea was relatively flat and placid. The Mark V made the most of the conditions and settled into cruise at fifty-seven knots.

Our radar could only see twenty miles, but thanks to Dominic's geek squad, we had a real-time, over-the-horizon, satellite view of everything within two hundred miles of our position, as long as the National Reconnaissance Office satellites didn't fall out of orbit.

The R/V *Lori Danielle* came into crystal-clear focus on the multi-function display seventy-two miles off our bow. That meant I had an hour and fifteen minutes to formulate a plan.

I didn't need the full seventy-five minutes. At twenty miles out, I tuned on the satellite uplink and hailed Captain Stinnett's ship. A communications officer answered my hail. "Calling the R/V *Lori Danielle*, go ahead."

"*Lori Danielle*, we're an American-flagged Mark V patrol boat twenty miles southwest requesting permission to come alongside."

He answered quickly, obviously not consulting anyone else. "Roger. Lay alongside to port amidships. We've been expecting you."

"Port side amidship, aye. Don't expect a radar return."

Twenty-five minutes later, Singer laid us alongside the ship, making the eighty-foot patrol boat look like a child's toy. I yelled at the sailor on deck above my head. "Permission to come aboard?"

"Come aboard!" came his reply.

I climbed from the starboard rail, up the rope ladder, and onto the deck of the massive research ship. The white-bearded skipper in a Gaspar's Revenge T-shirt stuck out a hand. "It's good to see you again, Chase. Last time you came aboard, you were at death's door. Welcome aboard on your feet."

I shook his hand. "Thanks, Captain Stinnett. It's good to see you, as well, but I'm not on my feet this time, either. It's just one foot, I'm afraid." I raised my pants leg, exposing my robot.

He gave me a nod. "I'm looking forward to hearing that story. Have the rest of your crew come aboard. We'll secure your boat alongside. I think our accommodations might be a little more comfortable than that old SEAL's tub. How'd you score a Mark V anyway?"

"It's a long story, Captain."

He motioned toward a hatch. "Come inside. We've got a fresh pot of coffee on. And call me Wayne, would you? Too many people already call me Captain."

Chapter 29
The Family Plan

Captain Stinnett was right. His accommodations were significantly more posh than our tactical appointments aboard the Mark V. The officer's lounge boasted leather recliners, a small galley, a conference table to seat six, and a pair of big-screen displays on the forward bulkhead.

He handed me a cup of coffee and motioned toward a lounger. "Have a seat, Chase. Something tells me you're just full of questions."

"I've got a few," I admitted.

He took a sip of the steaming brew and looked across the mug. "Before we get into yours, I've got one. What happened to your foot?"

"Like everything else in my life, that's a long story, too. But I'll give you the *Cliffs Notes*. We were working an assault on a modified fireboat in Gabon in Western Africa. I started a fight in a stairwell. I guess you could say I won the fight, but it cost me a foot."

He furrowed his brow. "Was it a sword fight? Who loses a foot in a gunfight?"

I chuckled and raised my mug. "It wasn't a sword fight, but next time I tell the story, it will be."

He let out a seaman's belly laugh. "Now you're thinking like a spy. Go ahead and lay those questions on me. I'll do my best to tell you the truth . . . mostly."

"First, how did you get involved in this whole thing?"

He eyed the overhead for a moment. "The same way you did, Chase. It was an assignment." It was clear he recognized my disappointment with the non-revealing answer, so he said, "That's not really the question, is it?"

I shook my head. "No, sir. My real question is, why does the CIA care about a drug-running operation?"

He gave me a wink. "Now, that's the question I expected. Let's start with the Bay of Pigs. They probably called it the Cuban Missile Crisis in your high school history class and talked about it for ten minutes." He closed one eye and stared at me through the other. "It ain't no ten-minute affair, son. Have you ever seen a pair of snakes mating?"

The off-the-wall question took me aback. "No, I've never seen that."

"If you look at their heads, you can tell the female from the male, but by the time you get to their tails, they're so twisted and tangled up you can't tell who's screwing who and where one snake begins and the other one ends. Pick any page out of that high school history book of yours, and whoever you can identify as the bad guy is wrapped up with the CIA, just like those two snakes."

I studied the lines around his eyes and the white in his beard. Age may have carved some of those lines, but experience cut the rest. "Are you saying the CIA is involved with Macario Mateo?"

He took another sip. "You're looking at the wrong snake's tail, my boy."

"I'm not following."

"Think about it, son. What happens when you pull a weed out of your garden?"

I sat in silent confusion.

He said, "I'll tell you what happens. Two more weeds grow right back in the spot you pulled the first one. The CIA doesn't give a dead rat's ass about Macario Mateo. The DEA could pull that weed out of the ground anytime they wanted, but they won't do it because they know two more just like him will spring up next time it rains. It's the nature of things in Central America."

He stuck the coffee cup back into the crease between his mustache and beard. "It's the American we want, son."

I tried to control the pinball machine doing the full tilt boogie in my head, but I was growing more confused by the minute. I said, "Conroy?"

The disappointment on Captain Stinnett's face stung almost as much as the foot jokes. He said, "You're not working with that weasel on this thing, are you?"

Finally, a chance to score some points . . .

"No. He tried to stick his nose in it, but we brushed him off. I did some checking, and nobody had anything good to say about him." I paused, considering my answer, then said, "Actually, we didn't brush him off. We let him believe he was on board, but we ignored the intel he fed us."

Stinnett grunted. "I don't think I would've given that much. He tends to hang folks with their own rope if they give him enough."

My heart sank as I realized I was about to give back any points I'd earned. "His guys in Colombia did get at least one picture of my recon team."

Stinnett scratched through his beard. "Ouch. That's gotta hurt. But we're getting off target. Let's get back to the American, Simon Benoit."

"The engineer?"

"Among other things," he said.

The bells and bumpers kept ringing and thumping. I said, "So, we're doing all this to get to Benoit?"

He emptied his mug. "No. There's no *we* in this thing. You'll learn that someday, and all the world will start to make sense. You and your door kickers are capturing a submarine and stealing all the bang out of it. That's where the *you* of *we* ends. The *I* of *we* then takes the harmless metal tube full of uncut Colombian gold with a street value that'll pay my salary for a few hundred years. You see, Chase, men like you and me are just greasy cogs in a great big greasy machine we're never meant to understand. The longer we live, the more of that machine we get to see. I've been in the game longer than you've been on the planet, so don't beat yourself up. You're way ahead of where I was when I was a thirty-year-old case officer for the Agency."

"Sometimes it feels like I'm just one tooth on that greasy cog."

"Savor that, my boy. The more you see, the worse it tastes."

I silently digested the words of experience.

He stood, poured another cup of coffee, and held out the pot toward me.

I shook him off. "No, thanks. I still have half a cup."

He replaced the pot. "Have your men been fed?"

"They have, but it's been four hours."

He picked up a handset from a compartment I hadn't noticed. "Get some hot sandwiches out for our guests, and put together something nice for supper."

Apparently without waiting for a response, he replaced the handset in its cradle. He turned back to me. "Always keep your men fed, even if you go hungry. The only thing that separates us from the animals is our soul. That means we're still animals who have to eat. If your men see that you're not eating until they do, the most primitive part of their brain remembers that, and that's the part where loyalty is built. The wolf pack follows the leader because that leader proves day after day that the pack is more important than him."

I walked from the officer's lounge to the midship deck and saw a six-inch black hose leading from the *Lori Danielle* to the Mark V topping off our diesel tanks.

Captain Stinnett joined me on deck.

I said, "Thanks for the fuel."

"Everything's got to eat. I thought we talked about that."

"Speaking of eating. Where's my crew?"

He ignored the question and motioned toward the Mark V. "I'll give you a million bucks for it."

I smirked and slowly shook my head.

He leaned over the rail and studied the patrol boat. "A million five?"

* * *

We found my team in the crew mess two decks below, devouring grilled ham and cheese on sourdough. Stinnett stepped beside me, and I said, "Thanks for fueling my men, too."

He gave me a nod. "Of course, all of you will stay aboard tonight and tomorrow until it's time to go to work."

"We appreciate the hospitality. Will our boat be all right tied alongside?"

"As long as the sea cooperates, but if she gets feisty, we'll lay over a hawser and take her in tow."

We spent the night aboard the *Lori Danielle* and gathered the next morning in the crew mess for morning chow.

With an overflowing plate of eggs, bacon, and biscuits in front of me, I asked Mongo, "How'd you sleep?"

"A lot better than I would have on the Mark V. I think we need to get us a boat like this."

"The captain's been lusting over ours, so maybe he'd be up for an even trade."

Mongo froze in mid-bite. "If my vote counts, I'm in favor of the trade."

"Your vote always counts, my friend. Especially when it's the same as mine."

Captain Stinnett took a seat beside me with the same coffee cup from the day before. "Is that mug permanently attached to your hand, Captain?"

He laughed. "Sometimes it feels that way. How's your crew this morning?"

"Well rested, thanks to you."

He lifted his chin toward Tony. "What's that man's name?"

I followed his chin. "That's Tony Johnson. He'll be one of our divers tonight. He's former Coast Guard—a rescue swimmer."

"That's a good man to have in the water. Is he afraid of you?"

"Afraid of me? No. Why would he be afraid of me?"

"His leg is hurt worse than he's admitting. If he's critical to the operation tonight, I suggest we get him down to sick bay and let my doctor check him out."

"He's new," I said. "He's not afraid of me. He's afraid of letting me down."

The captain stood. "You've got to learn to pick up on things like that. Get him down to sick bay. I'll tell the doc to expect him."

I didn't like feeling inexperienced, and I liked being ordered around by Captain Stinnett even less. Of course, he was right, but that didn't make me like it.

I stepped behind Tony. "Let's go for a walk. We need to have a chat."

He crammed another bite of biscuit into his mouth and one last drink of coffee. "Sure. Did I do something wrong?"

As we walked side by side, I raised my prosthetic and gave his left shin a tap. He let out a guttural groan and took the next two strides hopping on his right foot.

"Why didn't you tell me your leg was hurting so badly?"

"Winners have to play hurt sometimes. Putting the pain out of our heads long enough to get the job done is a crucial skill."

"I don't disagree, but there's a difference in playing while you're hurt and hiding injuries from your team leader. We're going to see the ship's doctor."

"It's just a deep bruise. I've had them before. They're no big deal. Seriously, I'll be fine in a couple of days."

I stepped around him and gave him a shove against his right shoulder, forcing him to plant his left foot. The wounded animal sound came again.

"I don't need you well in a couple of days. I need you at your best tonight."

I pushed through the hatch into the old familiar sick bay and pointed toward the recompression chamber against the far wall. "See that?"

Tony said, "The chamber? Sure, I see it."

"That thing, and the doctor who ran it, saved my life a few years ago. Your brother and I were on a gig in Panama, and I got myself blown out of the water a little faster than the nitrogen in my bloodstream liked. If Clark hadn't gotten me aboard this ship and into that chamber, you and I would've never met."

A familiar face and voice stepped through a pair of curtains.

I stuck out a hand. "Hello again, Dr. Shadrack. It's nice to see you."

He shoved a stethoscope into his pocket and took my hand. "It's good to see you again, as well, Chase. Last time you were here, you thought you and I had been thrown into King Nebuchadnezzar's fiery furnace. It's good to see you on your feet."

I raised the right leg of my pants. "Well, on my foot."

He took a knee in front of me and raised my pants all the way to my knee, examining the prosthetic. "That's excellent work. You didn't get that done on a boat."

I chuckled. "It started on a boat. At least that's where I broke the ankle too badly to be repaired. The finishing touches happened at UAB in Birmingham."

He stood. "UAB is top-notch. They're doing some cutting-edge stuff up there. I'm sorry about your leg, but I doubt that's what brought you back to see me."

"No. I'm not the patient this time. This is Tony. He got himself into an underwater wrestling match with an experimental piece of hardware and hurt his leg. I'd like for you to take a look."

Dr. Shadrack motioned toward an exam table. "Pull your pants off, and hop up there. Let's have a look."

Tony reluctantly followed the doctor's instructions.

Dr. Shadrack leaned in and probed the massive black bruise running the length of Tony's left leg and let out a whistle. "Ouch. Is it tender to the touch?"

Tony eyed me and then flinched as the doctor pressed a finger into the flesh.

"I'll take that as an affirmative," the doctor said. "Come with me. Let's get a picture of that thing just to make sure nothing's broken. How long ago did this happen?"

"Maybe a week ago," Tony said. "I'm not sure what day it is."

Shadrack looked up at me. "I get a lot of those answers around here. What is it with you and your team getting hurt in the water?"

I said, "We're just lucky, I guess."

The doctor situated Tony on an X-ray table and stepped behind the partition. He took several shots from every angle. "Okay, we'll have some films in a few seconds." He tapped a few keys, and the X-rays appeared on a laptop screen. Dr. Shadrack studied the images and leaned back. "Which do you want first—the bad news or the worse news?"

Tony leaned toward the screen. "It's not broken, is it, Doc?"

"No, it's not broken, but I suspect you've got quite a bit of soft tissue damage in the knee. We'll shoot an MRI to determine how serious it is. You're on a mission, right?"

Tony looked up at me.

I said, "We are, and Tony's a major player. We need him in the water tonight."

The doctor grimaced. "We'll see."

He situated Tony with both legs inside the MRI machine. The process took about ten minutes, and Dr. Shadrack was, once again, in the business of reading images. He pulled off his glasses and deposited them into his shirt pocket. "So, tell me about this mission tonight. How far are you swimming?"

Tony again deferred to me, and I said, "Hopefully no more than a few strokes. The bulk of the dive will be done behind a DPV."

He spun the screen around for me and Tony to see and spent the next five minutes giving an anatomy lesson of the human knee. "The long and short of it is this . . . I'm going to shoot that knee full of so much stuff you'll feel brand-new, but the relief will be quite temporary. You need a good knee surgeon like the ones at UAB. The damage can be repaired, but it won't heal on its own."

Tony looked up in disbelief. "But . . . I don't have any insurance."

I laid a hand on his shoulder. "Sure you do, kid. You're on our family plan."

Chapter 30
Lady Luck

Tony got his injections, and the rest of the team got thorough physical exams by Dr. Shadrack. Just as expected, everyone passed with flying colors . . . except Singer. He had a blood pressure issue.

"High blood pressure?" I asked.

Singer grinned. "Not exactly. It's a little game we snipers like to play. I bet the monks would be good at it, too. If I've got twenty minutes to psych myself up for it, I can get it under a hundred."

"Under a hundred? That's just as dangerous as high blood pressure."

"You learn to lie perfectly still without making a sound for thirty hours, then you learn you can do all sorts of crazy things with your body."

"Speaking of doing things with your body. I want you up top on the *Lori Danielle* tonight. That'll give you some elevation and a much more stable platform than the deck of the Mark V."

"I was going to suggest that. I guess it's true what they say . . . Great minds do think alike."

I said, "No offense, but I think Mongo is the only great mind on this operation."

"I think you may be right."

With *mostly* clean bills of health for the team, we checked in with the ops center, and Skipper was in rare form. "It's about time you called. I see you've been on-site with the *Lori Danielle* since yesterday afternoon."

I played a little game of diversion. "We've been undergoing our annual checkups with the ship's doctor, and Tony had an issue with his heart."

Her tone turned from sassy to concerned in an instant. "Oh, no! Is he okay? What's wrong with his heart? Can I talk to him?

I knew she was going to kill me when we got back to Bonaventure, but I couldn't resist. "It seems the doctor can't find it."

"Can't find what?"

"His heart. His best guess is that he left it with a beautiful young analyst in coastal Georgia."

"Chase Daniel Fulton, I'm going to kill you in your sleep. Don't do that to me."

I said, "I'd like to apologize . . . I'm not going to, but I'd *like* to. So, seriously, everyone checked out fine except Tony. He did a little more damage to his knee than we suspected. He's going to need to see an ortho doc when we get home, but Dr. Shadrack patched him up for now."

"Chase, you promised me you wouldn't let him get hurt."

"No, I promised you I'd do my best to keep him from getting killed. That's not the same thing. He's young and tough. He'll be all healed up in no time. Now, let's talk about tonight. Is everything still on schedule?"

"Actually, the timeline has moved up about an hour. There's a current we didn't expect, and the new model puts the sub at your location fifty-five minutes ahead of schedule. Are you ready for the intercept?"

"We are. How's the satellite availability for our over-the-horizon capability?"

"Not great. I'm afraid you're going to have to rely on the surface radar."

"That's all right. The radar antenna on the *Lori Danielle* is about fifty feet higher than the rig on the Mark V, so that'll give us at least double the range."

"That's great. What's the plan for the afternoon?"

"We're going to check out any boats within twenty miles before it gets dark so we'll have a database of possible intercept vessels. If we find anything with guns, we'll run up the Jolly Roger, lay along broadside, and shoot it out."

"Cut it out, Chase. This is serious."

"I'm just messing around, but we are going to take a look at anything in the area. The more we know, the better chance we'll have of coming out of this thing unscathed."

"Okay, be careful and tell Tony—"

"You tell him." I handed the phone off to our newest recruit.

I briefed Captain Stinnett on our plan, and he approved. He said, "We'll act as the center of the hub, and we'll track everything within forty miles. That's a lot of water to cover, but you've got a lot of boat."

"Let's focus on targets from the west. If they're operating out of Mexico, they'll come from that direction. It's a long way to anything dry to the east."

"Agreed," he said. "Do you want to start now?"

"There's no time like the present. Let's go hunting."

I left Singer on Captain Stinnett's ship so he could find just the right spot to practice his meditation—or whatever snipers do before an overwatch.

With the rest of the team aboard the Mark V, we set a course for the closest stationary radar return—a craft lying just twelve miles to the southwest that hadn't moved in two hours.

It took less than ten minutes to get the vessel in sight. "Tony, you've got the youngest eyes on the boat. Put some peepers on that thing and tell me what you see."

He lifted his binoculars and peered across the bow rail. "It appears to be a fishing vessel in distress. They've got a rectangular flag and a ball up."

"Great . . . just what we need. Okay, I'll take us in for a closer look, but if you're right, we're committed to rendering aid."

I added power and moved us within a mile of the vessel.

Tony reported, "They've definitely got the distress signal up, and there's hanging nets."

I picked up the mic and made the broadcast in both English and Spanish. "Fishing vessel displaying distress, say nature of emergency."

The radio crackled, and a voice spoke in broken English. "We are fishing vessel *La Diosa Fortuna*, and engine is gone."

I turned to Hunter. "*La Diosa Fortuna* is *Lady Luck*, right?"

"I think so, but my Spanish isn't great."

"It wasn't bad in Colombia."

He shrugged. "When in Rome . . ."

I keyed up. "Is your crew injured?"

"No. Crew is fine, but engine is no good."

"Stand by, *Lady Luck*."

I radioed the *Lori Danielle* and briefed them on the situation.

Captain Stinnett said, "Take a good look, and if you think they're really in distress, we'll call the Mexican Navy for them."

"Roger. Stand by for the report."

"We're going in for a closer look," I yelled. "Somebody get on the deck gun."

Mongo hefted the M2 fifty-caliber machine gun onto its base, and I headed for *Lady Luck*. We approached from her stern with Mongo scanning for anything or anyone who looked hostile. The transom of the vessel was charred black with smoke, and she was clearly adrift. We circled the vessel, and everything about her looked like a decrepit fishing boat that should've been in the scrap-yard years before.

"What do you think, Mongo?"

Without taking his eyes off the vessel, he yelled back, "I think she's exactly what she claims to be."

After I called Captain Stinnett, he radioed the Mexican Navy, then I lifted the mic to my lips and put my Spanish to use. "*La Diosa Fortuna*, we've notified the Mexican Navy of your position and condition. If no one is injured, that's all we can do for you."

They answered immediately. "Gracias. We are not injured. Only bad engine."

I took a mental snapshot of the vessel, but nothing about her concerned me. The fact that she wasn't resistant to the Mexican Navy getting involved only strengthened my belief. I called Captain Stinnett, and he gave me the coordinates of the next contact.

Our afternoon continued with my confidence growing stronger with every contact we investigated. Of the nine vessels we saw, none gave me any reason to believe they were the intercept vessel for the Colombian narco-sub.

As the sun plunged toward the western horizon, we returned to the *Lori Danielle* and refueled both our boat and our stomachs.

Night fell on the Caribbean Sea, and everything was in place. Singer was perched high atop the R/V *Lori Danielle*. Hunter and Tony waited in their dry suits and rebreathers. The EMP sled rested in its cradle with the crane's cable affixed to the pad eye and ready to deploy the machine. I hovered the Mark V a hundred yards to port of the *Lori Danielle* with anticipation beating in my chest.

The expected window for the sub's arrival came and went. With the secure satellite uplink and our comms system working flawlessly, I said, "Ops, One. What's going on? We expected the sub half an hour ago."

It was Clark who answered. "Be patient. There are a lot of variables in play. Double-check the receiver, and remain ready for interception."

I cycled the receiver and performed a systems check. Everything was functioning as designed, but *La Diosa Fortuna* wouldn't leave my mind.

"All systems are go."

Clark said, "Roger. Stay on your toes, College Boy. The sub could surface any minute."

I ran through all the variables and tried my best to use Singer's technique to slow my heart rate, but it wasn't happening for me. As the math involved in plotting the sub's course played out in my head, I flashed back to the countless hours I'd spent learning navigation and chart-plotting. That's when it hit me, and I almost shouted into my mic. "Skipper! We're at the wrong coordinates!"

Our analyst's voice filled my earpiece. "What are you talking about?"

"The unexpected current won't make the sub pop up sooner. It'll make it surface farther north. The current adds distance. It doesn't turn up the clock."

The silence on the line confirmed my theory, and I radioed the *Lori Danielle.* "We're moving north. Stay with us."

When Skipper's voice sounded in my earpiece, the anguish in her tone was almost palpable. "I screwed up the calculations, Chase. I don't know how it happened. I'm sorry."

"Don't be sorry," I demanded. "Just fix it. Plot the new position, ASAP."

Seconds ticked by like hours as we moved north at ten knots.

Skipper said, "I've got the new coordinates. Advise ready to copy."

"Send it!"

I wrote furiously as she read off the lat and long. When she finished, I read back the coordinates, and she said, "Read back, correct!"

After plotting the lat and long on the GPS and measuring the distance, I keyed my mic. "*Lori Danielle*, we're fifteen miles from the revised rendezvous point. What's your top speed?"

"Twenty-six knots," came the reply.

"We'll make twice that speed," I said. "Pour on the coal, and try to keep up!"

Chapter 31
Splash the Divers

It would take us sixteen minutes to cover the fifteen miles with the throttles buried against their stops. That would leave us with no overwatch and without the support of the *Lori Danielle* for twenty minutes, plus the time it took Captain Stinnett to accelerate to full speed.

Reading the radar display while pounding across the waves at fifty knots was not only impossible but also irrelevant. Regardless of what the radar returned, I wouldn't divert from course. I'd deal with the fallout with the deck gun if it became necessary, but I would *not* let anyone or anything beat me to the rendezvous point.

I silently begged the twin diesels for a few more knots. If the sub surfaced and the surface-support vessel arrived before us, the only two options were to bug out and start the whole operation again with the next sub, or fight the support vessel for the sub. I didn't like either of those options.

With three minutes to the predicted rendezvous point, I tried to focus on the radar screen, but something else caught my eye. The red overheat warning on the port engine shone like a beacon in the night. Instinctually, I turned to look for smoke from the engine, but the darkness and the EMP sled blocked my view.

Disco yelled, "What's wrong?"

I pointed toward the red light. "Overheat on the port—"

Before I could finish my sentence, the starboard engine overheat warning joined the first red light, and our speed started bleeding off. Both engines were overheating, and the only plausible cause was an obstruction in the raw water intake. The massive seawater pumps had picked up a plastic bag or some other scrap of garbage in both intakes. If I continued at full throttle, the quarter-million-dollar engines would cook themselves into oblivion, but if I shut the engines down to save them from destruction, we'd fall three miles short of the sub's likely position.

In the middle of a fight, sometimes the lesser of two evils is the worst decision a battlefield commander will ever have to make. It was my turn to make such a decision, and the clock was running out.

I yanked the port side transmission into neutral and reduced the throttle to idle. I would run on the starboard engine until it melted to the deck, then I would bring the other engine back online and milk it all the way to the rendezvous site. With any luck, we'd make the site, grab the sub, and wait for Stinnett and the *Lori Danielle* to show up before the rendezvous ship arrived and wanted to fight over the booty I wasn't willing to surrender.

My plan worked, but not long enough. The starboard engine turned itself inside out in ten seconds and gave up the ghost. I shoved the port side throttle full ahead, and the tachometer rose as our speed continued bleeding off. The engine produced less than half the RPMs it should have, but we were still making way. Our speed fell below twenty-five knots, and the radar screen came into focus. Two vessels approached from the southwest.

I shouted over the roar of our single failing engine. "Mount the second deck gun!"

Once our port side engine failed, we'd be a sitting duck with only our twin electric bow thrusters for maneuvering. I wanted every angle of fire covered.

Disco wrestled the gun from its locker and stumbled toward the bow. Mongo stepped into him and relieved him of his burden. The big man had the massive gun mounted, locked, and loaded seconds later.

Hunter came forward as our speed continued to diminish. "What's going on, Chase?"

"We lost the starboard engine, and now the port side is taking a dive. I think it's a cooling issue."

He said, "Shut it down before you cook it! The kid and I will go in and clear the intakes."

I pulled the throttle back and shut down the port side engine. It rattled and shuddered on its mounts but finally stopped turning. Before the silence had overtaken the night, both Hunter and Tony were over the side.

I left the pilothouse and ran astern, praying they'd surface with a wad of garbage bags in their hands, but just like the engines, our divers let me down. Both surfaced simultaneously while shaking their heads.

Hunter shucked off his mask. "Both intakes are clear."

"Did you clear them, or were they already clear?"

He pulled himself over the transom. "They were clear when we got to them."

I suddenly wished Earl were on board. If the raw water intakes weren't clogged, the obstruction had to be inside the lines, but what were the chances of both raw water intakes ingesting garbage at the same time?

Desperate for a solution, I threw open the consoles and thumbed the buttons to open the hatches to the engine room. I checked my watch in a near panic. Time was accelerating, and my world was melting around me.

I yelled at Hunter, "I'm going to restart the port side engine. Watch for water flow."

He climbed down into the engine room with his dry suit dripping salt water. The engine turned and groaned itself to life, but the overheat warning illuminated almost immediately.

Disco ran from astern yelling, "There's water flowing!"

My brain churned. Water was flowing to cool the engine, but it continued to overheat.

What's left? What else can possibly be causing the engine to broil itself?

A glance back at the radar display showed the two vessels still approaching from the south. The second target was making twenty-six knots, and her AIS identified her as the *Lori Danielle*, but the other boat was making just over thirty-five knots and closing on our position much faster than I wanted. She gave no AIS return.

Getting to the intercept point was more important than saving the engine, so I sent up a prayer and laid on the throttle. We accelerated slowly and finally settled on eighteen knots. I was doing half the speed of the vessel I believed was the support ship, and for the first time, Stinnett's ship was gaining on us.

The radio tuned to the expected frequency of the narco-sub's locator transmitter came alive with a roar and spat out lat and long coordinates. I typed them into the GPS, and the magenta rhumb line appeared, indicating the sub was on the surface just over a mile due east.

My eyes shot back to the radar display just in time to see the vessel turn directly toward the beacon. There was no question I'd identified the surface-support vessel and we were in a race to the thirsty sub. I worked out the intercept in my head, and it didn't look good. It was going to be close, but only if my failing engine could continue to produce fifteen knots or more.

I grabbed the mic and called the *Lori Danielle*. Captain Stinnett answered instantly, and I said, "We're down one engine, and the second is quickly failing. I need you to intercept the target two miles southwest of your position before he beats me to the sub."

His two-word response gave me the only good feeling I'd had all night. "Roger. Engaging."

With smoke pouring from our dying engine, our speed bled off gradually, and Tony yelled over the roar, "Chase! The crane won't work without an engine!"

What else could go wrong tonight?

I pulled the throttle to idle and grabbed Tony by the sleeve of his dry suit, then I shoved him toward the GPS chart plotter and jabbed my finger into the screen. "That's your victim, rescue swimmer! Don't let him die!"

When we reached the stern, Hunter had the EMP sled in the air and dangling beneath the arm of the crane.

I said, "Swing it overboard!"

He manipulated the arm of the crane, sending its load over the gunwale and hanging six feet above the water's surface.

He and Tony donned their full face masks and waited by the stern.

I yelled, "I'm going to push her until she lies down."

The dying engine slowed more by the second as if it were sinking in heavy mud. There was no way to know what I'd done to destroy both engines, but at that moment, it didn't matter. We were within half a mile of our target, Captain Stinnett was running interference for us, and our sled was ready to fly.

Another glance at the radar showed the *Lori Danielle* crossing the other ship's bow, east to west, but the maneuverability of Stinnett's ship was limited. Stopping, turning, and accelerating a ship of that weight and size required incredible forces and a skilled hand at the helm. As our remaining engine coughed her final death throes, Hunter hit the clutch on the winch, and Mongo's EMP sled fell six feet to the waiting Caribbean Sea. Hunter and Tony followed the sled into the water, and instantly, Mongo, Disco, and I were alone and dead in the water. We had electrical power as long as the batteries held, but if Captain Stinnett couldn't get the support ship stopped, things were going to get even uglier by the minute.

I reached for the mic to the secure satellite uplink. "We're dead in the water, and I splashed the divers six hundred yards west of the beacon."

Stinnett's stressed voice filled the speaker. "Roger. We're in one hell of a fight back here. We're head-to-head with a Mexican Navy Cape-class patrol boat. He's got us in speed, firepower, and maneuverability, but everything else is on our side."

It took me several seconds to realize the captain had a warped, dark sense of humor. I said, "If you can lure him to me, I can put some fifty-cal down his throat."

"How do you expect me to find you?" Stinnett said. "I can't get a radar return on you."

"Give me sixty seconds, and I'll leave the light on for you."

I pulled the mortar tube from its locker and loaded an illumination round. To avoid wasting time cranking up the elevation, I braced the tube against the deck and pointed the muzzle straight up. When the round fired, the shock wave blew me backward and left my ears ringing like church bells.

The round flew straight up for a thousand feet until its parachute deployed and the phosphorus ignited, lighting up the night sky like a Braves game at Turner Field.

Captain Stinnett's voice filled the speaker again. "Even an old guy like me can see that. Here we come."

The disadvantage of the illumination round was that I'd given away my previously stealthy position and essentially hung out a sign telling the bad guys to "Shoot Here."

I ordered, "Load the API!"

Disco and Mongo dropped the ammo cans full of tracers from their weapons and loaded the silver-tip, armor-piercing, incendiary rounds in their place.

"Locked and loaded," came the reply from both gunners.

"I'm going to bring us about with the bow thrusters and keep us bearing on the bogey on Stinnett's six. As soon as he gives us a shot, cut their navigation bridge in half."

Mongo acknowledged the order first, and Disco followed. "Yes, sir."

My heart pounded as if it were trying to leap through my ribs and join the fight, and everything in my world moved in sudden slow motion. The bow of the *Lori Danielle* loomed ever larger as she broke a thousand yards and continued bearing directly on our bow. I had no means to move the boat in any direction other than spinning her where she lay. The bow thrusters provided no forward propulsion, so I was essentially the commander of a fifty-ton, immoveable, double-barrel gun turret.

The speaker came alive again. "I'm bringing her right down your gullet, General Custer. If you miss, you can consider this our Little Bighorn."

At three hundred yards, with tracer rounds flying in every direction and the bow of the *Lori Danielle* looking like a mountain peak plowing through the water at twenty-five knots, Captain Stinnett threw the helm hard over to starboard, exposing his broadside to us, but only for an instant. He continued the maneuver, looping back on the Mexican patrol boat, barely a third her size. Every gun Stinnett had lit up and poured thousands of pounds of lead into the hostile vessel.

I yelled, "Light 'er up, boys!"

The two Ma Deuce fifty-cal machine guns thundered, sending their silver-tipped devils into the navigation bridge until the superstructure of the Mexican boat burst into blooming orange and black flames, lapping at the sky like the tongues of a thousand demons.

Just as my heart reclaimed its place in my chest, the realization of my deadly situation loomed over me as the flaming patrol boat continued directly at us on an unavoidable collision course.

"Kill the waterline!" I shouted over the roar of battle, and both of our guns peppered the craft where her hull met the water.

I'll never know what our high-explosive rounds struck inside the hull that sent the ninety-five-foot warship to hell in an explosion so massive the shock wave rolled our Mark V forty-five degrees to starboard, but whatever it was, I'll remain forever grateful it was flammable enough to destroy their ship and save ours.

As the remnants of the Mexican patrol boat floated and burned in a thousand small fires spread across the surface, Captain Stinnett laid the *Lori Danielle* alongside the Mark V, and two crewmen unfurled a rope ladder over the side.

Mongo and Disco left their guns and joined me on the starboard rail.

Mongo said, "The guns are too hot to touch, but we can't abandon them with the boat. Are we going to scuttle her?"

The thought of opening the seacocks and watching the Mark V melt into the deep blue Caribbean sickened me, but I feared we had no choice. I looked up to see Captain Stinnett joining his two men on deck.

He said, "Turn your anchor light on, and get up here. We'll pluck your men out of the drink and come back for the boat."

Disco climbed first, followed by Mongo, and I stepped from my ship last. Something about that step felt like I'd been run through with a white-hot blade. I swallowed the shame of abandoning my demolished ship at sea and followed my men up the ladder.

Chapter 32
Look What We Found

Disco, Mongo, and I moved to the bow of the *Lori Danielle*, and the captain brought every searchlight he had to bear on the water in front of us. We motored through the water at dead slow, searching every inch of the surface for Hunter, Tony, and one particular submarine that had caused a lot more trouble than it was worth, regardless of the street value of its cargo.

It was no surprise when it was the eagle eyes of our sniper—who was still nested high in the rigging—that were the first to spot our prize.

He radioed from his overwatch position. "Lights ahoy. Ten o'clock and five hundred yards."

The bow of the supposed research vessel came twenty degrees to port and continued slow ahead. To my relief and amusement, my partner and his protégé sat straddling the surfaced sub like bull riders and waving their dive lights over their heads.

As we drifted alongside the sub, Tony said, "Hey, Chase! Look what we found. I told you I was a rodeo cowboy."

Captain Stinnett ordered a tender to be lowered and a cargo net rigged to offload the sub's payload. Hunter and Tony tossed plastic-wrapped bails of cocaine from the sub until their arms were ready to fall off. We hauled them aboard, and Mongo finished the job with a little help from Disco, his gunner's mate.

With the cocaine locked securely in the *Lori Danielle*'s hold, a pair of engineers lowered a cradle from the ship's crane, and two of Stinnett's divers hit the water to rig the lifting cradle.

Half an hour later, the neutered narco-sub rested on blocks of wooden dunnage on the ship's stern deck. My team leaned against the sub and breathed a long sigh of relief.

I threw an arm around Hunter, who was still in his dripping-wet dry suit. "Are you sure you zapped this thing? I'd hate for it to cook off and ruin our night."

In true Stone W. Hunter style, he shrugged. "I guess we'll see."

Captain Stinnett ordered the ship's chief electrician to inspect the sub's systems, and he reported, "There's nothing to inspect, Captain. It's melted like chocolate in a pocket."

I gave Mongo a slug to the shoulder. "It looks like your gadget worked, big man. Nicely done."

He peered over the rail. "I'm glad it worked, but I'd be happier if we could get it back."

Tony and Hunter laughed in unison.

Hunter gave Tony an elbow. "Not even the rescue swimmer could get that thing off the bottom. She's gone for good."

We motored back to the crippled Mark V, and the seamen in the tender rigged a hawser to bring her in tow.

Even though there was no chance of anyone surviving the explosion on the Mexican boat, we scanned the water for any sign of survivors or bodies, but we found none.

With the search complete and the adrenaline finally slowing its race through our bodies, Captain Stinnett joined us on deck. "Well, men, it didn't go as we planned, but it looks like the mission is complete."

We took a moment to savor the victory as I watched the battle-weary Mark V trail behind. "Hey, Captain. I'll take that million five now if you still want our boat."

He joined me at the rail and said, "I've got a better idea. I'll send a couple of men to take you and your crew back to Isla Mujeres in my tender. A little birdy told me you could find a ride home from there."

"Thank you, Captain."

He threw up a finger. "I thought I told you to call me Wayne."

I shook his hand and saw him smile for the first time. At least, I think it was a smile behind that long white beard that could hide a family of ducks if they needed a spot to stay warm.

He pointed his chin toward the Mark V. "If you'll buy the MDO, I'll tow that thing anywhere you want."

I froze. "Did you say MDO, as in marine diesel oil?"

He nodded. "Yeah, that's what ships at sea burn."

"And that's what you pumped into my tanks when you refueled us the day we came aboard?"

"Yes, we bunkered four thousand pounds for you."

I leaned back against the rail and almost cried. "Our mechanic had those engines tuned to perfection on land diesel. The semi-heavy fuel you piped aboard was too much for them. Now it all makes sense, and I'm an idiot for not asking when I saw the hoses."

The captain let out a long, low whistle. "Ouch. In that case, just tell me where you want the thing, and I'll cover the fuel cost."

We offloaded the weapons from the Mark V and stowed them securely on the ship, just in case she broke free and drifted ashore on some island where fully automatic fifty-caliber machine guns aren't welcome.

The ride back to Isla Mujeres aboard the tender took three hours, and that was three hours of well-deserved downtime for my team. Even though Captain Stinnett—Wayne—wouldn't approve, I shoved a wad of cash in the hands of the crewmen who brought us ashore.

Warm, dry, and back on the Island of Women, Tony asked, "Do you think it'd be all right if I called my girlfriend and let her know we're okay?"

I panicked and yanked my phone from my pocket, but Singer grabbed my wrist. "Relax," he said. "I had the ops center on open channel the whole time. They already know, but Skipper would probably appreciate a call from her boyfriend now that he's a full-grown veteran of an honest-to-goodness sea battle."

"I can always count on you, Singer. What would we ever do without you?"

He laughed. "You wouldn't have any trouble finding another sniper, but you might have a tough time finding another Southern Baptist one like me."

"You're one of a kind, my friend, and I never want to do this without you having my six."

* * *

We opted for a good night's sleep and breakfast before climbing aboard our magic carpet masquerading as a Cessna Citation jet. Disco had us back on the ground in Saint Marys in no time, and I made the decision that we all deserved an extended vacation. Mongo had Atlanta Ballet Company's newest prima ballerina and a beautiful Russian woman who couldn't wait to get him home. Singer had a lot of thinking and praying to do. Disco and Tony had phase one of Clark Johnson's introduction to covert ops. Hunter opted for a long cruise with Tina Ramirez aboard *Aegis*. And I had some classes to attend at UGA if I was ever to follow in Dr. Richter's footsteps and earn a graduate degree—or two—in the study of what happens between the ears when the human mind departs from normalcy.

The classes went well, and the cruise was a dream come true for my partner and the woman he loved. Just when I started itching to see something other than the inside of a classroom, Hunter and I scored a couple of set passes to watch Penny's latest movie being filmed on a soundstage in L.A.

As fate, and our bad behavior on set demanded, Penny revoked our passes and sent us packing. The cross-country flight gave Hunter a few hours in the front seat of the Citation and gave me time to think about how the phantom pains from my missing foot never entered my mind while in the heat of battle off the Yucatan Peninsula.

Perhaps I was still in the fight. Maybe my Statement of Demonstrated Ability bled over from my flying life and onto my fighting life, as well. I resolved to get back in shape no matter how much it hurt or how boring the stationary bicycle became. I was back, and at least inside my head, I was better than I'd ever been. That's the leader my team deserved, and that's the leader they would have as long as the blood flowed through whatever remained of my body.

"Let's fly a pass over the house," I said. "It's become a tradition."

Hunter said, "You have the controls."

I overflew the downtown waterfront of Saint Marys and up the waterway to Cumberland Sound.

Hunter peered out the cockpit window. "I think that's Captain Stinnett's boat anchored in the Sound."

I rolled to the right in a lazy three-sixty. "I think you're right. That's a nice surprise."

I completed the turn and lined up for the runway. I loved seeing Bonaventure pass beneath the wings of whatever I happened to be flying. There's no feeling like home, regardless of it being an address or a hodgepodge of misfits who've become family.

"It looks like Kenny finished the boathouse."

Hunter stretched to see out my window. "It looks nice from up here. I can't wait to see it from the ground."

I surrendered the airplane back into Hunter's hands, and he painted an airline pilot's landing onto the runway. It was a thing of beauty.

When we taxied clear of the runway, he dusted off his shoulder. "And that's how that is done."

We taxied to the hangar and shut down on the tarmac. Hunter opened the hangar and motored out on the tug. We hooked up to the nosewheel of the Citation, and Hunter said, "There's something wrong with the lights in the hangar. They wouldn't come on, but the power's on because the door opened when I hit the button."

"Hmm. It's probably just a breaker," I said as I stepped away from the tug.

He positioned the jet in its appointed spot inside the hangar and hopped off the tug. "Thanks for letting me fly. I want to get my multi-engine rating and eventually check out in the Citation."

"We'll take care of . . ." Before I finished my sentence, the massive hangar door began its slow descent.

Hunter asked, "How did you do that?"

"I didn't do it," I said. "There must be something going on with the electricity. I'm too tired to deal with it tonight. We'll figure it out tomorrow."

When the door reached its stop and eliminated the natural light from outside, a Spanish-accented voice cut through the darkness. "For you, mi amigo, there won't be a tomorrow."

Chapter 33
The Human Shield

The voice had come from behind me, but the punch came from the front. It was a crushing blow to the center of my face, and I was on my back before I could draw my pistol. The sound I made when I hit the concrete floor was repeated as Hunter was knocked from his feet.

I scampered backward as I pawed for my Glock, while the taste of blood and the thunder of broken cartilage filled my senses. When the pistol cleared the leather of its holster, I was bombarded with a light that felt like the sun itself. Shielding my eyes with my left hand, I continued kicking backward across the floor. I raised the pistol in the general direction of the blinding light and felt the trigger begin its travel beneath the pad of my index finger.

I yelled, "Hunter!"

"Yeah," he let out in a pain-filled exhalation.

His voice came from my left, so I kept pressing the trigger, but a booted foot met my gun hand before the firing pin could fall. My pistol slid across the polished floor, and the boot returned. This time it was on my chin and forcing my head to the floor.

Through gritted teeth, I growled, "Shoot, Hunter . . . shoot!"

I grabbed the foot crushing into my face and twisted with every ounce of strength I possessed. The ankle gave way, and the cry of a wounded animal filled the air.

I pulled the broken leg toward me with the intention of using the man's body as a shield to keep his partners from drilling me with a dozen bullet holes. The man was small but strong. Even with his broken ankle, he fought like a wild man. We wrestled, squirming and twisting until I found the hair of his head, giving me something to grab. I pounded his face into the floor with two powerful thrusts and then pulled his unconscious body on top of me.

The pair of blinding beams had suddenly become one, and I could barely make out the silhouette of a man . . . or maybe two. With the dead weight of the first man on my chest, I stretched and slid my hand across the floor in a desperate search for my pistol. Just as my fingertips felt the polymer form of the weapon, the deafening report of a shot echoed from my left.

Still disoriented and confused, I shouted for my partner again. I needed to hear his voice. I needed to know the shot hadn't silenced him for all eternity.

The next sound I heard was Hunter's furious tone. "I'm still here, but this bastard just broke my hand."

I finally wrapped my hand around my Glock and raised it toward the remaining light. In a hasty attempt to gain at least the beginnings of the upper hand, I pressed the trigger. My pistol bucked in my hand, but the light didn't fall. I pressed again, and the trigger cycled, but the gun didn't fire. At least not my gun . . .

Two rounds fired from somewhere in the hangar, and I felt the body of the man on my chest buckle and the heat of blood pour across my abdomen.

Having trained for a decade on how to clear a jammed weapon, I slammed the butt of my pistol against the body on top of me, hoping to reseat the magazine if it had come partially dislodged in the fight. With my left arm still holding the human shield in place, I rolled my pistol over and stuck the slide against his shirt. I shoved the weapon forward, grinding it into his flesh. The slide cycled, and I raised the pistol to bear, once again, on the light.

An undeniably American voice cut through the chaos. "Don't kill them! We need them alive!"

Whoever he was talking to was not on my side, so I buried the trigger with my muzzle trained on the light. The firing pin fell, and the Glock clicked, but nothing else.

Realizing my weapon was little more than a pistol-shaped rock, I threw it as hard as I could directly toward the light. My throw was on target, and the man swatted at my flying pistol, losing his grip on his flashlight. As the beam swept across the floor, I caught a glimpse of Hunter grabbing for his pistol with his left hand, and the mystery of my misfire was solved. A few feet to my right lay my magazine still loaded with nine-millimeter rounds that should've been lodged in our attackers' chests.

The American voice came again with the same command. "Don't kill them!"

I tried to focus my attention toward the voice, but my eyes still burned from the blinding light. I couldn't see the man, but I did see one of the most beautiful sights of my life. The walk-through door beside the huge overhead door swung open, and two silhouettes stepped through.

I yelled at the top of my lungs, "Chase and Hunter are prone. Kill everybody else!"

The beams of the weapon-mounted lights cut through the cavernous space and fell on our three remaining attackers. The first silhouette double-tapped the man closest to him, and he melted to the floor. Silhouette number two downed the two remaining men with four perfectly placed shots.

I rolled over, shoving the dead man from my chest as the overhead lights came to life. Slowly, the darkened space brightened, and Tony's form appeared, kneeling over the source of the American voice. Tony had his pistol pressed beneath the man's nose with blood dripping from his lips.

"Don't kill him, Tony. He's got a lot of questions to answer."

As the man whimpered in terror that his ambush had fallen apart around him, Tony kept him pinned to the hangar floor.

I yanked up my shirt, feeling for entry wounds in my gut, but none of the blood was mine, and I didn't have any new holes. "Are you okay, Hunter?"

My partner groaned, "He broke my hand, but other than that, I'm okay."

We scrambled to our feet and crossed the floor to the spot where Tony was giving one unknown soul the worst day of his life.

I stuck my prosthetic in the man's crotch and eased about a fourth of my weight onto the fake foot. "What's your name?"

The terrified man stammered and spat something incoherent.

I doubled the weight on my prosthetic. "What's your name?"

He cried out in agony and surrender. "Benoit . . . Simon Benoit. Please don't kill me."

Epilogue

Simon Benoit, the brilliant engineer and mastermind behind Macario Mateo's narco-subs, cried like a frightened child and spilled his guts. Clark recorded the confession, even though Benoit would never see the inside of a courtroom. He told the story in brilliant detail of how Mateo had enticed him away from the Central Intelligence Agency's Office of Technical Services with the promise of untold wealth, and of course, the lives of his entire family.

As fascinating as that revelation was, the story turned even darker and more riveting when Benoit detailed how DEA Supervisory Special Agent Michael Conroy had been feeding the cartel volumes of intelligence for the previous two years, including the final report of his life about the tactical team from Saint Marys, Georgia, who captured one of their submarines alive.

When word of Benoit's capture, interrogation, and whimpering confession made its way to the slimy halls of Washington DC, SSA Michael Conroy's body was found floating in the reflecting pool between the Lincoln Memorial and Washington Monument, with twenty-one surgically precise incisions placed perfectly throughout his body to have caused the most agonizing death imaginable. The official press release from the public affairs office at the DOJ labeled the incident a ". . . heinous attack and murder of a well-respected, senior government agent with a stellar service record." The unofficial position of Supervisory Special Agent Ray White was that Conroy's death was ". . . the damnedest case of suicide he'd ever seen."

I secretly hoped they'd bury his corpse beside Benedict Arnold so the two birds of a traitorous feather could rot side by side for all eternity.

The ship anchored in Cumberland Sound wasn't Captain Stinnett's boat, after all. It turned out to be a prototype vessel being developed by an unnamed government agency for the purposes of covert operations on the waters of the world. I hoped Mongo's desire for a ship of our own was on the verge of becoming a reality.

Post-graduate study in the field of psychology at the University of Georgia's satellite campus bordered on mind-numbing after having spent nearly a decade studying some of the world's most depraved minds through the sights of my weapons of choice. Real-world depravity can't be captured in a three-hundred-dollar textbook, no matter how many professors wrote it. Just like Dr. Richter told me a lifetime ago: "We don't learn how the human mind works in this compost heap of intellectual garbage. We learn the ways of the mind by observing the behavior of its keeper."

Penny's movie was another blockbuster, and she was quickly becoming Hollywood's goose that laid the golden eggs. Offers came in from every direction, pleading to get her under contract, but just like me, she needed a little vacation, so the two of us pointed *Aegis*'s bow out to sea and left the whole world astern.

Author's Note

It is my sincere hope that you enjoyed Chase's latest adventure. The creation of this story took me down some dark roads as I explored Chase's depression and recovery following the loss of his right foot. As dramatic as Chase's story felt, I believe the most impactful drama in this book unfolded between Singer and Mongo. Arthur Quiller-Couch said, "You must kill your darlings." It's not easy to inflict pain, especially psychological pain, on the characters who've become my darlings. I love them all, and it breaks my heart to see them sink into darkness, but I like what we learn about them when they're at their most vulnerable. I hope you feel the same.

Originally, the subject of suicide arose three times in this story, but after Melissa's reaction to the book, I cut the number down to two. The horrific act of suicide touches so many lives and leaves countless victims behind to ask questions to which there are never any answers. I used the suicides in this book to demonstrate the scars left on the lives of those still living when someone they love is forever gone. How people react, mourn, and heal is fascinating and unique to every individual. If you have been scorched by suicide's terrible flame, I pray you receive the same peace and reassurance Singer realized in this work of fiction. If you have thoughts of taking your own life, please seek help. If it can't be found in the form of friends or family, please call The National Suicide Prevention Lifeline at 800-273-8255.

I have a few things to explain and even a few more confessions. I know absolutely nothing about the movie production business. Everything I described surrounding the filming of Penny's screenplay was one hundred percent made up. If I screwed it up, I apologize. I needed a scene in which Hunter and Chase could behave like spoiled children and get thrown out of Hollywood.

Likewise, the funeral ceremony at the monastery is purely the product of my imagination and based on nothing real. I don't know if Trappist monks perform funerals. I don't know if people are buried on the grounds of monasteries. Even though the scene is pure fiction, I used it to symbolize Singer's delivery back into the arms of his team and chosen family. I hope I accomplished my goal.

Finally, I must make an enormous confession. When I wrote the loss of Chase's leg in *The Smuggler's Chase*, I had no idea how I would get our hero back into the fight. I should've had more faith in the voices in my head. They did a marvelous job of leading me down the path to Chase's physical and psychological recovery. Taking risks like chopping off the protagonist's foot are done by only three types of writers: those who are self-destructive by nature; those who have a plan for a huge turning point in the storyline; and those who aren't smart enough to know what's wrong with the idea. I know which one I am, and I'm thankful not to be either of the first two.

I made several insensitive jeers and jokes at Chase's expense in this story, and I hope I didn't offend anyone while doing so. They were written because that's the kind of humor and comradery people like Chase and the team turn to when they don't know any other way to demonstrate concern and sympathy.

Writers, in general, are strange birds. We see stories where none exist and find characters in people who have none. The world through the writer's eye is a much different place than most people will ever see. I spend a great deal of time thinking about how to say thank you to the hundreds of thousands of you who buy my books and support my writing habit. I'd write the stories anyway, even if no one read them, because I'm a writer, and that's what writers do. I receive a couple hundred emails every week from people who claim to be fans. I always write back and thank them for taking a moment out of their busy day to write a letter to someone they don't even know. Mostly, though, I write back to tell them I've never wanted fans; I only want friends who enjoy what I write, and that's the magnificent gift you give me every time you open one of my books and step inside the world as I see it through my writer's eye. I believe I may have finally come to know how I can thank you for making my wildest dreams come true. I think I've already done so twenty-one times, including this story, by writing a love letter from me to you in the form of a novel and inviting you to come outside and play with my imaginary friends and me. From the depths of my heart, thank you for taking me up on that invitation, time after time.

—Cap

About the Author

Cap Daniels

Cap Daniels is a former sailing charter captain, scuba and sailing instructor, pilot, Air Force combat veteran, and civil servant of the U.S. Department of Defense. Raised far from the ocean in rural East Tennessee, his early infatuation with salt water was sparked by the fascinating, and sometimes true, sea stories told by his father, a retired Navy Chief Petty Officer. Those stories of adventure on the high seas sent Cap in search of adventure of his own, which eventually landed him on Florida's Gulf Coast where he spends as much time as possible on, in, and under the waters of the Emerald Coast.

With a headful of larger-than-life characters and their thrilling exploits, Cap pours his love of adventure and passion for the ocean onto the pages of the Chase Fulton Novels and the Avenging Angel - Seven Deadly Sins series.

Visit www.CapDaniels.com to join the mailing list to receive newsletter and release updates.

Connect with Cap Daniels:

Facebook: www.Facebook.com/WriterCapDaniels
Instagram: https://www.instagram.com/authorcapdaniels/
BookBub: https://www.bookbub.com/profile/cap-daniels

Also by Cap Daniels

The Chase Fulton Novels Series

Book One: *The Opening Chase*
Book Two: *The Broken Chase*
Book Three: *The Stronger Chase*
Book Four: *The Unending Chase*
Book Five: *The Distant Chase*
Book Six: *The Entangled Chase*
Book Seven: *The Devil's Chase*
Book Eight: *The Angel's Chase*
Book Nine: *The Forgotten Chase*
Book Ten: *The Emerald Chase*
Book Eleven: *The Polar Chase*
Book Twelve: *The Burning Chase*
Book Thirteen: *The Poison Chase*
Book Fourteen: *The Bitter Chase*
Book Fifteen: *The Blind Chase*
Book Sixteen: *The Smuggler's Chase*
Book Seventeen: *The Hollow Chase*
Book Eighteen: *The Sunken Chase* (Summer 2022)

Books in
The Avenging Angel – Seven Deadly Sins Series

Book One: *The Russian's Pride*
Book Two: *The Russian's Greed*
Book Three: *The Russian's Gluttony*
Book Four: *The Russian's Lust* (Summer 2022)

Other Books by Cap Daniels

We Were Brave
I Am Gypsy (Novella)
The Chase Is On (Novella)